LEGACY
✦ of the ✦
CLOCKWORK
KEY

ALSO BY KRISTIN BAILEY

The Secret Order · Book Two

Rise of the Arcane Fire

The Secret Order + Book One

LEGACY
of the
CLOCKWORK
KEY

Kristin Bailey

Simon Pulse

New York London Toronto Sydney New Delhi

SIMON PULSE

An imprint of Simon & Schuster Children's Publishing Division

1230 Avenue of the Americas, New York, NY 10020

First Simon Pulse paperback edition February 2014

Text copyright © 2013 by Kristin Welker

Cover photograph of bird copyright © 2013 by Scott Nobles

Cover photographs of London and clouds copyright © 2013 by Thinkstock

Book design by Angela Goddard

All rights reserved, including the right of reproduction in whole or in part in any form.

SIMON PULSE and colophon are registered trademarks of Simon & Schuster, Inc.

Also available in a Simon Pulse hardcover edition.

For information about special discounts for bulk purchases, please contact

Simon & Schuster Special Sales at 1-866-506-1949 or business@simonandschuster.com.

The Simon & Schuster Speakers Bureau can bring authors to your live event.

For more information or to book an event contact the Simon & Schuster Speakers

Bureau at 1-866-248-3049 or visit our website at www.simonspeakers.com.

The text of this book was set in Granjon.

Manufactured in the United States of America

10 9 8 7 6 5 4 3 2 1

The Library of Congress has cataloged the hardcover edition as follows:

Bailey, Kristin.

Legacy of the clockwork key / by Kristin Bailey.

p. cm.

Summary: An orphaned sixteen-year-old servant in Victorian England finds love while unraveling the secrets of a mysterious society of inventors and their most dangerous creation.

[1. Secret societies—Fiction. 2. Orphans—Fiction. 3. Love—Fiction. 4. London (England)—History—19th century—Fiction. 5. Great Britain— History—Victoria, 1837–1901—Fiction. 6. Science fiction.] I. Title.

PZ7.B15256Le 2013

[Fic]—dc23

2011049871

ISBN 978-1-4424-4026-5 (hc)

ISBN 978-1-4424-4027-2 (pbk)

ISBN 978-1-4424-4028-9 (eBook)

For Mom and Dad.

Thank you for everything you are and everything you've done for me.

I love you.

CHAPTER ONE

SIX MONTHS. IT HAD ONLY BEEN SIX MONTHS.

Heavy flakes of snow drifted past the black iron bars of the front gate. I watched one flutter and land on the muzzle of one of the enormous bronze lions standing guard. His glassy eyes caught the first light of dawn breaking over the eastern garden wall.

In that moment he seemed alive somehow, watching me with a grimace that displayed his awful teeth. I didn't recall noticing the statues the first time I'd walked through the gate, but now I stared, transfixed by the guards holding me within my beautiful prison.

On the quiet London street beyond the gate, time brushed

past like the flakes of falling snow. I could no longer feel the cold breeze making the snowflakes dance. My whole body felt frozen, frozen in place, frozen in time.

Before I arrived here, I thought I had known frustration. As it happens, I knew nothing.

A distant conversation rumbled through my memory. "I have an offer of employment for you, Miss Whitlock." Fateful words from the mouth of my late father's solicitor. At the time they had brought me hope. I hadn't imagined they would lead to this.

The solicitor had leaned back in his chair, stretching his too-tight waistcoat until his buttons nearly popped off. "Lord Rathford sent me a letter after hearing of the tragedy. He claims to have been a good friend of your family and has offered you a respectable position under the supervision of his housekeeper, Mrs. Pratt."

"A housemaid?" My voice had cracked as I'd said it. I had hardly spoken in the weeks after the fire that had claimed the clock shop on Oxford Street. The flames had taken my home and the lives of my parents, leaving my life in ruins.

"You'll be paid, fed, and clothed, and you'll have a roof over your head. Seeking respectable employment is your best option, child." He had tried to pat my hand as if he were placating a little girl who had dropped her favorite poppet in the mud.

Pompous old boar. I was not a child, and he had had no inkling of what he was sentencing me to. Lord Rathford was a stranger to me.

"It's your only option. I suggest you take it." His final words to me had felt as immovable as the brass lions at the gate.

That was six months ago. Only six months. It seemed like six lifetimes.

I shook the snow from my starched white apron, then gently lifted out the blackened pocket watch I kept on a chain around my neck. It was all I had left, a broken timepiece I had found next to my father's charred hand.

It twisted on the chain, tarnished and black against the snow. I knew I should polish it, but every attempt I made felt wrong, as if I were trying to undo the past. I looked back at Lord Rathford's house.

I had moved into a place where time had stopped altogether.

It was my job to make it certain it never moved again.

As was my habit, I touched the watch to my cheek, feeling the kiss of cold metal, before slipping it back into place behind my bib. Gathering my skirts, I shook off the snow then hurried back to my master's house. My thin boots and stockings did little to save my feet from the sting of the cold as I stepped lightly down the snow-filled stairwell that led to the servants' entrance to the kitchens and cellar.

If I didn't have the fires lit before Agnes, the cook, woke, she'd have my hide. Every day was exactly the same, and I had worked the routine into my bones.

With an effort that would have appalled my delicate mother, I cleaned the kitchen grate, thankful I didn't have to blacken it with the foul-smelling polish I had to use on all the other grates in the fireplaces throughout the house. I started the fire, set the tea, and prepared the kitchen for breakfast.

As soon as the tea steeped, I carried a pot of it into the sitting room. On the table near the window, a cup rested on its side, the spilled contents drying on the marble top. I cleaned the mess, carefully polishing the cup before setting it on the saucer and filling it only one third with the piping hot tea.

Then I reached over and tipped the cup, carefully spilling the tea on the table, making sure the handle rested to the left as always. Only then could I dust the room no one would ever sit in.

In the upstairs bedroom, I tugged at the freshly laundered linens, pulling them over the soft feather mattress, so much like the one I used to have. How I wished to fall into the bed, let my eyes close, and sleep. Perhaps I could wake from this nightmare.

I smoothed the rich red fabric of the bed cover until the bed was perfect. Every morning I ached and strained to make it neat, then I yanked the cover down, creasing the blankets. With my fists I pounded a deep indent into the pillow and tugged it askew.

Everything in each room of the enormous house had to remain exactly as I had found it the day before. Nothing in the house ever changed. It was my job to make sure of it, and I did my job well.

It was infuriating. At times all I wanted to do was walk along the tables and sideboards with my hand out, knocking everything over until I created such a mess no one could possibly put it right.

But I couldn't. I didn't dare. If I lost this job, I would have no home, no food. I'd be out on the streets. So every night, in an intricate exchange, I rotated each candle in the house to ensure that in the morning they'd all seem as if they had never burned.

For all the polishing and dusting, the baron's house remained quiet, cold. It had been frozen as deeply and surely as the ice-covered garden still gripped by the cruel hand of the lingering winter.

I descended the stairs feeling the slow burn of my frustration. Soon enough, Mrs. Pratt would order me to polish five dozen sets of silver spoons no one would ever use.

As I reached the bottom of the steps, I nearly tread on a piece of the broken vase that remained shattered at the foot of the stairs.

I let my boot hover over the delicate shard. Oh, I was tempted, so tempted to kick it straight into the sitting room. Or stomp on all the pieces until there was nothing left but dust. Then perhaps I could finally stop dancing around them every time I had to go up or down the stairs.

In the end, disturbing the shards would only cause me grief, and I knew it. I placed my foot to the side and turned away from the vase. The soft chink of the porcelain on the polished wood floor broke the oppressive silence of the house. A curved piece of the broken vase spun slowly, like a ballerina caught in a dream.

"Bloody hell."

Hands shaking, I scrambled to rearrange the pieces as they should be. I was always too careless when flustered, but never had it hindered my efforts as much as this. The edge of a triangular shard sliced into my middle finger and I let the piece fall to the floor. I cringed as it clattered against the wood, but thankfully it didn't shatter.

My eyes stung as I brought my finger to my mouth.

"Heaven's mercy, Meg. What happened?" Mrs. Pratt's voice sounded like a tree limb breaking under a heavy burden of ice.

The housekeeper fell to her knees by the shards, her full skirts billowing around her.

"They moved." I took a step back to give her a better look. "My skirt brushed them."

"How could you be so careless?"

I felt the flush of anger heat my face. "It was an accident. Why can't we just leave them? It's not as if anyone would notice."

"He's watching," the housekeeper warned, glancing over her shoulder, her pinched expression growing tighter. "You must take care at all times, Meg. He is always watching."

I'd never met the baron, or even seen him, but the thought of him watching every moment crept through my mind like a rat in the dark.

I struggled to my feet, clenching my bleeding hand in my skirts, then ran down the back stairs into the kitchens. Once inside, I took a deep breath and pulled my mop cap from my head. This was insanity, sheer insanity. I'd had enough of it.

I concentrated on stanching my bleeding finger, but a

shifting shadow caught my eye in the flickering light of the cold, empty kitchen. I hoped it wasn't a rat.

The house was modest in comparison to some of the city palaces in St. James, but with its high-walled garden, courtyard, and carriage house, it used to be a stately gem. Now it was dour and faded.

The enormous labyrinth of kitchens, pantries, cellars, and laundry had once provided every conceivable comfort for the elegant family living above. Now the servants' world beneath the stairs remained dark and empty except for the main hearth and a single pantry. How humble the kitchen seemed with rosemary hung by the frosted window, racks of unused pots and pans, a dented teakettle, and the itchy tick filled with straw that served as my bed.

Eerie shadows swayed, cast from the hanging pots clinging to the exposed girders. The kitchen was the only room that was allowed to age, clinging to the last vestiges of vibrancy while the rest of the house remained as lifeless as a tomb.

I reached for the broom, keeping a wary eye on the corner. Two luminous green eyes stared back at me, reflecting the fire in the hearth.

I sighed. It was only Old Tom. The distinguished silver tabby emerged from the shadows with the grace of a duke.

He lifted his chin in a haughty feline acknowledgment of my existence.

Putting down the broom, I turned my attention back to my sliced finger, grabbing a rag to clean the dried blood.

"Meg!" Agnes the cook flopped a meaty hand onto the door frame and pulled her ample body into the kitchen from the passage that led to the pantry beyond. "Meg, could you be a dear and fetch me one of those icicles hanging near the steps?" she asked.

She moved toward the table with her eyes closed, like a great ox stumbling forward while half asleep.

Gracious, she was hungover again. Yet another thing that never seemed to change in this household. With a heavy groan, she fell onto a stool, then let her head fall back and heaved a dramatic sigh.

I snapped the rag away from my cut as I opened the door to the stairs that led up to the small kitchen garden and the courtyard beyond. A new dusting of snow already softened the trail of footprints leading to the garden pot. I stepped in one to save my foot from the cold. It didn't take much effort to knock down one of the brittle daggers of ice and gather it in the rag.

"Thank you, dear." Agnes took the rag then smashed

it against the cooking board with all the delicacy of an axe-wielding executioner.

"Should I track down a hairy dog?" The one that had bitten her had gotten her good. Its name was stale rum, and it wasn't the first time the beast had unleashed its fury on poor Agnes.

Agnes laughed as she placed the ice-filled rag on her head. "Nay, I'm afraid I ran the poor mongrel off last night."

"You drank it all?" Heavens, no wonder she was in a state.

"Don't you fret. A bit of tea will straighten me up."

I crossed the kitchen and carefully closed the heavy oak door that led to the servants' stairs. Mrs. Pratt would be in a fearful mood after having to rearrange the shards. I didn't want Agnes to suffer for it.

"Last night, Pratt had the gall to remind me that I should cook beef stew for this evening's meal," Agnes lamented, placing the lump of icy rag on a new part of her forehead. "As if I haven't made bloody beef stew every Wednesday for nearly eighteen years."

Eighteen years? Had this started so long ago?

What could have driven the baron to wish this on himself for a good third of a man's life? Curiosity gnawed at my thoughts.

No one was supposed to talk about it, so I kept silent. Instead I poured the tea, trying not to think about why these strange souls had decided to remain in this madhouse for longer than I'd been alive. No wonder Agnes stewed herself in swill every night. And poor Mr. Tibbs. The butler wandered around the house as if he were a resident spook of the Tower of London. What had happened so long ago?

Agnes shook her head. "Never you mind."

"I didn't ask," I protested.

"You didn't have to. You had that look about you. This is how the baron wants things, and our purpose in life is to make sure this house is exactly as the baron wants it." Agnes offered me a withered smile. "Best keep curiosity in your pocket. It killed the cat, you know."

I stoked the fire, flinching when a log rolled forward, sending out a spray of embers onto the hearth.

"What's the harm in curiosity?" I asked, though it was more of a thought for myself than a true question. I turned away from the fire and looked up at the cook. "Other than an overabundance of dead cats?"

"Meg." Agnes flopped the ice over her eyes.

"When was the last time you actually saw the baron?" I persisted.

"Oh, I daresay it's been close to seven years now." Agnes leaned back in the chair.

"Seven years? And you never once questioned—"

She sat up, crooking her brow into a deep scowl. "I said, never you mind!"

"This is madness." I turned my attention back to the fire.

"Aye, the madness of our betters, so we must abide it. Get to your chores. I'll save you some tea."

Resigned to the inevitable, I broke off a chunk of stale bread from the remainder of yesterday's loaf and set to my day. Clean the grates, tend the fires, trim the candles, pull the drapes, dust, dust, dust, polish, polish, polish. On and on it went.

Late in the morning, I found myself in the study. I threw open the shutters and pulled back the heavy velvet drapes, letting cold light into the lifeless room. Large flakes of the early spring storm continued to drift past the swirls of frost on the windows. The remnants of the bleak and mournful winter had laid the world under a blanket of white.

I watched the quiet snowfall, wondering if light and happiness had simply abandoned England. Queen Victoria remained in mourning after the death of Prince Albert. She was no longer the queen I remembered from my childhood.

She had been solid, regal. So long as she reigned, all in the world was right and steady. Now she was gone too, hidden away. I didn't know if she'd ever return. Somehow I felt that even if she did, it wouldn't be the same.

Time was supposed to heal all wounds, but what was one to do when time stopped? My life had ground to a halt before it had a chance to begin.

There simply was no way out. Only one month shy of sixteen, I could marry, but whom? I had neither the means nor opportunity to leave the house. Even if I did, I was now a housemaid. Whom should I marry? A servant?

I was raised better. Before the fire, I'd been preparing for my introduction into polite society. Now no man of my true class would ever look at me.

All my education, my talents, had fallen to waste. I could read and write German and French thanks to my Swiss mother. I had a talent for the pianoforte and a good mind for numbers, thanks to my father, who seemed to enjoy teaching me the intricate nature of computation. Now my options were few. I couldn't even find better work. I had no one to recommend me. Since my employer hadn't shown his face in seven years, I doubted anyone ever would.

Escape was impossible. Where would I go? One day I'd

end up silent and dour like Mr. Tibbs, drunk and frustrated like Agnes, or just plain barking mad.

I was of half a mind that Mrs. Pratt maintained her rigid schedule only to keep herself from admitting she was no longer needed. Perhaps the baron had withered and died in one of the upper rooms and Mrs. Pratt was covering up the tragedy to keep her sense of purpose.

Then again, there was no hiding the stark fear in her eyes every time she mentioned our employer.

Her voice slithered through my mind.

He is watching.

An unsettled feeling crept across my shoulders and I looked up, noticing a carved wooden angel in the upper corner where the cornices came together. It had glassy black eyes like the lions at the gate. I didn't know why I stared. It wasn't as if the statue would start to waltz before my eyes. Its cherubic expression never changed. I needed to know things could change.

I needed it like air.

Letting my gaze fall, I moved toward the ornate clock resting in the center of the large mantel. The early spring sunlight glinted off the crystal face.

Its hands had stopped long ago, and the whole of the house had frozen in time when that pendulum came to rest.

I wanted to open the clock, wind it somehow, but I had yet to find the mechanism for bringing it back to life.

Something in my life had to change, but there was only one thing I could call my own. I pressed my hand to my bib, feeling the broken watch push against my heart as I silently left the room.

That evening I sat at the table drying and stacking dishes, thinking about my broken watch while Agnes lumbered around the kitchen like an arthritic goose. Strands of her dark gray hair peeked out from beneath her worn cap as she set the kitchen right for the evening.

"Did you enjoy the stew?" she asked as she straightened the shelves.

"I don't believe I've ever tasted anything quite like it," I teased.

Agnes guffawed. "It's my specialty."

I smiled. "Do you think the groom would be willing to perform a small task?" I asked. It was time to do something about the watch. Every time I touched it to my cheek, I longed to hear it tick.

A knife clattered on the cooking board. "Good heavens, Margaret. Don't you dare go near that carriage house. Do you hear me?" The cook's words boomed in the kitchen, rattling the pots above.

My hand slipped on the dish I was holding. I wasn't expecting so much vehemence. I only wished to repair my watch. "I have something that's broken. Doesn't the groom tend the pots and harnesses?"

"Aye," Cook said, drawing the word out as if it had some deep importance. "He's a *tinker*." Her eyes widened as her mouth set in a frown. She gave me a serious nod.

"Is he dangerous?" I didn't know much about tinkers, nothing at all really. Once again my head started spinning with curiosity.

Agnes threw up her hands and grabbed the old jug she kept near the basin. I wondered what was in it this time, but thought better than to ask. She was agitated enough. "He's a traveler, dear, and a bleedin' Scot at that."

I tried to follow but still didn't see how that should make him some vile creature. "I don't understand."

Agnes sighed and rested her elbow against the cooking board. She used her other hand to bat her apron. "You wouldn't understand, living the way you did."

Now at that, I took offense. "My father's shop on Oxford Street was very respectable."

"Aye, that's the problem. Tinkers have naught to do with respectable. They're wanderers, no better than Gypsies. A good girl like you should stay far clear of such associations. Why the good baron decided to take in a mongrel like that, I haven't a notion. That tinker holds a candle to the Devil, you mark my words."

The thrill of fear coursed through me. I'd never seen the groom. He lived in the carriage house and hardly ever came into the main house. If he did, he was like a shadow, passing silently before I ever caught full sight of him. In my mind he took on a beastly quality that I found strangely compelling.

"How did he come to work here?" I asked.

Agnes flopped onto a stool and leaned forward.

"The baron found him wandering down a road near Blairgowrie years ago. The whelp was calm as anything, just walking, covered in blood. Several miles down the road they came upon his family's wagon, ransacked, the horse gone, and his father murdered in a ditch. Lord Rathford took him in and set him in the stables to help poor old John, God rest his sweet soul." Agnes crossed herself and stared up at the ceiling beams with a wistful look on her crinkled face. Then her eyes turned as sharp as a hawk's. "He is naught but trouble, mark my words."

I couldn't say anything for a moment. All I could think about was a lost and frightened boy wandering down the road alone.

"How old was he?"

"No one knows, exactly, but he was thin as a stick. He couldn't have been more than six." Agnes crossed her arms over her bosom and leaned back.

A deep sadness gripped me and didn't let go. I knew what it was like to feel so alone.

"And he didn't cry at all?" I had cried. I had cried until I had made myself sick with it. I hadn't known how I would endure without the sweet patience of my mother or the cheerful wit of my father. I'd cried until I couldn't cry any more.

Agnes shook her head, the ruffles of her cap swishing against her forehead. "It was unnatural. He couldn't mourn proper for his own family. He didn't talk, neither. Thought he was dumb for years. He's a fair groom, good with horses, but you hear me right, child. He's not to be trusted. You stay far away from that carriage house."

I nodded, but it was an empty promise I already knew I wouldn't keep.

CHAPTER TWO

THE NEXT MORNING WELL BEFORE DAWN, I STOOD AT THE threshold, my fingertips touching the cold brass handle. Every moment I hesitated was another secret moment wasted.

I knew I didn't have much time. If Agnes caught me sneaking off to the carriage house the morning after she told me not to, she would make my life miserable.

There was one rule every kitchen maid knew to the marrow of her bones. Don't anger the cook.

Agnes had a hot temper and knew how to hold a grudge. If she petitioned Mrs. Pratt, she could have me sacked for my cheek. After the incident with the shards, it wasn't as if I were in Mrs. Pratt's good graces either.

The thought of being turned out onto the street terrified me.

A girl with no prospects could end up in the workhouse. Or worse, I could end up working as a dollymop on the street corner, something a proper girl shouldn't even know about, let alone consider.

I shuddered.

Was it worth the risk?

Yes. I pulled the door open. Violent wind buffeted the mounds of snow piled against the ice-covered skeleton of the hedge near the back stairs. I gathered my shawl around my neck, but it was of little use. I shook as I stumbled up the steps and ran across the bleak gardens still shrouded by the thick veil of night.

I kept my head down, but the skin of my cheeks burned with the bitter cold. In the dark I managed to find the large curved handles of the carriage house doors, and struggled to push them open. They didn't budge until I threw all my weight against them, and even then I only managed to squeeze through the gap.

The wind whistled through the door as I pushed it shut. It closed with an ominous boom, leaving me alone in the dark. My hands burned from the cold, so I tucked them under my shawl. A dim light flickered from somewhere deep in the carriage house, outlining the form of an elegant old landau coach that probably hadn't moved in years.

"Is anybody here?" I called into the empty dark.

A bit of ice melted into my boot, sending a shock of chill down to my ankle. I took a moment to shake the rest of the snow off my skirt.

"What are you doin' here?" a low, calm voice asked, though there was no mistaking the subtle edge of anger.

I wheeled around but lost my footing on the damp stone and fell against the door.

A horse neighed, the sharp sound ringing off the stone walls. I stood and faced the man. He held a lantern in front of him, casting him in shadow.

"Are you the groom?" I asked as I stood straighter. Yes, it was early, but no earlier than a groom is expected to rise.

"No," he answered with a very subtle Scottish lilt in his voice. "I'm the horse."

Now I was the one who was vexed. I had come for help, not for biting retorts. I gripped my skirts to keep my hands from shaking as I deliberately ignored his comment. I stared into the light of the lantern without blinking. As my vision adjusted, I caught a glimpse of dark, shadowed eyes beneath thick hair unkempt from sleep. Though clearly strong and tall, he had a long-limbed look of youth. I had thought he would be a grown man, but a shiver ran down my spine as I realized he was not much older than I.

"I need your help," I stated calmly. Aloof civility would be my weapon, and I intended to use it.

He lowered the lantern and leaned against the ornate carriage wheel.

My breath hitched. I couldn't help it. A fluttering began within my heart and took the strength from my legs. Indeed he couldn't be more than seventeen or eighteen years. He had a rugged look, made more so by the deep bruise on his cheek and the cut on his upper lip. Had he been fighting?

Gracious. Agnes was right.

"What?" he asked.

I forgot what I had been talking about. "I beg your pardon?" I responded. He scowled, then touched his knuckle to the cut on his lip.

"Do you need my help, or not?" He set the lantern down on the footboard of the carriage then crossed his arms over his loose shirt.

Heaven's mercy, I had woken him. No wonder he was in a surly mood. At least he'd had the decency to put on some trousers and boots, though his shirt hung out at his waist and his bracers remained slack, hanging by his thighs instead of being properly strapped over his shoulders to keep his trousers up.

I swallowed the lump in my throat. "I need you to repair my watch," I explained.

"You woke me for a watch?"

"Yes, it's important."

"If you need to know the time a'day, 'tis early," he huffed, and I had to grip my skirt tighter to keep from throwing the watch at him.

"It is important to me. I wish to make it work. Now will you help me or not?"

He turned away from me, lazily pulling one strap of his bracers over his shoulder. "What are you willin' to pay me?"

His question stopped me short. "Pay?" It slipped out before I could stop it. I didn't want to reveal that I hadn't thought of payment, but the word had left its mark.

"Aye, pay. You think I work for free?" He cocked his head. I suddenly felt like a beggar clinging to the hem of a rich man's cloak.

"I thought out of kindness, you might—"

"Kindness." He chuckled, but never in my life had I

heard a more bitter sound. Then he turned and walked away.

"Wait!" I demanded, but he continued walking. I lunged forward and grabbed his sleeve. My hand met the unyielding strength of his arm. The fluttering returned, but I stamped it down with all my will. I had to make him see me. I had to make him understand. I needed his help, and I was willing to do just about anything to get it. I tried to bargain.

"I don't know what I can pay, but I'll help with your work when I can. I'll do whatever it takes."

"Whatever it takes?" One of his dark eyebrows rose.

I let go of his arm, incensed that he might think I meant to suggest something improper. "You know what I meant."

"Do I? What would Mrs. Pratt think if she found you here?" He snatched the handle of the lantern and swung it in front of him. I backed away from the hot light. "I'll tell you what she'd think," he continued, though there was no need. "Young foolish ninny, good-for-nothing groom, loft full of hay . . . Are you followin' me?"

Oh, I was already ahead of him. "I will not have you question my moral character."

He chuckled again. "Spoken like the queen herself. You certainly have airs. For as much as you're a prim and proper *maid . . .*" he intoned. I caught his insinuation and it infuriated me. Whom was I supposed to have ruined myself with? Mr. Tibbs? "If Mrs. Pratt finds us," he continued, pressing forward enough that he forced me to take a step back, "we'll both lose our jobs. Did you think about that at all before you ran out here to beg a *kindness* from the tinker?"

He turned his back and strode to the far end of the carriage house, carrying the light with him.

"Arrogant bastard." The vile curse fell too comfortably from my lips as I watched him go.

I managed to get back to the house without arousing any suspicions, then set about my chores with extra vigor. As I unmade the bed again, I poured my frustration into the simple act of yanking the linens out of place.

One thing. I only wanted this one thing. Surely, it was a simple enough task to repair a watch. But no.

I pulled it out and examined the tarnished silver.

What would it have cost him to take a look?

Nothing.

The knowledge that he was my age only made it worse. I had gone for six months feeling all alone in the world, and not fifty feet from the steps was another person I could have talked to, could have become friends with.

If he weren't such a toad.

He was a fellow prisoner of this madhouse. Why didn't he understand?

I tucked the watch back in its place and sat on the bed.

The house was so silent.

He had the horses, living, breathing things to care for. I had an unmade bed, a spilled cup of tea, and a broken watch.

Feeling the heat of my ire in my cheeks, I had to stop thinking of him. I had to go back to the pointless drudgery of my existence. If only I could return to the way it was before, when I didn't know who the groom was.

That night I sat alone in the kitchen watching the fire slowly die on the charred stone of the hearth. I took out the watch once again and let it spin in the dim light of the fire.

Could I repair it? I had spent hours as a child watching my father work with his delicate instruments. He had such remarkable hands. Unbidden, the sight of his blackened hand in the ash came to mind. I shook my head, but my eyes suddenly stung.

He had made the most amazing things with those hands and his simple tools, but he had forbidden me from touching anything in his shop. As a child, I had a tendency to use his tools to take things apart, yet never managed to set them right again. It drove my father to fits. I couldn't bear the thought of dismantling the watch in my attempt to repair it, and having it in pieces.

I rubbed my thumb over the tarnish. I could clean it.

My heart pounded even as I thought about polishing the watch. Cleaning the watch wouldn't undo the destruction of my life. It couldn't be undone.

Of course it couldn't be undone. That didn't mean the watch had to remain as I had found it. It could be beautiful, even if it never worked again. I could do that. I could change that.

My hesitation seemed silly. I was clinging to something that barely made sense to me anymore. I needed to change something. I could change this.

No, it would not bring my parents back. No, it would not make me feel as if things had returned to the way they had been.

But I knew in my heart it was time to move forward.

I took the cloth I used to polish the cutlery and rubbed the watch.

A glint of silver shone through. It caught the light of the fire and gleamed as if it were alive. Dark ash clung to the grooves of the etchings, painting each line in dramatic black. I took a closer look, compelled. The etchings almost looked like an ornate compass rose with four sharp points for each direction and a second set of smaller points between.

I held it firmly in my hand, vigorously rubbing the life back into it. The silver grew warm in my palm, as if it belonged there.

It was no longer my father's watch. It was mine. I would care for it. I would keep it, and I would make it work again.

Turning it over, I began to clean the back. With the first rub of the cloth, I noticed the tiny imprint of my grandfather's mark. An anchor with two chains, there was no mistaking it. Papa had made this watch.

Swirling lines danced around the outer edge of the watch. In the center a circular design that reminded me of a three-petal flower had been engraved on a raised button of sorts. It was askew somehow. It seemed to me that one of the petals should have pointed toward the latch, but it did not, not by any means.

Still, it was beautiful.

I thought about my dear sweet grandfather, and found myself wondering if he had done all the etching himself. Papa had died about three years before the fire. I still mourned him as deeply as I mourned my parents.

Holding the watch, I settled in for bed. I tucked myself under my worn blanket, but I couldn't find comfort. Every bone in my body ached with soreness from my work.

Shifting on the lumpy sack of straw, I tried to find a bit

of relief, but something pressed into the small of my back. I turned. It still pressed into my side.

Blasted lump.

Climbing out of bed, I lifted the edge of the tick and reached beneath it with some trepidation. It wouldn't be the first time I found a nest of rodents in my bed. My fingertips brushed something soft, fabric. I pulled the lump of material closer and the warm scent of leather surrounded me.

Shirts!

Someone had hidden them where only I would find them.

With haste, I pulled them from beneath the bed and inspected them. There were six total, worn, handmade, and very old.

My finger poked through a hole beneath the arm of the one I was holding. Another had a missing button. On another, the seam at the collar had begun to unravel. They all desperately needed repair and laundering.

I smiled. I couldn't help it. The tinker had given me a challenge and I accepted it gladly. I couldn't fetch my sewing kit soon enough. Hope threaded through my heart as I began to stitch the first shirt.

Perhaps I'd hear the watch tick after all.

CHAPTER THREE

I STAYED UP AS LATE AS MY EYES WOULD ALLOW AND mended the shirts. Working past the point of exhaustion, I tied off my final knot, then washed the shirts and hung them before the fire. I smiled. It was done. I must have stabbed my poor fingers more than the fabric, but it was worth it. Utterly spent, I fell asleep.

I didn't know what woke me, only that I'd started awake with my heart in my throat. Good heavens. It was morning and Agnes would be up at any moment. Something clattered in the corner of the kitchen. The tinker's shirts hung proudly before the fire, proclaiming my insurrection like a bloody Jolly Roger.

I leapt to my feet desperate to stash the shirts. In a kitchen filled with nooks for things to hide, I couldn't settle on a single place to be rid of them.

There! I grabbed the washtub, threw the shirts underneath, and turned it over.

I snatched my dress off the peg by the hearth. Thankfully, I was in the habit of sleeping in all my underclothes, even my corset, for warmth. I pulled the stays tight and threw my dress over my head, my fingers flying up the buttons on the front.

"Have the tea on yet?" Agnes asked, rolling her shoulders and yawning as she emerged from the passage.

"Not yet." I dropped to my knees by the fire and jabbed at the embers trying to get them to spark. My eyes drifted to the tub.

I tried to look away. If I looked at it, Agnes might notice.... One of the sleeves peeked out from beneath it!

The fire flared to life and I jumped away, backing toward the tub, but Agnes beat me to it.

"Wait." I held my hand out to stop her. Then I bit my tongue as she turned around and sat on the tub like a great bullfrog on an awkward toadstool.

"My, you've gotten impertinent. Best mind yourself, girl,

you don't wish to lose this position and I'm your superior. I shouldn't have to wait for my tea."

"Yes, missus." I ducked my head even as I felt the flush of heat in my face. I tried to look submissive, but on the inside my relief and the tickle of absurd laughter nearly choked me.

She was sitting right atop them.

How would I ever get them out from beneath her enormous . . .

"Thank the dear Lord it's market day today," Agnes declared as she grabbed a pail and began peeling potatoes.

"Indeed." I coughed. The urge to laugh had gripped my ribs, and I found it difficult to breathe. It felt good to have a secret. And the secret was certainly safe beneath Agnes's voluminous—skirts.

I felt more alive than I had in months.

Mrs. Pratt burst through the door and marched across the kitchen like a stuffy Beefeater. All she needed was a Tudor bonnet, a halberd, and some poor prisoner to guard at the Tower.

If I wasn't careful, that wretched prisoner would be me.

"I'm off to the butcher," she announced. "We haven't enough beef for the stew."

That just about did me in. I choked, and then coughed

until tears came. I felt I would burst of laughter if I couldn't escape soon.

"Heavens, Meg. Are you well?" Mrs. Pratt asked.

I sniffed, then held my breath. "Quite," I forced out.

She crinkled her thin nose as she looked to Agnes. "Make sure all is in order by the time I return."

Agnes nodded. As soon as Mrs. Pratt thumped up the stairs, Agnes turned to me. "I'll be stepping out for a bit, if you don't mind. Keep to your chores, will you?"

"Yes, missus." I couldn't believe it. Freedom was within my grasp. I'd be able to return the shirts that morning.

Trembling with excitement, I waited for Agnes to abandon her post on the washtub. I had no idea what she was up to, but I enjoyed the knowledge that I wasn't the only one who wished for a brief escape.

After Agnes had been gone more than half an hour, I gathered the mended and laundered shirts and bounded up the stairs, nearly slipping on the ice.

The sun shone bright, so bright I couldn't see, but the kiss of it felt warm and welcoming, a sign that perhaps winter would not last forever.

Careful to tread in the boot prints of the others who had passed to and from the carriage house, I made my way across the snowy garden. Icicles dripped off the roof, glittering in the sunlight as they reached down over the twining branches of dormant ivy clinging to the stone. They shone as silver as my watch, the ice catching the light and transforming it into something breathtaking.

I pushed open the heavy doors with less trouble now that there was no wind to contend with. Within the sanctuary of the carriage house, the faint rhythmic sound of a brush kept time as a soothing melody floated through the air. It came from the stalls at the far end.

I listened for a moment to the clear voice of the groom. The melody was sad, haunting in that lonely way that makes all things fall quiet and listen. I didn't understand the strange language he sang. I didn't have to.

There was no time to dally. Agnes or Mrs. Pratt could return at any minute.

I needed to leave the shirts and get back to the house. Another confrontation with the surly groom would ruin what progress I'd made in our unspoken agreement.

But I couldn't leave the shirts anywhere. Mrs. Pratt would see them when she returned with the cart. Biting my lip, I crept deeper into the carriage house.

When I reached the corner that separated the stables

from the main body of the carriage house, I paused, peeking around the worn stone.

The groom's large hands slid down the neck of the old seal-colored gelding with affection and care. My heart hammered in my chest as I watched the sleepy-eyed horse tilt his back hoof up in utter contentment. At least the groom was dressed this time in a proper, if faded, brown waistcoat, though he had his shirtsleeves rolled up to his elbows.

"Like sneaking around, do you?" the groom stated without ever looking up.

"If that's my greatest shortcoming, I'm hardly the worst sinner in this household." I lifted my chin, determined not to let him get the better of me this time.

He chuckled as he tossed the brush into a bucket. Patting the swaying back of the gelding, he turned and looked at me.

"Do you want your shirts, or not?" I managed to say the words without much of a tremble in my voice, though I couldn't quite move my feet without fear I'd stumble. Finally, I composed myself and stepped around the corner with a confidence I didn't feel.

"What's your name, lass?" He grabbed a cloth from the bucket and rubbed the gelding's face.

"Margaret Whitlock. Everyone here calls me Meg." As

soon as I said it, I questioned the familiarity of letting him use my given name, but this was hardly proper society. He was the groom. I was the maid. There were different rules in this world.

The beginning of a smile pulled at his wounded lip. "William MacDonald. No one here calls me anything at all, but you can call me Will if you want." He wiped his hands as he approached.

I fought the urge to step back as he strode toward me. He didn't stop until he'd forced me to look up at him. A lock of his dark hair had fallen over his forehead and he pushed it away from his eye with his knuckle.

"I brought your shirts and some of the treacle tart from yesterday's tea." Why did I find it so hard to speak? I had to force myself to remember that he'd been rude and insolent to me the last time I'd seen him. I thrust the bundle of shirts toward him with stiff arms, but he didn't move back a step.

"Treacle?" He smiled fully, and I almost dropped the shirts. They slipped out of my hands and I bent forward to catch them, crumpling them together until his hand caught mine.

I held my breath.

Slowly he helped me rise. Then he took the small rag-wrapped tart that I had crushed somewhat inelegantly against my chest.

My gaze met his. "Consider it a kindness," I mumbled. He just stared, his dark brown eyes so deep, I . . .

I dropped the shirts on the floor and retreated toward the door. My face felt on fire as I heard the heavy beat of my heart in my ears.

"Meg, wait," he called.

His voice stopped me, trapping me in the spot like a wild bird in a snare. My heart fluttered, beating wildly as I clung to the heavy latch.

He crossed the distance between us. With a gentle touch, he lifted my hand from the door. "Let's take a look at your watch."

I took a deep breath to steady my nerves. "Mrs. Pratt will be home soon."

Will smiled. "Aye, but Old Nick knows when Little Nancy is near. He'll give us fair warning." He winked, then pulled me deeper into the carriage house, leading me back toward the stables. "Come, Meg. Share a bit of tart with me." He motioned to a worn chair by a small fat-bellied stove in the corner.

I perched on the end of it but found my toe tapping in

a rapid and unladylike way. I stepped on it with my other foot. He only wanted to help. It's what I'd asked of him. I gathered my skirts, bunching the fabric over my apron. Will rolled over a barrel that had been cut in half to form a large tub and turned it down to make a small table near the stove. He grabbed a stool with a mismatched leg and eased down beside me.

We sat in silence as I watched him break the tart and hand me a piece. It was a bit of a mess without any proper plates or utensils, but it tasted heavenly.

I closed my eyes. "This is good," I murmured through my mouthful, then immediately looked at him abashed, until I noticed his cheek overstuffed with tart. I laughed.

"Aye," he agreed, eating what remained of his portion with another single bite. "You're lucky."

"You think so?" I broke off a dainty piece of mine and tried to look elegant while eating in such a barbaric manner.

"You get to eat this every week." He shrugged. "I get left over beef scraps and whatever I can manage on my own."

"I've never had this before," I admitted.

"Why not?" He picked up a cloth and wiped his hands.

"We're not allowed to eat it. The cook makes one every Thursday, and I have to throw it away uneaten every Friday."

I finished the last of my piece then wiped my hands on my apron.

"Why?"

"I thought you'd know." I certainly couldn't find an excuse for such a waste of food and effort.

He looked down and scuffed the floor with his shoe. "John never talked about it. Not once. Told me not to mind what goes on in the house, so I didn't."

That was the crux of the matter. No one ever spoke of it. I felt as if all the pieces of a great puzzle were laid out before me, but I couldn't see the picture. "All I know is this is how the baron wants it."

Will sighed as if he understood. "So, do you have the watch?"

I reached to my neck and his dark eyes followed the motion of my hand. Slowly I pulled the watch out from beneath the front of my apron, but his gaze remained fixed on my bib. I tilted my head and he snapped his eyes to the timepiece spinning between us.

Will reached up and stopped the hypnotic movement with the tips of his fingers.

I paused. I hardly knew the groom at all. Could I trust him? He'd clearly been in a brawl, and he'd just admitted that he had to scrape for his own food. What if he took the watch and sold it to some seedy duffer?

I hesitated, pulling the watch back just enough that it broke from the tips of his fingers.

Will dropped his hand. His gaze turned icy.

"Go back to the house, lass." He placed his hands on his knees and stood, towering above me.

"Wait." I couldn't repair it on my own. "Please, I'm sorry."

I quickly placed the watch on the barrel and pulled my hand back, but I couldn't fight the urge to reach toward it again. I had to stop myself. Pulling my fingers into a tight fist, I brought my hand to my lap, but I couldn't take my eyes from the watch.

Will walked away. I felt my heart twisting. He loosened Old Nick's cross ties and led him back to the stall, then slammed the stall shut and turned on me. I'd never seen such anger in a face. "Either you trust me, or you don't."

Everything Agnes had said about him rushed through my mind. But it didn't matter. I had no choice. I had to trust him. He'd given me no reason not to. Still it was difficult. The watch was all I had.

Enough. I had to stop thinking before I drove myself clean out of my mind. "I apologize. It's very precious to me. I have a hard time letting go. I need your help." I looked him in the eye, determined to show him the sincerity of my words. "I can't repair it on my own."

"Have you tried?" He crossed his arms.

"I can't bring myself to. I don't want to break it." I looked down at the watch. "I break a lot of things."

Will huffed. "Mrs. Pratt must be fond of you."

I tried to quell my nerves as I looked up at him. "Immensely."

He chuckled as he grabbed the stool and sat down again. I tried to gather my wits, but when Will reached out and took the watch, I felt an empty hole open up inside me, as if he'd just picked up my beating heart and was holding it in his hands.

Will turned the watch over and over, smoothing his finger across what appeared to be the latch, or the hinge, I wasn't sure. He pulled a short knife out of his boot and I winced.

"Easy." His voice dropped to a low and musical tone he probably used on the horses. His hands closed over the watch as he set the edge of the knife in the seam. With a swift *pop*, he cracked it open as if he were shucking a clam.

I felt as if I'd just been jabbed in the ribs, but I forced myself to remain calm.

His expression turned quizzical as he squinted in the dim light. "I don't think this is a watch."

"What else could it be?" I reached forward to grab it then pulled my hand back. My fingertips came to rest on his, but he didn't look up. Instead we both stared at the strange mechanism unfolding in his hands.

Like an odd shining blossom, three silver structures rose up on a short brass stem as Will opened the cover. Each petal's edge had a different pattern of irregularly shaped teeth. The shape resembled the flower embossed on the back, but with sharper edges and minuscule gears.

"What is it?" I had never seen anything like it before in my father's shop.

"I don't know." Will delicately flipped the device over. "Look at this."

The round nub had protruded out of the back, lifting the image of the three-petal flower out from the casing to create what looked like a button.

"Press it," I urged. My shock had dissipated in favor of raw excitement. I had no idea what would happen, but I felt like a child waiting for the jack to spring forth from the box. Will pushed the button, and with a click, the gears began to move. They twisted and spun as the mechanism turned in a slow circle.

Music, the clear tones of tiny bells, reached out to me. Though the tune was delicate, it was as if I could hear my grandfather's rumbling voice singing to me and only me.

"Do you know the song?" Will asked, but his voice barely broke through the haze of my memories. I could see my fingers awkwardly pressing the keys of the pianoforte while Papa laughed. I could feel white skirts swirling around my legs as I stood on my grandfather's feet and danced.

It was a song we had created, a song only the two of us had known.

"It's my grandfather, my Papa," I whispered. "He must have made this for me."

"'Tis a sweet music box," Will offered. I couldn't say anything in response. The song faltered and he inspected the tiny gears. After removing a bit of grit, he closed the musical locket again. It folded elegantly, the flower sinking neatly into the heart of the locket as the cover closed over it.

He handed it back to me and I brought it to my chest. What had been important to me was now priceless. Will had given me something no one else ever could.

"Thank you."

A shy smile spread over his face. "It were nothin'."

He stood and replaced his knife in his boot. Old Nick lifted his head and whinnied.

"You'd better get back to the house."

I touched my eyes with the back of my wrist and nodded even as Will opened the side door. Keeping the locket pressed tight to my chest, I ran back to the steps.

The bright sun felt warm on my back, soaking into me as I thought about Papa and his precious gift.

I nearly slipped down the stairs to the kitchens, catching myself on the door. With shaking hands, I placed the locket back around my neck and tucked it under my apron. My brief freedom was over.

I opened the door and ducked into the kitchen.

A meaty hand caught my shoulder. My legs almost gave out as Agnes slammed me back against the closed door.

"Where have you been?" she demanded. Her bloodshot eyes bulged out of her ruddy face, laden with accusation.

I was caught.

CHAPTER FOUR

"YOU WENT OUT TO THAT CARRIAGE HOUSE, DIDN'T you?" Agnes barked, and the sound rattled my bones. She'd never shouted at me before. Her grip tightened, squeezing my arm until I feared it would break. I tried not to breathe as the foul odor on Agnes's breath nearly choked me.

"I ate a bit of the tart, I'm sorry!" My mind worked furiously as I tried to think through the lie. I prayed a bit of crumb from the tart clung to my dress. "It crumbled on my apron and I went outside to shake it off for the birds."

I held deathly still, like a pup caught by the scruff. The suspicion in Agnes's eyes burned, then her gaze whipped to the window.

My heart beat once, twice. A cart's wheels rumbled on the stones of the drive.

Agnes paled, looking uncertain, then eased her hold on my arm. Tucking her nose against her shoulder, she smelled her own dress. She reeked of cigar smoke and liquor. I'd never been more thankful that the cook had her own demons to hide.

"Prigged some tart, eh?" She released my dress. I took a step to the side trying to move clear of her arm's reach. "That tart is not for eating."

"But it's such a waste." The more I could get her to focus on the tart, the more likely she'd forget about her initial suspicion. "You work so hard to make it, shouldn't someone enjoy it?"

She let out a heavy breath, and I had to stifle a cough from the odor. "It's not for eating because it wasn't eaten." Agnes shook her head. "You should know this by now. Nothing can change from that day."

"The day the baroness died?" I didn't know where the question came from. It just burst out of me.

Agnes's eyes grew wide, her gaze more clear and sober than I'd ever seen it. "What do you know of it?"

I felt my heart drop into my boots. Dear Lord, I was right. It was as if all the pieces had suddenly arranged themselves before my eyes, and it was only in this moment of shock that I could see clearly. The bed I'd made every day, the vase, the teacup, the bath, the rose petals, the powder lid. All the things that were to remain askew in the house, they were all a woman's things. I'd been playing lady's maid to the memory of a woman who had been dead longer than I'd been alive.

"I know nothing," I whispered. I just wanted to leave, to think about this new revelation on my own.

"Listen, girl. We never speak of that day. Never. Do you hear me?"

I nodded.

"You'd best get to your work and stay at it," Agnes warned. I hurried toward the door, my mind reeling. "Don't come down for tea. You've taken more than your share already."

The rest of the day, thoughts of the baroness consumed me. Every room I wandered through, all I could see was her touch. The teacup that had spilled in the sitting room, it was hers. It looked as if she could have just overturned it, not as if eighteen years had passed.

She was at the heart of all of this, and for the first time I began to feel I understood my employer.

What had happened to his wife that terrible day? My

racing thoughts kept sleep away that night. The house creaked and groaned. I felt the shadows fill with the presence of the dead.

I didn't know what drew me out of bed, but I couldn't ignore my restlessness. Gathering my petticoats, I threw a shawl over my shoulders. I lit a candle from the glowing embers of the fire and crept through the dark house.

As I passed the study, a flash of something pale caught my eye. With trepidation, I entered the dark room. The light of my candle caught the crystal of the ornate clock on the mantel, but my eyes were drawn to the portrait hanging above the clock.

A young woman with lovely dark hair and deep soulful eyes rested her hand on the back of a chair. Elegant in a white ball gown, she stared into the room with a sad smile on her softly painted lips.

I'd seen her a hundred times. There were a lot of portraits of stuffy aristocrats in the house. I hadn't paid much mind to any of them until now. Now I could *see* her, the baroness. She was the reason that time had stopped and I was bound in servitude to madness.

What a strange thought, that this woman had the power to stop time. She was beautiful, truly lovely. I was a mouse by comparison, with my dust-brown braids and gray eyes. She looked delicate, like a porcelain doll on a shelf, the kind no child plays with for fear it will break. I opened the shutter to let in more light. The full moon shone on the snow in the garden and cast a haunting silver light across the mantel.

My grandfather's musical locket fell against my heart as I looked at the baroness.

"What happened to you?" I asked. I waited for a long moment as if the portrait could tell me. She only stared. It was foolish, and I was foolish for being up so late. I placed a hand on the mantel and looked at the clock as if it could still tell me the time, but its hands remained frozen.

That's when I noticed it.

The gold medallion in the center of the clock had an etching on it, a flower with three petals.

Just like my locket.

My heart beat heavy in my chest, flooding my ears with the sound. A chill raced down my neck as I reached up and touched the medallion on the clock.

It swiveled to the side, revealing a brass wheel with an indent the size and shape of the structure that had risen out of my locket.

I dropped my hand and took a step back. My throat tightened. I tried to swallow. What was this?

The clock drew me back like a flame beckoning a hapless moth. For the first time, I noticed my grandfather's mark on the base. Papa had made this clock. The baron had said he'd known my family. He must have commissioned the clock when Papa still ran my father's shop.

The locket wasn't merely a locket. It was a key!

I grabbed the locket from about my neck and cracked it open. The silver flower rose up, and I knew immediately what to do. I fitted it into the brass wheel and pressed the button on the back of the locket.

The song played as the wheel turned. To my astonishment a panel rose just beneath the medallion, revealing a very small set of keys, like a tiny pianoforte.

As each note of my grandfather's song rang clear and bright in the darkness, I looked over my shoulder, worried someone might come through the door at any moment.

With a click, the song stopped right in the middle of a musical phrase. My heart stopped too, even as my mind continued the melody of the song.

What was I supposed to do?

Like a ghost whispering in the room, I could almost hear my grandfather's voice.

Finish it.

One by one I delicately pressed the keys in the clock. I hesitated as my finger hovered over the last note in the phrase, and I wondered what would happen if I pressed it. I could feel the tension in my hands. My fingertip quivered. That final note rang through my mind, daring me to play it.

I let my finger fall.

A heavy clunk echoed from somewhere within the wall behind the clock. I jumped back, pulling my key out of the clock.

What had I done? Whatever I had broken wouldn't be easily restored. I spun around, certain the noise must have woken someone in the house. Then I heard the groaning of gears moving and a grinding sound like an old millstone turning.

I stumbled away, ready to run to the kitchens. A soft puff of ash floated up from the fireplace. I shut the key and the flower folded, hiding itself once again.

Before my eyes, the stones in the back wall of the fireplace retreated, almost as if they were melting into the wall, opening up a hidden passage. I inched forward, grasping my candle tighter. A chilling breeze like a dying breath escaped from the opening.

It ruffled my petticoats as I leaned under the mantel. I

gasped as the light from my candle illuminated a narrow spiral staircase descending into the inky shadows below. The dank scent of mold and dust wafted up from the depths.

I paused, listening again for any sound, any sign that I had disturbed the sleeping household. There was nothing but stillness, and I felt an irresistible urge to explore the passage.

I ducked through the fireplace, bending low to keep from brushing against the cinder-blackened walls. The smell of ash clung to my skin as I found myself standing on the edge of the first stair. It felt like ice beneath my stocking-clad feet.

There were probably rats.

I took a step, sheltering my candle, my only source of light.

It could be a passage to an old catacomb.

I took another step.

There might be skeletons and all sorts of unpleasantness.

My foot moved forward again.

I would be trapped in the dark, buried forever. No one would hear me. No one could help.

With each step into the darkness, my mind wandered farther and farther down horrifying paths, yet my feet continued their steady descent.

Secret passages were secret because people wished to hide

something. Whatever lay so far beneath the house, my grand-father must have known about it. His clock was the unlock-ing mechanism for the entrance.

Somehow I knew my Papa wouldn't have gone to such intricate trouble to hide some rats and a bunch of rotten bones.

Yet as the darkness pressed around me, I had only my small flame to ward off the complete and utter blackness. With the cold stone walls of the narrow stair pressing me in, I felt as if I were descending into my grave.

The stairs ended at a narrow tunnel with a vaulted stone ceiling. It wasn't even wide enough for two people to walk abreast.

My hand brushed the wall as I slowly stepped forward. After the twisting stair, I'd lost all sense of direction and couldn't tell if the tunnel led beneath the basements of the house, or to another place altogether.

I looked back but could no longer see the stair. With no other direction to go, I continued until the tunnel ended at a heavy wooden door that was slightly ajar.

Pushing it as hard as I could with my shoulder, I peered inside to the room beyond, unable to believe my eyes.

CHAPTER FIVE

AT FIRST, ALL I COULD SEE WAS THE GLITTERING OF hundreds of tiny lights. They seemed to float in the darkness, dimmed as if by a thin veil. It took me a moment to realize they were reflections of my candle shining back at me from metal and glass coated in a fine layer of dust.

An ornate lamp sat on a small table just inside the door. With haste I lit it, grateful that it still held oil. I replaced the large red glass globe over the flame as the room filled with warm light.

"Good heavens," I whispered. I couldn't help myself. I'd entered some sort of workshop. The room was filled with fantastic machines, their form unlike anything I'd ever seen. Great wheels, some larger than I, rested against the wall amid elegantly formed arms of brass and great curved plates of copper.

I felt as if I'd just stepped within the inner workings of one of my father's clocks and was caught amid the gears.

I crept deeper into the workshop, drawn toward the machines. Shelves cluttered with odd bits and parts lined the walls. I peered at each beautifully and carefully crafted trinket, trying to determine its purpose.

An imposing armchair was nestled near two bookcases in the corner. Just to the other side of the chair rested a lovely bassinet lined with delicate white lace.

How odd.

A large table ran along one wall, its surface covered with dusty papers. I lit a second lamp on the table and peered at the documents.

They were drawings, hundreds of intricately detailed designs of some great machine. It looked a bit like an egg. Only the egg had windows all along the top and sat within an imposing cage of wheels and gears.

One of the drawings caught my eye. It showed the layout of the interior of the egg. I marveled at the instruments and controls. It looked as if the egg were some sort of vehicle. Where would one go traveling by egg?

A twisted contraption, like a nest of brass pipes, squatted

at the edge of the table. A large oval peering glass as black as obsidian was nestled in the center, and a turn-crank jutted from one side. No cobwebs had formed between the crank and the machine, and the light glinted off the polished glass orb.

I drew closer. With some trepidation, I reached out and turned the crank. A light flickered deep within the smoky glass, and as it grew brighter, I saw a clear but colorless image of the study and the fireplace. Confused, I leaned in to inspect the image more closely. I couldn't figure what use it would be to have a picture of the study. Then I noticed the back of the fireplace. It was open.

My blood ran cold. I didn't want to believe it, but as I looked at the image, Mrs. Pratt's words echoed over and over in my mind.

He's always watching.

It couldn't be. Such things weren't possible. Just below the glass was a knob. I turned it. With a hushed *snick* the image blinked out, then returned. This time it showed me the area before the front gate and the entrance to the carriage house.

My fear turned to dread as I realized I was peering through the eyes of one of the lions at the gate. I turned the knob again, and the image switched to the perspective of the other lion, the one staring toward the street.

I watched as a man in a dark overcoat lingered near the gate as if studying the wall. His collar was turned high, and a top hat pulled low to obscure his face. Then he walked with a jerky gait, and the glass revealed his movement.

Dear God, with an invention such as this, Rathford could see everything.

I would be discovered. In a rush I turned the knob and reset the image to show the study. Grabbing my candle, I turned from the table, but in my haste, I brushed a piece of paper. It fluttered to the ground.

Snatching up the paper to replace it near a smudged handprint, I caught a glimpse of the writing.

In my shock, I nearly dropped the candle. It was my grandfather's handwriting. I was sure of it. He'd taught me my letters, and the script was as familiar to me as his voice.

My hands shook as I read.

Rathford,

I cannot begin to express my distress over recent events. You've opened Pandora's box, and it will not easily be closed. In my heart, I still do not believe you wish it closed, and so I fear I cannot trust you. You once confessed that I was your most beloved instructor. You claimed me like another father to you. With such sentiment in your heart, please heed my advice.

Four of our number are now gone, and more may follow. There's already been one attempt on my life, and I refuse to stand here and wait for death. There's a traitor among us, someone willing to murder all those who know anything of the abomination you manipulated us into creating.

In spite of your letter protesting Charles's accusations, I find logically, you are the one with the most at stake. While I do not wish to believe you capable of murder, I confess my mind has turned to such dark conclusions.

There's something I must do for Simon Pricket in the West of London. After I finish, I shall disappear in earnest. I find being dead has certain uses. As you are the only one who knows I am indeed alive, if anyone searches for me, I shall know you are the one who betrayed us. The matter of the traitor will be settled.

You cannot open the box again, my friend. It's time to say our goodbyes and let the dead remain so. Relinquish the heart. It is the only way.

Sincerely,

Henry

For a long time I couldn't move. All I could hear was a loud rushing in my ears, as if I'd suddenly been thrust into the center of a storm.

The letter was dated August 17, 1858. My grandfather had died in June of that year. I flipped the letter over, inspecting it for any detail that could tell me more. On the back, a seal had been pressed in red wax, the now familiar three-petal flower with the letters S.O.M.A. imprinted just beneath it.

I placed the letter back on the table before I could give in to the urge to rip it to pieces.

How could he? How could he let me believe he was dead? How could he abandon me?

My eyes stung as I extinguished the lamps and ran out the door, through the tunnel, and up the stairs. I would not cry. I had mourned for my grandfather, and I would not cry again.

He was alive, and he hadn't cared about the fire. He hadn't cared about the death of his own son. He hadn't cared that I'd been left alone with nothing.

I ducked out the secret door and burst into the study. Yanking the key from around my neck, I threw it into the ashes of the long-dead fire.

I didn't want to see it again. I didn't ever want to hear that song again.

A hollow whistle drifted up from the stairs.

I glanced up at the cherub with the glassy eyes. I had no way of knowing what Rathford could see, or when he was using his glass. I couldn't leave the door open. If the baron knew I'd been sneaking around his secret workshop, that I'd read the letter, and that I knew my grandfather suspected him of murder . . .

Fear closed in, and the air itself seemed to grow heavy.

With haste, I pulled the key from the ashes, gently rubbing it with the hem of my petticoat. It didn't feel right not to have it around my neck. It'd been important enough to my father that it had been the one thing he'd tried to save from the fire. It was possible he had died for it.

It was mine now, and I was the only one who could use it.

I placed it in the clock and pressed the button. The song played and keys revealed themselves as before.

I played the notes without hesitation this time, and with relief watched the fireplace return to normal.

As I entered the kitchens, the house remained still. Nothing had changed. I stopped on that thought—outwardly, nothing had changed, but in truth I felt everything had. I eased onto my tick and pulled the blanket to my neck, but my mind found no comfort.

I couldn't believe my grandfather was involved in such a scheme. He'd always been so sweet and odd. He was the type to hide trinkets and draw maps to them, not the type to be involved with murderous plots.

There was no way to know if he was alive or if the murderer had found him. I never knew the details of his supposed death. I only knew that his carriage had gone into the river. They'd never found the body. That must have been the first attempt on his life that he mentioned in his letter. It had happened three years before the fire struck the shop on Oxford.

Papa could have traveled anywhere by then, and he likely had never heard about the fire. If he had left the country, how could he know? He could be out there still thinking we were safe and happy on Oxford Street. If he returned, he wouldn't know where to find me.

Then there was the question of why the baron took me in. Perhaps he felt guilty and wanted to make up for whatever falling-out they'd had. Unless he was keeping me to lure my grandfather back.

The memory of the giant clock wheels and arms filled my mind.

What was S.O.M.A.?

Endless questions plagued me until nearly dawn. I still hurt. Deep in my heart I ached. In the end, the one thought that rose above all the others was that my grandfather might be alive out there somewhere.

He was the only one who could answer the swarm of questions buzzing through my mind. I had to find him, but where to start?

Asking the baron was out of the question. I had to begin with the last person who had seen my grandfather alive, Simon Pricket.

How was I to find this man in all of London? How could I begin such a search? I had no clue to his occupation or location. The only way to start was to leave the mansion and ask questions about town. I had no opportunity to do so.

I needed help.

I needed Will.

CHAPTER SIX

IT WAS A FULL THREE DAYS BEFORE I COULD ESCAPE TO the carriage house. At every moment I felt I was being watched. During the day, Agnes scrutinized everything I did. Whatever friendly rapport we had shared was gone, vanished under the dark glare of suspicion.

Day and night, thoughts of the baron haunted my every move. I still didn't see him. In all respects, nothing in the house had changed, but I felt the threat of his presence now in a way I never had before. I found myself searching out glints of black glass and wondering if they were part of the spy glass. My only recourse was to work hard and diligently to disappear into the routine of the house, so no one would notice me or think to question what I knew.

It was well past midnight of the third day when I finally dared to sneak out of the house. The weather had grown warmer, bringing with it heavy rain that melted the snow and turned the path to the carriage house into muddy soup. It was dark, too dark for the lion's eyes to see me move across the courtyard in my black dress. I held my skirts with great care, fearing the mud would mark my guilt on my hem.

All was still as I pushed through the carriage house door. I hurried to the stables, holding my candle high.

"Will?" My voice came out as a hushed squeak. A horse swished its tail. "Will?" I tried again.

A hand grabbed my shoulder, spinning me around. I tried to scream but another hand clamped over my mouth. I slammed against the stall door, a hard body pinning me to the wood. My candle fell to the floor, the holder clattering to the hard bare stone. The stable plunged into total darkness.

"Have you gone barking mad?" Will whispered near my ear. I felt his hot breath slide over my neck as he eased his hold and lowered his hand from my mouth, but he didn't back away.

His body pressed against mine, and even through the layers of clothing, I felt the heat of him.

"Will . . . ," I stammered.

"Hush," he scolded. "You're going to get us both sacked. Get back to the house."

"Please," I whispered. "I need your help."

He stiffened, then let go, retreating from me. I grabbed the front of his shirt. My fingertips brushed smooth warm skin, and I nearly lost my grip on the fabric.

"Let go, Meg." His hand closed over mine, his touch gentle in spite of the warning in his voice.

"I can't." I dropped my head and my forehead touched his shoulder. "Hear me out. I'm not here to cause trouble."

He took a step back, shaking off my hold and leaving me alone in the dark. "You've caused enough trouble. I'm not going to lose the only home I've known for you."

"Did Lord Rathford discover us?" I held on to the stall door to steady myself.

"No."

I almost collapsed to the floor in my relief. For as frightened as I'd been the last few days, I didn't want to be thrown out onto the street either.

I could see the outline of Will in the dark. He turned.

"That doesn't mean he won't. Coming here in the day is one thing, night is another."

"I had no other choice." I took a step toward him, leaving the safety of the door. Adrift in darkness, I took another step to close the gap between us.

"Why are you here?" he demanded, and I retreated, flattening my hands against the worn wood.

"There's a man named Simon Pricket." I wished I could tell him more, but I couldn't bring myself to. I felt I was in danger for knowing what I did. I didn't want him to be in jeopardy as well. "I need you to help me find him."

Even as I said it, I feared I was drawing Will in too far, asking for his help to pull me out of a net that could easily catch him, too.

"I don't believe this." He crossed his arms.

"You can leave here any time you want, and no one minds. You can take the horses." He had freedom I didn't have. I couldn't do this without him.

Will kicked a pail, sending it crashing against the stone wall. It clattered along the floor. The horse behind me kicked the stall door and neighed. I jumped away, startled by the sound. Without anything to cling to, I felt lost in the darkness.

"No," Will insisted.

It felt as if the horse had landed a second kick to my chest. Fine.

He was right. I shouldn't have expected any more from him, and I shouldn't have taken the risk to come.

"I'll have to search myself," I whispered.

I moved toward the carriage house door, resigned. I had to find a way to do this alone.

Will sighed. "Dammit, Meg."

Stopping near the coach, I turned toward his voice. A small slant of dim moonlight cut across the empty dark and fell on him. He hung his head. "I'm such a fool."

A lightness came over me. He'd help.

"Who is he?" Will asked. I could hear the irritation in his voice.

"A man who knew my grandfather. His name is Simon Pricket. He's in the west of London. I don't know any more than that." The words came out in a rush.

"Get back to the house. If I find anything, I'll come to you."

I fought the urge to run forward and embrace him. "Thank you." He held up a hand and retreated into the shadows.

I felt along the floor to gather my candle, then stumbled out of the carriage house and returned to my bed.

Every day that passed felt like a lifetime as I waited for Will to leave me some sort of sign that he'd found something. Every quiet moment alone was a moment of hope, then disappointment.

I obsessed over the key around my neck and the clock on the mantel, taking extra care when polishing them to ensure I hadn't missed some clue to the connection between the baron and my grandfather.

After two weeks of torment, I had begun to give up hope that Will could help. Perhaps he'd offered to help just to make me leave, and he'd never searched for Simon Pricket at all. Or maybe Simon Pricket didn't want to be found.

What was I to do? I could hardly start making inquiries on my own. I could ask to accompany Mrs. Pratt on market day and try to discover something, but it was unlikely that Mrs. Pratt would allow me to come when I had so much work to do in the house. Besides, I knew she wouldn't let me speak with any of the vendors.

The sack of hay beneath me felt thin and worn as I watched the embers glow in the fire. Agnes snored from her bed in the pantry. The rest of the house remained quiet.

Perhaps I needed to return to the secret workshop. I

had left in a rush after discovering my grandfather's letter. Maybe I could find another clue if I looked more carefully, but I had no way to know if Rathford was working within it. There must be a way to close the entrance to the passage from the inside. In fact, there had to be some other way in. The large gears I had seen could not have fit down the stair. I didn't wish to think about what might happen if he caught me there.

I had to take the chance.

I clasped my key in my hand, crossed the kitchen, and opened the door.

Will stood in the doorway like a wall, his hair damp from the rain. It fell across his brow in dripping curls, while the wet shirt I'd mended clung to the muscles of his chest and arms.

"Will." Breathless, I looked him in the eye, trying to gauge whether he had good news for me. His dark brown eyes looked as black as the stormy night.

Suddenly I realized I was standing before him in nothing but my underclothes. My skin felt as if it had just caught on fire as I grabbed my blanket and covered myself.

"You could have given me some warning." I sat down at the table, holding the blanket tight under my chin.

He smiled. "You didn't give me any last time you visited."

He eased down across from me. "Fair enough," I admitted, though I had a feeling my modesty meant slightly more than his. "What have you discovered?"

He shook his head. "I'm sorry. Pricket is dead."

My heart pounded. "How? When?"

Will ran his hands through his hair, slicking it back over his head. He wiped his face, then clasped his hands on the table. "He died in July nearly four years ago. Shot in the back. The murderer wasn't caught."

I brought my hand to my mouth and fought to tamp down my thundering heart. Simon Pricket had died a month before the date on my grandfather's letter, one month after Papa's supposed death.

My disappointment felt as heavy as a leaden blanket. None of this made any sense.

I looked at Will and time seemed to slow as I watched the low firelight flicker over his stoic features.

"My grandfather said he visited Simon Pricket in the west of London that August." I stood up from the bench and retreated to the fire. I watched the embers slowly dying. "But that's not possible."

"You mean the cemetery?"

I turned to Will so fast one of my braids swung over my back. I nearly dropped the blanket. "Pardon?"

"People call the Winchester cemetery over in Brompton the West of London."

I felt like I'd been struck by lightning. That was it. Pricket was one of the men who had been murdered, and my grandfather had promised to do something at Pricket's grave.

That was where I'd find the next clue.

I looked at Will in earnest. "I have to go there."

CHAPTER SEVEN

WILL PUSHED AWAY FROM THE BENCH AND HEADED straight for the door. I ran to him.

"Will?"

"No." He grabbed the handle and opened the door to the stairs. A damp wind swirled into the kitchen. "I'll have no more of this."

He slammed the door loud enough to rattle some of the hanging pots. I stiffened, afraid that if I ran back to my bed it would only increase the disturbance. Had the others woken? I listened for the harsh rumble of Agnes snoring, but heard nothing. A single *tick* cut the silence, but it was only the house settling. Agnes choked, coughed, and her familiar snore resumed. Only then did I ease onto my bed. Each crinkle of the straw sounded like the crackle of snapping kindling in my ears.

I let my head fall onto the musty pillow.

He didn't need to storm out of the house. I hadn't even asked anything of him yet. Surely helping me visit a cemetery wouldn't be so difficult. I nursed my sore mood with a heavy sigh.

I was on my own.

Sneaking away and walking to the cemetery was both dangerous and impossible. I could barely make it to the carriage house—not that I planned on ever going there again. Brompton was all the way out near Chelsea.

Inspiration struck, and I nearly shot out of my bed. I hadn't gone to visit the graves of my parents since entering this house.

Perhaps it was time.

The following day just after tea, I sought out Mrs. Pratt. She pinched her already thin lips tight as she looked up from her ledger. On the morrow she'd be leaving for the market, and I didn't want to miss my opportunity.

Dropping my gaze to the floor, I bobbed a short curtsy in respect.

"What are you about, child?"

I straightened and tried to fix my expression to some semblance of abject misery. "I have a kindness to ask, missus."

She blinked, but otherwise gave me no indication that my plea for sympathy was working. I folded my hands in front of me to try to calm my shaking nerves.

"Well, what is it? Speak up." She scratched at the ledger with sharp, hard strokes then blotted the ink with fierce stamps that shook the desk.

"My mother's birthday is recently past and I have found myself thinking on my parents of late. I wish to assuage my grief and tend their graves."

The tightness in her mouth eased. "So that's the cause of your recent mood."

A shiver tingled down my back. I'd tried hard not to be noticed since finding the letter. It worried me that Mrs. Pratt suspected something.

"Yes, missus," I answered, tucking my head again so she couldn't read the prevarication in my eyes.

"Very well. If you are done with your morning chores before I leave for market, you may accompany me. But you must finish all your regular tasks after we return."

"Thank you, missus." I bobbed another short curtsy.

"You may go." She returned to studying the ledger as I exited the room.

I worked hard all through the day and well through the night to get my chores done. I didn't want to give Mrs. Pratt any excuse for leaving me behind.

The next morning I stood dressed and waiting for her at the stairs that led from the kitchens to the garden. Though I'd barely gotten two hours of sleep, I didn't feel fatigued. Excitement coursed through my body. Mrs. Pratt marched past the table, once again putting the queen's guard to shame.

Agnes gave me a couple of sprigs of lavender to tend my parents' grave and a wary look, as if she still suspected I was up to something. She didn't say a word as I ascended the stairs after Mrs. Pratt.

I stopped short. Will stood by the cart holding the reins of Old Nick. He blinked once from under the short brim of his cap. His expression reminded me of cold stone, his face giving away nothing of our secret meetings. He was angry. It didn't show, but I could feel his displeasure lingering in the air between us.

Immediately, I dropped my chin, hoping to hide the burning flush I could feel coloring my cheeks.

I hardly had to bother. Mrs. Pratt didn't spare me a glance.

Will gave her a hand to help her into the cart then climbed up beside her. While he took the reins, Mrs. Pratt ordered me into the back. She didn't have to tell me twice. I clambered into the cart and seated myself in a little heap just behind her.

Will never looked at me. He was the picture of calm as he sharply snapped the reins. He acted as if I didn't exist. Perhaps it was for the best. He wore an old gray coat with a patch on the elbow right where I'd mended a tear in one of his shirts. I had mended his tattered clothing, and now I didn't warrant any acknowledgment at all, not even a conspiratorial glance. The cart rumbled forward. I felt each bump and jostle in my bones as we lumbered along through the sleepy streets of London.

The sun slowly rose, painting the east in pink and orange, but the rest of London remained under a heavy blanket of gray clouds. The air felt damp from the cold spring rains. They had melted all but the most persistent lumps of snow, leaving the landscape bleak, soggy, and dead.

As we neared the markets, more carts rambled down the street. Vendors laid out their wares in open stalls. The staffs of the privileged families of London wandered through the crowded square looking formal and dour in their crisp blacks, whites, and grays. From his perch on an old crate, a scraggly brown mongrel eyed the sausages. He nearly snatched one before a fat man with a tattered broom chased him away.

Will helped Mrs. Pratt out. She straightened her bonnet while inspecting the quality of a sack of onions.

"Take the girl to the cemetery, then return here to help me load the cart."

"Yes, missus."

I climbed to the seat of the cart. Mrs. Pratt skewered me with a harsh glare then flicked her gaze in the direction of the groom.

"I expect you to honor the memory and reputation of your parents well," she warned. I swallowed. Doing my best to look humble and innocent, I nodded. "You have three hours."

Will snapped the reins again, and we rumbled on. As we turned a corner the sounds of the market faded into the clatter of London's busy streets.

I looked longingly down the neat lanes as we traveled west and entered the quiet neighborhoods and wealthy shops of Mayfair. Oxford Street was just north of us. I felt as if I'd stepped back into my old world. We were merchants, but my family had done well. I belonged here, not under the stairs.

We'd had our own housekeeper, a sweet woman named Mrs. Cobb who always made my favorite currant scones in the summer.

We drove south, near the edge of Hyde Park. In my mind I again wandered down its stately paths. On pleasant mornings, mother and I would walk through the park, and even the most well-to-do ladies would stop to greet us kindly. She seemed to know everyone in the West End.

I swore I could hear my mother's voice as she taught me about the trees and gardens, then shared the latest gossip about the parade of gentry before us. The trees and the gardens remained. The nobility still strutted about. It wasn't the same. My mother was gone. Mrs. Cobb was gone. Yet the West End looked as if nothing had changed at all.

Will drove the cart west down Brompton toward the Earl's Court, and I found myself wishing I were going to lay flowers on my mother's grave. She deserved them. I suddenly felt bad for my deception, but it was too late to change course now.

"What are you about?" Will asked, breaking the silence between us.

Funny how he could ask a question and not have it sound like one. "I'm visiting the graves of my parents." If he didn't want to be a part of my quest, he didn't have to.

A muscle in his jaw ticked. "If you were clever, you'd stop trying to find Pricket." He snapped the reins and

Old Nick tossed his head as he picked up his step.

"I don't see how my business is any concern of yours." It wasn't. I'd decided.

"'Tis my concern when you do something foolish. Are your parents even buried here?" He gripped the reins tighter, his knuckles blanching under the pressure.

"I'm never foolish, and yes," I blatantly lied. After all, the cemetery at Kensal Green was practically the same as Brompton. It was a matter of perspective, really.

He laughed, and it reminded me of how he'd chuckled when we first met. It was a hard and bitter sound.

I rounded on him. "Look. Either you wish to be within my confidence, or you don't."

"Your confidence is a dangerous thing," he observed.

He was a rat. I clasped my hands in my skirt and counted to ten as he drove the cart past a milkman with a braying mule. A short distance ahead I saw the gate of the cemetery. The tall stone walls, set with narrow windows in close pairs, rose up from the street. The gate loomed higher than the walls and was built from larger blocks of stone that had a golden hue in the weak light of the overcast sky. Four thick columns stood beneath the heavy crown of the gate. The sharp, clear letters cut into the stone had a grim finality.

"I think it's best if you stay with the cart," I said as I tugged on my mop cap. I didn't need him. I knew what to do, and I could do it just as well without him.

He pulled Old Nick to a stop.

I jumped down from the cart on my own and marched to the gate. Heavy iron bars lurked within the thick arch, a severe warning that this was one place that had no escape.

I didn't look back. Whatever I found, Will would have no part in it, and that suited me splendidly.

He could sit in the dust and dark of the carriage house and rot for the rest of his life. Clearly that's what he wished to do. It was not my place to get in the way of so profound a destiny.

I shivered as I passed through the arch to the long open path beyond. The cemetery was enormous. The path continued on and on beneath trees lined up like soldiers, their skeletal branches reaching over the rows of stone crosses and sculpted angels.

It had taken us a half hour to reach the cemetery, and it

would take another to return. I didn't have much time to find Pricket's grave.

It seemed impossible. The graves were jumbled together in crowded rows, leading to the colonnade at the end of the stand of trees. I had to start somewhere. Within the colonnade was as good a place as any.

I ran.

I didn't stop. I didn't look up until I reached the center of the circle at the heart of the graveyard. Out of breath, I turned, surrounded by angels, crosses, and death.

All around me, the colonnade stretched, enclosing the circle in its grim arms. The series of arches in the corridor reminded me of an endless row of doors that all led to the same lonely path. The arches gave the illusion of escape, but through them, all I could see was the solid wall beyond. I felt completely closed in. No one else wandered the cemetery save a raven roosting atop the silent bell tower that guarded an entrance to the catacombs below.

Dropping the lavender, I gathered my skirts and marched to the circle of graves. I swept past the headstones and monuments without really seeing them. I only looked at the names as a picture. What had once been people, death had transformed into nothing more than a series of letters on a stone.

I didn't have enough time. There were too many graves. The world seemed to spin as I passed the domed chapel over and over again, time sliding past as quickly as the names on the graves.

On and on, names flashed before me, but I couldn't find the one I was looking for. How many people had died in London and why did they all seem to be buried here? After searching the circle, I continued on through the graves crowded between colonnade walls, working toward the stand of trees leading to the gate.

Several times I looked up expecting the bell tower to be on my left, only to find it on my right. I was twisted around, confused, and out of time.

I fought the clenching in my chest as the hope caught within slowly died.

I heard a rustle behind me, and the unsettling feeling of being watched crept down my neck. Glancing back, I thought I saw someone in a dark coat pass through an archway in the colonnade.

"It's over here."

The familiar voice drew my attention from the stranger. My heart fluttered as I turned. Beneath one of the trees, Will stood with his arms crossed. He scowled, but he inclined his head toward a large pedestal gravestone with a cross. The halo circling the center of the cross resembled a gear wheel.

He found it.

I ran to the grave, stopping short as Will speared me with the intensity of his gaze. What was he about? One moment he took great pleasure in chastising me, the next he helped. I didn't understand. "Thank you," I said, unwilling to think on it further or give him any more than that.

"Whatever you're after, I hope this puts it to rest for both our sakes." He flicked a small rock at a tree across the path, hitting it with a sharp *snap*.

I fought the urge to huff at him as I knelt and carefully inspected the grave. The pedestal below the cross was smooth marble with a single name carved in crisp block letters.

PRICKET

A darkened brass plaque was attached to the front. I felt along the thin edge of the plate as I read. The first inscription was for Georgiana Pricket, wife, mother, so on and so forth. Then came Harold Pricket, husband, father, yes, yes yes . . . Finally my eyes reached the one name I had hoped to find.

SIMON PRICKET

BELOVED HUSBAND AND TRUSTED FRIEND

WHO DEPARTED THIS LIFE ON THE 8TH OF JULY 1858

AGED 22 YEARS

Etchings of overturned torches marked the plate on either side of his name, a symbol of a life cut short. I touched them lightly, knowing in my heart they did not lie. Simon Pricket had died too young.

I couldn't let myself dwell. I was here for one thing. My grandfather had been here. He had to be alive somewhere. I knew it.

I ran my fingers over the brass plate, looking for a button or lever, something that would reveal the three-petal flower I'd found on the clock.

Nothing.

I stood and circled the grave.

"What are you looking for?" Will stepped away from the tree, but didn't uncross his arms.

I didn't bother to answer. I checked the base, the cross, the gear-like crown of the memorial.

Nothing.

"It has to be here." My hands slid over the gritty stone.

There had to be some sort of groove or chink that would reveal the flower medallion.

Pressure mounted in my head until I couldn't think. I was wasting precious seconds. I felt the heat in my face as I clenched my hands. All around me, death. Nothing but dirt and rotting bones beneath my feet.

I kicked, the heel of my boot connecting with the corner of the brass plate.

"Meg!" Will grabbed me from behind, locking his arms around my chest as I struggled against him. He pulled me back, but I continued kicking. I couldn't help it. Death, it was all death. Everyone that had cared for me was buried and gone, rotting in the grave. Only my grandfather remained, but the dead wouldn't give up their secrets.

Will placed my feet squarely on the ground and spun me, then grabbed my face and forced me to look at him. His eyes were filled with worry, worry that shouldn't have been there. Not for me. I felt a tear slide over my cheek. He brushed it with his thumb.

"They're dead, Meg." His voice was clear, reasonable, and I couldn't speak. "Let them go."

He brought me into the circle of his arms. I tucked my chin and allowed him to hold me. I couldn't stand on my own.

85

Will's threadbare coat pressed against my cheek. I nodded against his chest. He was right.

He was right.

"Let's go home," I whispered.

I collected myself and pushed away from him. "I'm sorry. I'm usually not completely daft."

He shrugged. "Are you sure?" He gave me a hearty thump on the shoulder, as if I were a friend. I don't know why but I was both heartened and disappointed by it.

He stepped to the grave. "You knocked the plate out of its setting. Wait, what's this?"

I wiped my eyes on the backs of my hands. Will carefully lifted the plate, prying the metal pegs in the back out of the fitted stone slots in the pedestal. As the plate came free, sunlight filtered through the branches of the barren trees and the light glinted off metal.

Embedded in the pedestal, set in the exact center of the slots for the brass plate, the three-petal medallion clung to the stone.

"Good heavens," I whispered.

It was here. It was actually here!

I fumbled as I tried to pull the key from the front of my apron. I yanked it over my head, opened it, and fitted the petals of the key into the wheel. I fumbled a bit with it in my agitation but managed to slide the petals into the lock.

"Meg?" Will knelt beside me. I pushed the button and the key began to play its familiar song.

The grave rumbled. A slab of marble on the base shook. The seam along one edge cracked as dust crumbled out of the gap. It shuffled to the side the way a heavy curtain reveals the stage. The small compartment held a tiny set of pianoforte keys, the same as the clock.

Will leaned forward.

The clockwork key stopped in a different musical phrase than it had the last time, but I knew the song and it was just as easy to play the tune on the tiny keys.

"I'll be." Will reached out to press a key, but I landed a sharp smack on his fingertips before playing the end of the phrase.

As soon as my finger pressed the final note, I heard a *chunk*, then the *tick tick tick* of gears coming to life somewhere within the grave.

I watched in wonder as the stones just beneath the medallion shifted, moving out and down like bewitched puzzle pieces. They opened up in the same manner as the back of the fireplace, stacking themselves out and away, sliding on hidden gears until a small slot opened up.

Will's mouth hung agape.

With great care, I reached into the slot, not knowing what my fingers would discover. They slid along the smooth edge of what felt like leather, then I drew them down over the crinkling ridges of . . .

"It's a book!"

With both hands I pulled the book out of the slot, captivated as it emerged from the dark hold of the grave.

The sun shimmered on golden letters embossed in rich leather, then caught in the three-petal medallion embedded in the cover.

I traced the letters with my finger.

The Illustrious History
of the
Secret Order of Modern Amusementists

S.O.M.A. I'd found it.

CHAPTER EIGHT

I COULDN'T MANAGE TO DO ANYTHING BUT STARE. I certainly couldn't speak. I shook myself out of my stupor. I didn't have time to be dumbfounded. Mrs. Pratt would be waiting, and I couldn't afford to risk her ire now that I'd found another clue.

Will stared as I played the set of notes to close the gravestone again. After affixing the brass plaque back on the pedestal, I rose and offered him my hand.

He took it.

I helped him to his feet and his brow knitted as he looked from me to the grave. I took a step toward the path, but he didn't move.

"Mrs. Pratt will be waiting. I'll explain in the cart." While I could sympathize with his shock, we didn't have time to dally.

He nodded, though he took one last look at the now unremarkable grave.

We ran out of the cemetery. I barely noticed the rows of tombstones as we hurried to the cart. He lifted me onto the seat before I had a chance to climb in myself. "What is going on?" he demanded, taking the driver's seat.

My words tumbled out without a thought. I was too swept away by the excitement of it all. "After you helped me restore the locket, I discovered a mechanism within the clock on the mantel of the study. I thought the locket might be the key to wind it, since my grandfather also made the clock." If only the story were as simple as that. Then perhaps I would have believed it. The truth was far too extraordinary.

"It *is* a key, Will. It's the key to everything." A cab raced by too closely in a clatter of hooves and wheels on stone.

"What do you mean?" Will worked the reins as Old Nick tossed his head.

It felt good to finally have a confidant, so I told him all that I had discovered. The secret workshop, the letter, everything.

"If your grandfather's alive, where is he?" Will shook his head as if this whole mystery were beyond the pale.

"I told you. He's in hiding. My grandfather, Pricket, the baron, they're all members of this Secret Order of Modern Amusementists." I smoothed my hand over the embossed seal on the book.

"What is an Amusementist?" We turned a corner and I heard the din of the market in the distance. I didn't have much time.

"I haven't the faintest," I admitted. "I'm sure I'll find the answers when I read the book."

Will slowed Old Nick and looked at me, his expression serious. "Whatever this is, you'd better stay out of it. These are secrets, deadly secrets if Pricket is any example. They're also the baron's secrets. He won't appreciate you digging in 'em."

"This is my grandfather, Will. My only family." I tucked the book safely under my apron. It felt heavy in my lap, comforting and terrifying at the same time. "I'm not going to stop until I find him."

"At what cost?" Will asked, but I knew he wasn't expecting an answer.

We fell silent as we approached the market. Once Will

stopped the cart, I climbed into the back just in time for Mrs. Pratt's return.

Her sharp eyes scrutinized me as soon as she reached the side of the cart. "Did you find your solace, child?"

I pressed my hand to the cover of the hidden book. "Yes, missus."

That night, I huddled near the light of my candle and opened the book.

Neatly elegant handwriting stretched across the pages. Like the papers in the baron's workshop, the book was filled with detailed drawings. They weren't designs so much as illustrations, a visual account of beautiful machines, some functional, some whimsical, and some purely terrifying.

The candlelight flickered across the page as I turned to the front of the book and found a list of hundreds of names. A few caught my eye, Henry Whitlock, my grandfather; George Whitlock, my father; Lord Rathford; Simon Pricket. My eyes skimmed past the rest, overwhelmed by them. From what I could tell, there were members of the House of Lords as well as common tradesmen. Even if only half of these men remained a part of the Order, the scope of it was enormous and, if the foreign-sounding names were any indication, far-reaching.

I turned to one of the early entries and began to read.

Headmaster Lawrence has accepted my proposal to record some of the most recent Amusements for posterity as part of my apprenticeship. I hope that after I pass my initiation, I will continue this venture, and this record will inspire and advise those who come after me. For my first entry I wish to speak with Charles about the use of Stonehenge as his inspiration. While the Brenington land was suitable for such a venture, the task of having the Amusement rise out of the ground proved daunting. Argus and the rest of the men from the Foundry outdid themselves crafting the gears needed to make the sculpture erupt from the ground in magnificent fashion.

Lord Brenington had died in a hunting accident not long after my grandfather. The rumor was he'd hit his head after a fall from his horse. But one did not have to fall from a horse to receive a crushing blow to the skull. My thoughts turned macabre. Gracious, someone murdered a titled man. I flipped through several pages of Pricket's writing on the aesthetics of the Stonehenge design. I paused as I read a single word, the word that was circling through my own mind.

Why?

It has often occurred to me that I do not know why we should invest ourselves so heavily in such a sport as this. As part of this journal, I feel I should address this.

Why did I accept the nomination to become an apprentice? I suppose I love the challenge. My work is enhanced by the creativity the Amusements inspire, and I enjoy the company of like-minded men who serve as guides and mentors for my growing business as well as my invention.

Mostly it has appealed to my boyish fantasies of being part of a secret order. We are truly a society apart. I find the politics and long-standing rivalries between old families within the order more complicated and fascinating than any of the goings-on in the House of Lords. Take the example of George and Elsa. One would have thought their names were Montague and Capulet.

A strange sickness settled in my heart. George and Elsa were my parents' names. I continued reading.

It is no wonder they have attempted to keep their young daughter apart from this. Their marriage certainly caused a stir. Now if only I can find myself as fortunate in both love and the ability to challenge the expected.

My fingers felt numb as I read the last part over and over. He was talking about me. My mother and father had tried to protect me from this, but now I was deeply entwined. And Papa! He used the song we sang together, and yet never once let on that it had a purpose.

I flipped back to the list of names. To my shock I found

the name of my other grandfather, my mother's father, as well. Gerhard Reichlin. I don't know why I hadn't noticed it before.

I let the book fall into my lap. The cover softly closed, leaving me staring at the Amusementist seal embossed on the medallion.

I couldn't read further, but I couldn't sleep either. My mind was full, reeling with a mystery so great, I felt as if it could sweep me away in an unforgiving tide. Everything I had thought I'd known, I now doubted.

This was a secret far greater than anything I ever had to bear. I tucked the book under my pillow, then a wave of doubt passed through me. Agnes could find it, or Rathford could be watching.

With haste, I wedged it between the wood frame of my bed and the wall. Only Will knew I had the book. I questioned my decision to tell him about the key and the plot against my grandfather. I realized I didn't know the depth of his loyalty to Rathford. He might confess what he knew.

Powerful men had died. I couldn't shake the feeling that I might be next.

All the next day passed by in a blur. Thank heavens my hands had become so accustomed to my daily routine, I could shuffle through my chores without thinking.

My mind was too filled.

That night I dared open the book again, but skipped to the back. I needed to know what had happened. What had driven the Amusementists to murder?

My grandfather's name caught my eye. I began to read.

Henry stopped by the shop today, concerned about Rathford's latest plans. What each of us has been given is beyond the scope of an exploration of a simple property of physics.

I admit it does seem suspicious, and I've been rather baffled by my part in what Rathford has proposed. Usually the larger scheme is included, but for this project, each of us has received only a part of the design to implement. I find it a dangerous way to work. One mistake and the whole of the design could go awry.

Henry is more concerned with the secrecy. He claims Rathford has been in a strange mood since the delivery of the designs. Henry intends to present the design in the next Gathering to seek approval from the Order to continue to work on the project. Surely, whatever Rathford's invented cannot be so dangerous as to require trickery to achieve it and he is not so bold to defy the rules of the Order. I'm certain Rathford is simply being impatient as usual. If we weren't allowed to explore new discoveries without the specific approval of the Order for each new innovation, no one would have the freedom to achieve anything.

Henry is not convinced. He is working with Alastair to surreptitiously gather all of the plans. They are attempting to discover the purpose of Rathford's strange machine.

The next entry was more hastily written. Pricket's neat handwriting became a jagged scrawl.

I cannot portray in words the horror of that which has been discovered. If what Henry believes is true, this machine, this terrible machine that we've all so carefully created, could destroy all we know and love.

How could a man even conceive of power so great as to challenge the hand of God himself?

I'm appalled by it.

Too much of the machine has already been delivered to the final site. We have disabled the locks. Only Henry's master key can open it now. We hope to force Rathford to relinquish the heart before it's too late.

The key.

I clutched it in my hand. My grandfather's song was random, not making any musical sense to anyone but a child.

Me.

I was the only person who knew the song, who could complete any section of it.

I was the master key.

My apprehension turned to a sickness within me. Did the baron know? Was this the true reason he'd brought me into his house?

On the next page, the handwriting degenerated further. Blots of ink stained the page in random splatters.

I was right. Charles's death was no accident, and now Henry's carriage was found in the river. We've had no sign of him. I fear he is dead.

The night air felt cold, and I pulled my thin blanket over my knees. Every shadow seemed a threat.

I flipped through the pages one by one, looking for the next clue. I almost missed the thin smudge of ink marring the crease close to the spine. Forcing the binding open as far as I could, I read the tiny scrawl hidden there.

Start with the Raven.

I didn't know what that could mean, but it had to be a clue.

I turned to the final page of writing, and my heart came to a painful stop.

Dearest Lucinda,

I expect I will die soon, murdered by one I trust. I only hope that you remain safe. The only thing I fear now is harm coming to you.

You are a light in my soul, my beloved wife. I will never regret anything, save that I could not give you the one thing you so desperately wanted. You deserve every dream of your heart.

I never deserved your love, and still find myself amazed by the gift of it. If I travel on through the gates of death, know I will carry your goodness with me, and so make Heaven that much brighter because of you. As I prepare to place this book in the gravestone of my family, I feel a fear more terrible than any I have known. Without Henry, I can't set my father's lock. I had asked Henry to set it should anything happen to me, but with his death, I fear I'm exposed. If I am right about my fate, I hope that no one ever reads these words, even you. The secret contained within could cost your life.

I must trust a gravestone is strange enough a hiding place that no one will find the book here. I can't bring myself to destroy it. If you never read these words, I hope you will feel them in your heart. If you do find the book, burn it. Take its secrets with you until we can meet again.

I love you. To the end of all days, I will love you.

With my heart,

Simon

My tear splashed on the page, lingering as a shining drop before soaking into the paper and spreading toward the calm and elegant handwriting.

I closed the book.

Raw and bewildered, I didn't know how to sort the thoughts spinning through my head. The baron was a murderer. I knew it. He was after the key. How long would it take before he killed me for it?

Except, he didn't know the song. That was the catch. He needed me alive.

Simon believed my grandfather was dead. The fact the grave was locked was further proof that Papa had been alive, at least for a time after he'd written the letter I'd found in the workshop.

What of Simon's wife, Lucinda Pricket?

Somewhere out there, his widow waited. I doubted she'd ever read her husband's final words. She deserved to have them, in spite of the danger he warned of.

I knew what I had to do, but it would not be easy.

"He's going to hate me," I whispered to myself even as I looked to the stairs that led out to the carriage house.

CHAPTER NINE

IT WAS LATE, JUST ON THE CUSP OF THE DEEP PART OF night where everything falls quiet. I listened to the house, but only the dying fire and Agnes's muffled nose made any sound at all. The last time I had visited Will at night, he hadn't been happy. I brought my fingers to my throat. The memory of his whispered words along my neck sent a quiver racing over my skin.

He'd probably throw me out into the garden on my arse.

And he'd be right to do it. I was taking a risk, a terrible risk.

The letter Simon had written to his wife had moved me. I couldn't let his final words remain unread by her, and I needed to know more. Pricket's widow was the only one who could shed light on the clues contained within the journal. As much as I loved my family, I now felt I didn't know them at all. I longed to speak to someone, anyone, who could tell me more about this secret part of their lives. A mystery lingered, a deadly one. I needed to reach the heart of it before someone took my life.

I crept up the stairs into the garden. It was a foggy night, with a thick mist hanging in the air. Halfway to the carriage house, a creeping suspicion woke within me. I stepped away from the lions, concealing myself in the fog and shadows.

My heart skipped. I thought I saw a light in one of the upper windows of the house, but when I turned, there was nothing.

I considered retreating to the kitchen.

A hush fell over the garden, as if an audience in a darkened theater was watching a terrible drama unfold. I hugged the book tighter to my chest and sprinted to the side door of the carriage house, away from the blank stare of the lion. I passed into the stables and was surprised to find a warm light flickering by the stove.

Will sat on the stool dressed in his shirtsleeves and waistcoat. He continued polishing the leather strap of a bridle and didn't bother to look up.

"You're still awake?" I took a seat beside him.

"I was expecting you sooner," he admitted, looping the bridle on an empty peg among the other straps, harnesses, halters, and saddles hanging neatly from the wall of a small storage room.

He wanted me to visit? I fiddled with my skirt to soothe the restless feeling in my hands. "You aren't going to lecture me about how we could lose our jobs?"

He leveled me with a cool glance as he returned to his seat by the stove. "It's too late for that, and clearly, reasoning with you doesn't work. So what's in the book?"

Here in the stable, my doubt of him eased. I needed someone I could trust. Will hadn't failed me. "It seems to be notes and drawings of inventions. There's a secret order of inventors who create these things in some sort of competition to outdo one another." I opened the book to the drawing of the mechanical horses. He squinted at it with a curious look.

"They invent things for fun?" A serious expression fell over his face, almost like longing.

"Strange, isn't it?" I traced my finger over the elegant arc of a horse's neck. "They have a whole system worked out, even an academy for apprentices to the organization, and a foundry somewhere up north that supplies all the parts for their machines. The scope of the organization is astounding, and yet, I've never heard anything about them until now, even though my family was a part of it."

Will wiped his hands on a rag. "That takes some doing." He tossed it in a pail. "Did Pricket say anything about your grandfather?" He collected the lid for the leather balm and fitted it on the small jar.

"He did." I swallowed my misgivings. "And Lord Rathford. My grandfather believed that the baron had invented something dangerous. Papa was helping the others disable it and lock it away so it couldn't be used. That's why they were all murdered."

The jar clattered to the floor. "What did you say?" Will stood and paced over by the stove.

"Lord Rathford murdered other members of the Order who were trying to prevent him from using his machine." My heart felt heavy even as the words fell from my lips.

"That's impossible." Will picked up the jar then crossed his arms.

"It's all right here." I rose, holding the book out to him.

"The baron isn't a murderer." His voice growled low.

"Yes, he is. He killed Simon Pricket. Pricket knew it was coming. He wrote it all down." I shook the book at Will, demanding he take it, but he only glared with more anger than I'd ever seen. "He even hid the book within his own gravestone knowing that Lord Rathford would kill him."

"The baron saved my life." Will's eyes flashed in the dim light. Old Nick whinnied, tossing his head. And then silence fell between us. "He's not a murderer," Will insisted, though his voice was now hardly more than a whisper.

I'd forgotten.

The baron had taken him in. Of course Will would be loyal to that. I was a fool to have trusted him with this. I had to convince him of the truth of the matter. "I'm sorry, Will, but it's all very clear."

He turned from me, walking down the row of stalls toward the uneven stairs beyond. Suddenly he rounded on me. "Is there any proof?"

"Read it for yourself," I insisted, holding the book out to him once again.

He shot me a look that could have boiled an egg. "I can't."

Now I was becoming angry. He was so stubborn, a blind and deaf mule couldn't compare. "Why not? You don't want to believe it?"

"Blast it all, Meg. I can't read." He stumbled on the words, as if he didn't want to release them.

I felt as if he'd just slapped me in the face. I even touched my cheek to be sure, but the sting was on the inside. I hadn't considered that. Good heavens, I hadn't meant to insult him.

"Not that, in any case," he continued. "John taught me letters, how to sound them. But the letters he taught me were all straight and clear. He said every good driver should know how to read signs."

"Will." I hadn't ever heard him string so many words together. I hadn't meant to hit a nerve. I certainly didn't want him to feel ashamed of himself. It wasn't his fault. "I'm sorry. I assumed. You're more clever than I."

He looked away, kicking the floor with the toe of his boot.

"You certainly have more sense," I added.

He huffed the beginning of a laugh, then looked at me. "Clearly."

I dropped my gaze to the floor, not sure if that last word was a jest or an insult.

"Is there any proof?" he asked again. This time his voice was calm, almost imploring.

I took a deep breath. "The baron invented something dangerous. I don't know what it was. Pricket and my grandfather both believed he was the murderer."

"But there isn't any proof." Will looked to me, but I didn't know what to say.

"I don't know, Will." I could see in his face, he didn't believe me, and he wouldn't. Not tonight. "There's only one way to know for sure." I took a step toward Will, and while he crossed his arms again, he didn't back away.

"What is it?" he asked.

"There's only one other person who could help us find the truth."

He held his hand out. "I don't want to hear it."

"Please, Will. Pricket's widow is out there, and she needs to see this book. Help me find her."

He shook his head. "No. I'm done. Go back to the house before you get into any more trouble. Some things are best left be."

He turned away from me, and I knew it was over. I wouldn't have anyone's help. I had to do this on my own. As I slipped out of the carriage house, the loss of my only ally felt like a crushing blow. Each step felt harder than the last. I wanted to go back, to say I was sorry, but I didn't know what I was sorry for, and so it was useless. Will was done. He'd made that much clear.

I was done with him.

The house loomed dark and menacing, shrouded in the dark fog. I took a deep breath, hoping that everyone still slept.

Creeping down the stairs, I gently opened the door and slid inside. With hushed care, I eased the latch closed and turned.

Mrs. Pratt stood by the table.

Bloody hell.

My heart stopped. I heard a rushing in my ears as she slowly turned the key on a lamp, filling the kitchen with light.

I couldn't move. I didn't know what to say. Maybe she'd believe I was out relieving myself in the garden pot.

No. The disappointment in her eyes burned with such glaring intensity the light seemed dim by comparison.

"Missus . . . I," I stammered. I gripped my skirts, holding the book slightly behind me. No matter how tightly I clenched the fabric, I couldn't keep my hands from shaking. The quake shivered through the tiers of my skirt down to the hem.

"I told you." Her voice was low, calm, but it cracked just slightly. "I told you, he's always watching." Her thin lower lip trembled as she threw a piece of paper at me.

Each beat of my heart felt like a stab in my chest. My limbs grew heavy. I managed to pick up the paper, but could barely hold it to read.

Dear Mrs. Pratt,

Please dispense of Miss Whitlock's services immediately as she has engaged in an inappropriate liaison in the carriage house. I will not tolerate having those with questionable morals residing under my roof. She will receive neither severance nor recommendation. She is to be removed from the property at once.

I dropped the letter to the floor.

The room blurred before my eyes, and I had to put a hand out to the cutting board to steady myself. Mrs. Pratt grabbed my arm, though her grip wasn't punishing.

"You've made this bed, Meg." She led me to the table and let me sit there. I couldn't speak, couldn't think. I looked at her. Were tears shining in her eyes?

"It's not what you think," I implored. "You can't believe I would do something shameful."

She shook her head. "It doesn't matter, child. Don't you see? It only matters how it appears. It appears to be an indiscretion."

Blast it! I pulled my mop cap from my head and threw it to the floor. "You can't possibly turn me out in the middle of the night! I didn't do anything wrong," I protested. This was so unfair.

Mrs. Pratt's shoulders sagged. "I'm sorry, Meg. This is how the baron wants it."

Damn him. I hated him. I hated him and his bloody house. I hated him and his dead wife, too. How could he take me in, only to ignore me, use me until I ached every single moment, only to throw me out into the night? I didn't care if Will believed he might be innocent. I knew the truth in my heart. The man was cold and ruthless. He was a murderer, and I had to escape. I'd be better off free of this place. Did he know I had been in the workshop? Had he seen me in the spy glass? Was that the reason for this?

It had to be.

"What of Will?" I demanded.

"What of him?" Mrs. Pratt answered back, even as she picked up my cap and wrung it in her hands.

"Did the baron say anything about him?" I tore off my apron and tossed it at Mrs. Pratt's feet.

"No." She stood and tucked a chunk of bread in a small satchel and handed it to me. I slipped the journal in with it and slung it over my neck. Damn him, too. Clearly he was Rathford's pet. No wonder he stood up for the baron. How could Will stand for a man who would throw me penniless into the street?

I hated Will in that moment. I didn't want to, but I did. Will still had his job. He still had his life.

Mine had just been crushed.

"I know it is unfair, child. But that's the way of it for women. Head for the church and ask for the vicar, do you understand?" Mrs. Pratt ordered in her usual gruff manner.

I nodded even as the tears began to flow from my eyes. Mrs. Pratt handed me her handkerchief.

If this was the baron's means of murdering me, he was doing a good job. The streets were dangerous.

I'd have to face them alone.

I gripped the key hanging openly in the center of my chest now that I no longer had my apron to hide it.

"Send me word through the vicar once you are safe." Mrs. Pratt lifted my chin. I looked her in the eye, and through the hurt, the disappointment, I saw something else there.

Sympathy.

I embraced her. She held me tight with the strength and rigidity she always carried.

"I'm sorry," I whispered. The truth was, I hated myself, too. I'd gotten so caught up in the book, I'd become careless.

She nodded. "Go."

I ran out into the night with nothing but my shawl, the

key, and the small satchel. In the mist, the wrought iron gate and decorative filigree along the top of the garden wall looked like the twisted gates of Hades. The lions appeared to laugh as I approached. I looked into their gleaming eyes and glared. If Rathford could see me, I wanted him to know how much I despised him.

With all my strength I wrenched open the heavy gate, the hinges creaking with my effort. I slipped through and let the iron bars swing shut behind me.

I found myself adrift on the side of the wide cobblestone road. For months I had longed for the freedom to stand on this side of the gate. Now that I was here, I felt sick with bitterness and fear. Large houses and garden walls boxed me in, creating a great and terrible maze before me. I found it difficult to breathe, impossible to run. The weight of my anger and sadness pressed down on my shoulders until I felt crushed by it.

My parents were gone, burned, along with everything I ever loved. For six months I'd worked to the bone, but I never had the chance to properly mourn them. I looked down at my dress, the mourning dress my neighbor had given me out of pity. It was supposed to show the world my sorrow for the loss of my parents. Beneath my apron, it had only showed my servitude.

To what?

To an insane murderer.

Now I had nothing.

The pain of it welled in me so strongly, all the loss. All the sorrow, it swallowed me whole, like a great dark whale, carrying me down into the depths.

The streets became a blur of darkness and glowing pools of light. Ornate houses leered at me. I had no home, no food, no money, no shelter. I'd have to throw myself on the mercy of the church and confess sins I'd never committed.

I had no one. No one I could trust.

I didn't know how long I walked, or how far. I kept blindly putting one foot in front of the other. Somewhere, people chattered at some fancy ball, their voices ringing like bells in my ears. The merry laughter seemed to mock me. Through the windows of the house, I could see the ladies in pretty ball gowns, drinking, flirting, not a care in the world as they bartered their reputations like a cheap bet in a game of cards.

Yet I, in my modest mourning dress, was the one turned out for my lack of moral character.

I turned down a side street where a row of hansom cabs lingered, waiting for the drunken revelers to emerge. I had barely noticed them as I hurried down the lane.

"What's this, lovely?" A cabdriver stepped out from behind one of the horses. "Hey, Bill! Take a gander at the pretty little pigeon what come our way."

I stopped in my tracks and looked up just as the cabbie lunged toward me. I jumped back and spun around as a second came up from behind.

He smiled and his tongue poked out from the gap of his missing tooth.

"What's wrong, miss? Lost? Just say the word and Eddie here'll give ya a ride." They laughed, barking like mad dogs.

"Leave me be," I snapped, trying to take a quick step around them. One grabbed me by the shoulder, his grubby fist catching my shawl.

He pulled me closer. "Maybe a kiss'll cheer you up."

I slapped him as hard as I could, my palm burning from the blow and his grubby stubble. Then I kicked him in the knee, but he held me fast. I couldn't escape.

"C'mon, miss. One little kiss. And if ya like that, there's more I can show ya." I froze as he pulled me toward him.

A shot rang out, the round crashing into the side of the cab with a loud *crack*. The cabbies jumped away, ducking for cover. They cursed as I regained my senses.

I ran, leaving my shawl behind.

My heart pounded. Never had I been so afraid. My feet flew over the paved stones. I didn't know where I was, but I had to keep running. A second shot rang out, this one whistling past my ear.

I screamed, nearly falling to the street, but I picked myself up and dodged down a narrow lane to the left.

Whoever was shooting, was shooting at me.

My corset was too tight. I couldn't breathe in.

The heavy sound of boots drummed on the pavement behind me. A rush of heat flooded up through my face to my hair. My head pounded with it. I could taste my fear like the sharp tang of blood. My lungs burned. I tried to keep running but I stumbled.

My head swam. I couldn't move my feet. I tried to breathe. The stays of my corset gripped too tight.

I just couldn't breathe.

Desperate, I ran down the lane, but the fog confused me. I found myself in a small, quiet square. There was no place to run. I turned to face my attacker.

A man in a dark coat stalked down the lane beneath the skeletal trees. His face remained hidden behind his high collar and the brim of his hat. Mist swirled around him as he slowly raised the gun.

I was going to die.

A shot rang out, and I shut my eyes, unable to find the voice to scream. I had expected the round to rip into my chest, but when I opened my eyes, I saw the man in black had turned, his coat fluttering as he ran into the mist.

One moment he was there, the next, gone.

I fought for breath as a second dark form emerged from the fog. He strode toward me with purpose. The glow from a streetlamp spilled over his face.

"Will," I whispered as I exhaled. A dizzy rush overtook me and I fainted.

CHAPTER TEN

I WOKE TO WILL JOSTLING ME AND URGING ME TO STAND.

A short gasp pushed much-needed air into my lungs as I struggled against him in my panic. He held me tight and helped me to my feet.

"Who was that?" I shook from head to toe. I hadn't been so close to death since the night of the fire.

"There's no time. Quickly now." Will pulled me forward and I stumbled along beside him, clinging to his arm.

His grip remained tight as he made a turn toward the trees peeking over the London rooftops. We must have been near one of the parks.

"The park isn't safe," I protested, as I stared at the pistol in his hand.

"Nowhere is." Will loosened his grip on my arm, sliding his hand into mine as he led me down the street. "There will be less light, and we can conceal ourselves in the fog."

We ran until we crossed into Green Park. Together we flew down the path and ducked behind a large tree. Heavy mist rose off the damp grasses and the lake, concealing us, but also giving perfect cover to the man in black.

"I think I scared him off," Will said. He was breathing heavily, and his face looked pale in the moonlight. "Are you harmed?"

"I'll be fine." Even as I spoke the words I didn't believe them. I didn't think I would ever stop shaking. "Who was that?"

"I don't know," Will admitted as he looked back over his shoulder.

"We need to find shelter," I insisted. Suddenly I missed the high stone walls of Rathford's house and the fearsome lions guarding the heavy gate.

"How did you know I had been sacked?" I asked.

Will took my hand and pulled me deeper into the mist. "Mrs. Pratt came to the carriage house and gave me a piece of her mind." He rubbed the back of his neck. "Then she threw the grooming pail at my head."

"At least you can go back. The baron didn't toss you out into the cold." I crossed my arms and rubbed them.

"I told you this would happen." Will turned suddenly at the sound of a snapping branch. "You should have listened to me," he whispered.

We settled into a brisk walk, fear driving each step forward. I kept glancing at Will's pistol, realizing I knew hardly anything about him at all.

A shudder racked my shoulders as I thought about the cabbies. I could feel them tugging on my clothing, smell the stench of rancid male sweat.

Sometimes a weapon could be useful.

In the distance I could see the glow from Buckingham Palace through the fog and the looming dark branches of the London plane trees.

Will started down another path, changing our direction. I still didn't know where we would find shelter.

"We've no place to go," he said.

"I think . . ." My voice cracked and I cleared my throat. "I think it might be a good time to find the Widow Pricket."

He turned on me. "Dammit, Meg. Someone just tried to murder you. You have to let it go."

"I can't." I threw my hands up and walked away from him.

What other choice did I have? "I have to see this through."

"I swear you are the most stubborn, willful, obstinate creature I've ever met," he muttered.

"You've been in the stable too long." I took the book out of the satchel. "I'm in this too deep. Will you help me see it through?"

He looked uncertain, as if battered about by two swiftly churning tides. He let out a resigned breath. "Pricket had a shop up on Bond Street. Perhaps his widow is still there."

The rush of elation and relief overwhelmed me, and I nearly threw myself into Will's arms. I felt the urge to embrace him as I gazed into his eyes. Suddenly I didn't feel so alone anymore.

Yet we were walking into the unknown.

Dawn broke as we made for Pricket's Toys and Amusements. I was exhausted. I didn't know how long we'd wandered through the mists in the park, but it seemed as if the night had passed too suddenly.

After skirting Hyde Park heading north, we had wandered down countless streets of terraced houses, all neatly conforming like obedient schoolchildren lined up in a proper row. The ornamental stonework put lacy frills on the otherwise boxlike squares.

We saw no sign of the man in black, and eventually Will put his pistol away.

When we reached Bond Street, only a short distance from where I grew up on Oxford, I sighed. Here each building had its own personality, but they still stood shoulder to shoulder, with no room for anything but stone and lampposts. Every awning felt familiar, even in the dark. This was my home, yet walking through it, I felt as if I had no place to enter.

My eyes burned and the skin on my cheeks felt tight and itchy. I needed someplace to rest, but as we approached Pricket's shop, I didn't think we would find rest there. During the night, the fog had cleared. Now the shadow of the buildings stretched over the street in the new morning light.

The shop was closed and dark, a thin layer of dust coating the carefully arranged toys in the window. A doll smiled at me, the weak sunlight dull in her lifeless glass eyes.

Did the widow even live here?

Will ran a tired hand over his face. If I felt tired, I had no right to complain. He'd been up all night as well.

I noticed a stylized flower with three petals incorporated into the uniform of the tin soldier painted on the sign above the door. A faded CLOSED sign had fallen askew in the window.

I knocked.

Nothing.

"Maybe she's not yet awake?" Will peeked in the window, but the interior of the shop was too dark to see.

I knocked again.

This time we heard shuffling within the shop. Slowly, the door cracked open. "We are closed until further notice."

I shot my hand in the door hoping she'd have enough mercy not to shut it on my fingers.

"Lucinda Pricket?" I implored.

The door opened a little wider to reveal a slender woman dressed from head to toe in a glorious full-mourning dress. Black lace hung from an elegant bonnet trimmed with jet and the shining feathers of a raven. It obscured her pale face, and I could barely discern her expression. Yet the veil couldn't hide the radiance of the beautiful lady before me. She couldn't have been much past twenty, with golden-red hair, eyes the blue of distant tropical seas, and the air of aristocracy.

"What do you want?" she demanded. Her voice, slightly husky, sounded as if she hadn't used it in years.

"My name's Meg Whitlock. I'm George and Elsa Whitlock's daughter." Even as I said it, I feared the man with the black coat was sneaking behind us on the avenue and in that instant another shot would ring out.

Mrs. Pricket placed a single finger under my chin and lifted my face. I looked her in the eye through the veil. Her eyes widened in shock. "Gracious, get inside!"

Her gloved hand clasped mine and pulled me in. Will followed, then the widow slammed the door.

A shiver overcame me as I looked around the dusty shop. Marionettes with jeering faces hung from the rafters. Cobwebs had collected between their strings. On the shelves, a plethora of wonderment sat silent and motionless. Music boxes, tin soldiers, clockwork animals, it was the magic of a thousand Christmastimes faded and still, lying lifeless.

My eyes lingered on a doll that looked just like one I had as a girl. Had my toys come from this very shop? The thought tainted my memories, like seeing an old friend in tattered rags and not knowing what to do to help.

We followed the widow to a cozy sitting room in the back. Will haunted the door as I gratefully sank onto the settee. A modest fire warmed a simple teakettle. It seemed only the shop had been neglected.

The widow swept across the room but did not lift her veil. It had been over three years since Pricket's death. Surely she wasn't still mourning him?

I cleared my throat. "I apologize for disturbing you so

early, but I fear we are in danger. A man shot at us in the park."

"Did you see his face?" she asked as I placed the satchel at my feet.

"No. But he was wearing a black coat and top hat." I twisted my fingers together.

"Along with half of London," the widow said as she poured the tea. "So, he wasn't some street ruffian. That is one clue at least." Then she turned to Will. "Now who are you?"

"William MacDonald, ma'am." He nodded to her.

"You're not part of the Order." Her posture stiffened.

"No, I'm not." Will met her challenge. He shrugged. "From how I see it, danger comes from within your Order, not outside it."

"Logical, I see," she commented, placing the teapot back on the tray. "Simon would approve. He was the logical sort as well. Unfortunately, you are incorrect. Anyone can be bought. It is not safe in these times. You're lucky you weren't killed."

"Do you know who is behind the murders?" I asked.

Lucinda shook her head. "If I knew, he'd have visited the gallows long ago."

"Perhaps this might help," I suggested as I pulled the book from the satchel.

I placed the book on the table. It was hers by right, but I felt unsure if I should trust her with more.

I looked at the Widow Pricket. She couldn't fake such deep grief. She hadn't killed her husband. But I was on the edge of a dangerous web, and I didn't know where she was caught in it.

"Will and I found this book locked inside your husband's gravestone." I touched the key hanging around my neck but didn't mention it. It felt heavy.

"In his grave?" She didn't seem shocked by the idea. "However did you discover it?"

"It was within a secret compartment in the stone itself, hidden behind the plate," I clarified. The last thing we needed was to be cast as grave robbers. "Have you visited the grave recently?"

"Every day." She dropped to the edge of a chair, her wide crinoline floating about her. "Why didn't he simply leave it with me?"

Her words sounded so soft, so hurt. We were opening old wounds.

"I think he feared what it contains could endanger you. He knew he was to be murdered." I didn't know what to do with my hands. I wanted to reach out to the widow. She seemed stricken.

"Too many people are either dead or gone into hiding. When will this end?" She took the book and opened it, letting out a shaky breath as she stared at the handwriting. "We were only married for two years before he was taken from me. It wasn't enough time. It wasn't nearly enough time."

I glanced at Will, then back at the widow. I didn't know Will's intentions, but in that moment, I knew mine. "Help us find the murderer. Let's end this together."

She looked to me. I could see she was struggling. "I don't wish to be involved. My life has already been destroyed by all this. I'll tell you what I can. But then you must leave me be."

CHAPTER ELEVEN

THE WIDOW EXCUSED HERSELF, AND I TURNED TO WILL. He shrugged but remained near the doorway, as if he didn't feel he was allowed into a lady's parlor.

I sipped my tea listening to the faint traces of hustle and bustle from Bond Street, hushed by the eerie shop and the dim interior of the parlor.

My eyes stung as I fought to keep them open. It had been a long night.

I blinked. It was so difficult to pull my heavy eyelids open again. I shook myself awake just as I felt the teacup slip from my lap.

Oh! Reaching out, I tried to right it, but only tipped it

more, spilling the contents down my skirt and onto the floor.

The cup fell on the opulent rug, and the tea eagerly soaked into the fine threads. I dropped to the floor and pressed the hem of my skirt into the stain to soak up the spill.

The widow returned. "What happened?" She placed an ornately painted tray laden with simple scones on the table.

"My pardon, I made a dreadful mess of things."

She knelt beside me, grasped my hands, and lifted me to stand.

"Leave it for now." She lifted her veil, and the full effect of her refinement awed me. Her honey-red curls rested in perfect coils along her neck. Her bright blue-green eyes searched mine. "You look exhausted. Have you been walking all night?"

I nodded.

"Come, you need to sleep." She gave a short nod as if the matter had just been decided and she'd hear no word against it.

"What of Will?" He needed to rest as well.

She looked over her shoulder at him. "He can stay in the mews in the back."

I pulled my hand from hers. "You're putting him out with the horse?"

"Meg." He shook his head, just a hint of movement, but I read it clear as day. *Not now.* He gave the widow a short bow.

"Thank you for your generosity, Mrs. Pricket. I appreciate your hospitality and trust."

Hospitality my boot. She was practically asking him to sleep on the front stoop. I owed him some measure of loyalty. He had just saved my life.

Lucinda pointed to a door in the back, and Will disappeared through it with a tip of his hat.

"Now then," the widow continued. "You may follow me."

She led me through the dimly lit house. As part of a row of storefronts, only the rooms facing the street or the mews behind the house had windows. I found it disconcerting to be in a tight space with so many oil lamps burning.

We began an ascent up a tight and steep set of stairs. "He's a handsome one," the widow commented.

"I beg your pardon?" The comment caught me completely off guard, and my heart thundered to life. I felt the rush of heat in my face. Why would she notice? She was a widow.

"It isn't seemly for two women to entertain his company within the house. I do have to maintain propriety." Her voice was cool, and she didn't bother to look back at me.

For whom? It didn't appear as if she'd entertained anyone in years, so I didn't see what good propriety would do.

"Have you maintained a sense of propriety?" She stopped and turned to me. I nearly stumbled backward down the stair.

"Yes, ma'am." I didn't appreciate the insinuation that I hadn't. I gripped the rail so tightly my fingers ached. Why was everyone so quick to assume I'd throw my moral character out of the window with the dishwater?

A curious look, a bit like that of a cat sniffing cream, crossed her face. "Do you fancy him?"

There was no trace of Agnes's harsh judgment in her tone, yet my face burned to the tips of my ears. I probably looked like a puffy radish. How was I to answer that? Did I? No.

My heart hammered again. Well, he *was* handsome, but that wasn't the matter at hand. Will was . . . Will. He was only the stable hand. I needed his help. We were clearly from different worlds. I could write in three languages, and he couldn't . . .

I didn't allow myself to finish that thought. I wasn't here to play the part of some sentimental trollop over a boy with a handsome face. Or strong body, or—

"I see." Her eyes crinkled in the corners in an aloof and knowing way that irritated me. See what? There was nothing to see. She turned again and continued up the stair as if she hadn't just fired a volley of cannons across my bow.

At the top of the stair she opened the first door to the right. A snug but neat little room with a small, cheery bed and a stand with a washbasin greeted me. A high window overlooked the roof of the mews. A flock of pigeons roosted there, cooing in the morning light.

"Get some rest. We have much to discuss when you wake."

I was exhausted to the bone, and the feather mattress felt like lying on a cloud, yet I didn't fall to sleep. My skin felt tight, warm and tingling, and I couldn't stop thinking about Will.

It shocked me when I woke, because I hadn't realized I had slept. I just jolted out of blackness, disoriented and frightened. It took me a moment to remember where I was.

The house was dark, yet my eyes adjusted in the slant of moonlight shining through the window. Sharp pangs of hunger bit at me.

Easing out of the bed, I crept with soft steps toward the stairwell. I didn't want to wake the widow should she be sleeping.

As I reached the stair, a faint melody whispered through

the sleeping house. Curious, I kept my hand to the wall and followed the sound. A light flickered on the other side of one of the doors. It was open only a crack, but it was enough for me to peer through.

The widow rocked in a creaking chair in the corner. Her strawberry-gold curls tumbled free down her back, but a heavy black shawl hung over her shoulders, covering her soft blue dressing gown. She sang a sweet lullaby and in the crook of her arm rested the smooth head of a baby.

She had a child? I brought my hand to my mouth as I watched her. She rocked it, cradling it with such love, it nearly broke my heart. Eventually she stilled, sighed, and lifted the infant.

That's when I noticed the stiff arms, the unmoving head. The utter silence. It was only a doll dressed in the most lovely white gown. She stood and placed it in a bassinet.

Her breath hitched as she looked at it. Her ivory hands drifted over her flat stomach in a circling pattern, as if soothing a deep hurt there.

I retreated a step, turning my back so I could lean against the wall. I couldn't quite make sense of what I'd just seen. I only knew it was something I shouldn't have witnessed. The deep sadness of it reached into my heart and wouldn't let go.

Racking sobs broke the silence as the widow grieved, the sound so aching and raw, it forced tears from my eyes. I felt my own grief so close, I had to grip my grandfather's key.

I retreated to my room, softly closing the door behind me, but I didn't sleep again that night.

The next morning, the widow looked as calm and collected as she had the day before. Elegant in her stark black, she had removed her veil, but the contrast of her dark attire with her bright hair and eyes only made her look more striking.

I felt like a dowdy sparrow next to a peacock in my own faded mourning dress and simple braids. Will came into the parlor and haunted the door.

The widow raised her cup to him. "I'd like to thank you for tending to Daisy this morning. She's very dear to me."

"'Twas my pleasure." He looked her in the eye and gave her a hint of a bow. She didn't break his gaze for a long time.

It made me uncomfortable. I did my best to convince myself it wasn't the stirrings of jealousy.

"I read the book last night," the widow began. "I assume you have as well, or you wouldn't be here."

"I read parts, Mrs. Pricket," I confessed.

"So you realize your grandfather faked his death." She

turned to me as if she were announcing tea was served in the parlor.

I felt as if a mule had kicked me in the middle.

"How do you know he's alive?" Will asked.

"Simple." She reached into her pocket and produced a key, a simple device a bit like a corkscrew with the three silver triangles at the end. It looked nothing like mine. "Every Amusementist has a key such as this. Each one is individual and allows a person to lock their inventions to prevent tampering. When I had Simon's name engraved, I discovered the medallion hidden behind the brass plate," Lucinda admitted.

So, that was the reason she hadn't seemed surprised at the idea of a hidden compartment within the gravestone. She continued, "I tried to open the compartment. Simon's key didn't work. Which means Simon did not set that lock."

Her gaze dropped to the pendant hanging around my neck. "Your grandfather invented the locking system for all the Amusementists. Many believed he had a key that could open any of his locks. If a master key does indeed exist, only Henry could have set the lock in Simon's gravestone, which means he was alive after Simon's death."

I dropped my gaze, feeling a bit like a criminal standing

before a barrister. It was time to confess. "Lord Rathford took me in after the fire. I recently found a letter among the baron's things. It was from my grandfather, dated after his death. I believe he's alive, Mrs. Pricket."

I took a sip of tea, but it tasted bitter. I didn't think another lump would make it any better.

"Lucinda, please. What did the letter say?"

"That my grandfather was going into hiding, and if anyone came searching for him, he'd know Rathford was the one who gave him away. He tried to convince Rathford to see reason before it was too late." I hoped my instincts were right about the widow. I didn't wish to put Papa in further jeopardy.

"Let me show you something." Lucinda rose with the grace of a born duchess and walked to the corner. She picked up a small frame and held it toward me.

I brought my hand to my chest. "It's Papa!" Reaching out, I took the picture to peer at it more closely. It was small, but clear. "He looks so young."

He was bending on one knee, smiling as he held a small box in his palm, above it a toy top floated in the air with nothing at all to support it. A lovely little girl with pale curls and a young boy with a missing tooth and shaggy hair clung to him with looks of delight on their faces. I knew that feeling. My grandfather had a way of making the ordinary magical.

"Is this you?" I asked, wonder filling my heart. The girl in the picture looked at my grandfather in the exact way I had looked at him as a child.

"Yes, it was my sixth birthday," she admitted. "You were a newborn. Your mother let me hold you that afternoon. She was a generous and kind woman. I missed her greatly when she decided to eschew our social circles. I'm sorry for your loss. Your father was a good man too. I saw him and your grandfather from time to time at gatherings. I was very fond of Henry. All the children were."

Will edged closer to look at the picture. It was a moment in time, captured. I wondered how it was made. It was unlike any sort of tintype I'd ever seen. "Is that your husband?" Will asked.

Lucinda sighed. "No." She bit her lip and her eyes darted for a second as if searching for what to say. "He was a friend."

"Why didn't my parents want me to know about the Amusementists?" I asked, clearing my throat.

Lucinda pinched her lips. "It's complicated. The Order is a culture unto itself, and has a way of consuming people."

"How do you mean?" Will spoke up.

"We don't follow the normal conventions. Take the names for example." Lucinda took a sip of tea. "There are certain rules of the Order. The first rule is that a man's worth is determined by the limits of his mind. Using Christian names instead of titles forces all the Amusementists onto equal intellectual footing. After all, inheriting land hardly makes a man a genius." Lucinda gave an inelegant snort.

"Always?" It was hard to imagine higher-ranking men like the baron would let go of formality.

"Usually. It forces men to rely on their wit and creativity to earn respect within the Order instead of the power of their family name, though certain members are more insistent on playing with a level field than others. And certain family names hold great prestige within the Order, though that has nothing to do with the gentry." Lucinda offered me a crumpet and I took it gladly.

"Take Rathford for example," she continued. "He rarely let anyone use his given name, probably because he didn't favor it much, but even he wouldn't dare insist someone within the Order address him as Lord. And for as powerful as some men are in political circles, the name Whitlock carries enormous weight within the Society. Reichlin did as well. I believe your mother didn't want to subject you to the pressures the Amusementists would have put upon you, Meg. In certain respects, I can't blame her. The unspoken rules for the Society of women associated with the Order are—restrictive."

"Are you an Amusementist?" Will's question surprised me and I almost choked on the crumbling pastry in my mouth.

"No woman has ever been nominated to become one. We are only part of the Society through our association with the men. You could say I have been part of the Society since birth." A hint of a wistful smile touched her lips. "Simon always claimed that was a shame. He once told me I was a more creative inventor than he was. He was lying of course."

"Tell me about the competitions." It was likely I would never know my parents' full motives for keeping the Amusementists from me, but I needed to know more. I was curious about the drawings in Simon's book.

Lucinda looked distant, as if remembering a fond holiday from long ago. "One person would issue a challenge to another, usually something whimsical, like make a clockwork rabbit. Then the men would try to make it. Over the years the clockwork rabbit turned into automaton fox hunts, and eventually the machines reached ridiculous levels of complexity and wonder. No one man could make them. All those interested in participating in the Amusements proposed at a Gathering of the Order would break apart into teams, each team contributing with the best of their talents and resources."

Will fully stepped into the room and took a crumpet, then retreated a pace, still unwilling to sit. "To what purpose?"

Lucinda sighed. "Fun, a challenge . . . to see if they could do it. Perhaps there was some pressure to impress the women of the Society. Occasionally a wager or two might have been placed."

She took a sip of tea, then stared at the liquid in her cup. "The men formed very deep bonds when working together on an Amusement. The craftsmen enjoyed the exclusive patronage of the nobility, and the nobility enjoyed thoroughly unique curiosities and profitable business arrangements with the craftsmen. Sons and daughters of Amusementists tend to marry within the Order. This is why the murders are so troubling. Whoever did this, he has killed his own brothers."

I didn't know what to say. The thought troubled me to no end. Lucinda placed her hand over mine. "If your grandfather found a way to stay hidden, it's because he had to. These men know him too well." She shook her head, a sad and unconscious gesture. "None of us knows whom to trust. There hasn't been a Gathering of the Amusementists since the murders. No one is willing to risk it. It won't be safe for Henry to return until the murderer is brought to justice."

The confirmation of my greatest fear sat heavy in my heart. I didn't know what the next step was. I only knew I had to unravel this mystery. It was the only chance of finding my grandfather alive, or returning to any semblance of my life.

"My grandfather and your husband believed Lord Rathford invented something dangerous." I placed my tea on the table. "Do you know what it was?"

"No," Lucinda admitted. "I knew nothing. I didn't even know Simon was working on Rathford's machine."

"In the back of the book, hidden in the blank pages, there's a message written near the binding. It says to begin with the raven. Does that mean anything to you?" I asked.

"The raven?" Lucinda visibly paled, then rose and hurried from the room.

She returned holding a large clockwork raven. Dark brass and copper gears swirled in the bird's breast, just beneath smooth dark wings. Two wheels instead of feet had been set on short brass legs. The body looked real, with real feathers, and the eyes were clear black beads. The brass beak had been so carefully crafted, the stately bird seemed as if it could come alive and steal the crumpet off my plate.

In the center of its chest was the flower medallion.

CHAPTER TWELVE

"HAVE YOU TRIED TO WIND IT?" I SMOOTHED MY fingertips over the fine feathers on the back of the bird's wing. The craftsmanship was amazing. If I hadn't known better, I would have thought the bird hatched with brass and gears in its body.

"It can't be wound," Lucinda said, folding her hands in her lap. A look of resigned longing came over her face. "Simon's key won't work."

"What does it do?" Will asked.

"I don't know." Lucinda ran her hand over the raven's head. A hint of a smile played at her lips. It reminded me of the way my mother would smile at my father when he burned the candles to stubs to keep fiddling with his gears for "just another moment."

"I'd love to see it work," the widow said and the hint of life and love that had come into her eyes died away again.

I lifted the raven into my lap. I was expecting it to be heavy, but it hardly weighed as much as a real bird. That alone was an astonishing feat.

Excitement rushed to my fingertips as I lifted the key from around my neck. I could bring the bird to life. I knew what to do.

I caught Lucinda's eye as I cracked the key open. Her brow knit together as her gaze dropped down to the circle of silver in my palm. I slowly opened the key, letting the flower unfold its elegant petals. Lucinda's eyes widened, and she brought her hand to her lips. "How extraordinary," she whispered.

She had yet to see what was to come. I slid the medallion to the side and fitted the key into the raven's chest, then bit my lip as I pressed the button. The notes of Papa's song rang out.

Lucinda gasped. "What is that strange music?"

"Your key doesn't play the tune?" I asked.

"No. Mine is a simple key, this is remarkable." Lucinda leaned closer.

If none of the other keys played a song, then my key was

truly the master. My grandfather had given me a wonderful gift, the gift of a memory, a song, one that had the power to unlock the impossible.

The song halted, but no door opened to reveal the keys I had to play. Where were they?

I tipped the bird over, looking for the hatch, but found none. A rush of panic seized me.

What if I couldn't get it to work? Where could the keys be hidden? As I turned the bird back over, my hand brushed the tail. I heard a soft *dink*.

Puzzled, I looked to Will. He nodded at me as if he knew what I should be thinking.

Of course, the tail!

The bird had twelve feathers, five short, seven long, in the pattern of a perfect octave.

I placed the bird on the table and stroked the tail feathers; each one rang with a tone that sounded like a spring being released. When I hit the final note, the bird blinked its eyes and let out a metallic caw. Pinwheels unfolded from the front edge of each of its wings as it spread them and lowered its head. A crank emerged from its back as it blinked again and trembled almost as if in anticipation.

"It looks as if it's about to fly." Lucinda's voice was filled with wonder. "How did he do it in something so small?"

"Let's take it outside and see where it goes," I suggested, lifting the bird by the chest, careful of the outstretched wings. I couldn't wait to see it soar.

"Have you lost your mind completely?" Will pushed on the back of my chair. I turned around.

"This bird could lead us to the next clue." I didn't know what the bird was made for, but with each new step I unlocked, my path seemed to become clearer. If the bird was going to fly, I wanted to see where it led.

"It could lead us into a trap." Will paced away from me, returning to the doorway. "Have you forgotten there's a murderer out there? One that clearly wants you dead?"

"Will . . . ," I protested. "We have to know." I stood and looked Lucinda in the eye. "If we don't unravel this mystery, I will have to live the rest of my days waiting for that man to kill me. This is the only way to discover his identity and bring him to justice. It's up to us."

Lucinda pressed her lovely lips together in an expression of pure iron. "I'll join you."

"No," Will cut in. "This is madness. You'll get killed."

Lucinda turned to him. "I'm already dead. I have nothing left to lose."

I took her hand. "Neither do I. I want to see this fly, and I'm going to follow it."

Will let out an exasperated breath and rubbed his hands over his hair, then interlocked his fingers behind his neck. Lucinda squeezed my hand tighter. In that moment, I knew we were of one mind.

"Fine. I'll hitch the horse. You can't chase a bloody bird on foot." Will snatched his cap out of his pocket and fit it on his head with a rough jerk.

My heart felt like it was growing in my chest. "Thank you . . ."

"Don't," he snapped. "Don't thank me. You should've thanked me if I'd talked you out of it." His accent thickened as he turned his back on us and stormed out the door.

"He can't help himself, can he?" Lucinda tilted her head in bemused consideration.

"Can't help being rude?" I had only wanted to thank him. If he didn't want to be a part of this, he could return to the baron at any time. He didn't have cause to lash out at us.

Lucinda chuckled then smiled as if she knew a secret. I didn't like that look. I felt as if she were playing some sort of game but I didn't know the rules. It left me with only one option: keep quiet.

"Come, Meg. Let's collect our things. It seems we're going for a ride." Lucinda gathered her skirts.

"I thought you wished to be left alone," I said, following her up the stairs.

"That was before I witnessed part of Simon come alive again. Thank you for that."

"You're welcome." If the Amusementists were family, I hoped she could consider me one. I would have loved to have had a sister.

We met Will outside behind the mews, where he'd hitched a light two-wheeled calash to a pretty little chestnut mare. She tossed her head and fidgeted as if she wanted to dance.

Lucinda stroked the horse's nose. "You ready to run, girl?"

I gingerly held the raven as I hunched my shoulder to keep the satchel from falling off my arm. It contained Simon's book, and a bit of cheese and bread. The raven vibrated with its wings outstretched, waiting. "Where should we let it go?"

"Here's as good a place as any," Will suggested, pointing down the long narrow alley. He collapsed the top of the carriage, folding it back behind the seat. "It's probably going to fly straight into a wall."

"Have some faith in my husband." Lucinda took the raven and wound it until the crank couldn't turn any more. It let out another caw. She placed it on the ground, adjusted her own feathered bonnet, and then pressed the button on the bird's back.

The crank sank back down into the body of the raven as Lucinda and I climbed in the carriage and Will jumped into the driver's seat.

The raven's wings jerked once, twice, then the pinwheels began to spin. The pinwheels gained speed and, with a caw, the bird raced down the alley then rose swiftly into the air.

"After it!" I shouted, taken with the excitement of the moment as Will urged the mare into a quick trot. We flew out of the alley and turned down Bond Street. Will snapped the reins and we charged into a run.

The raven kept climbing, sunlight glinting off its gears.

"It's turning to the west," Lucinda cried, clinging to her bonnet.

We raced up Bond Street and turned left on Oxford. Will expertly weaved through the street, leaving angry curses from fellow drivers hanging in the air as we passed. The clatter of hooves and wheels drummed out all other noise as we chased the raven along the north end of Hyde Park.

The tree branches blurred as I watched the raven gliding through the sky. Lucinda laughed as we surged forward again, Will pushing the mare into another swift canter.

"Hold on!" I clung to the seat as we swerved to avoid a cab crossing in front of us. The carriage leaned, and I fell against Lucinda.

"It's turning to the north!" Lucinda gripped my arm. Will turned to the right so suddenly, it threw me to the side of the carriage.

We chased the bird through Paddington, but it continued veering north, forcing us off the main roads as we headed into the countryside.

The wide avenues of London degraded to rutted paths and farm roads as we careened down the hills toward the creeks of Cricklewood.

The bird descended, and I nearly lost it in the trees. Spring rain had swollen the creeks, turning the country lanes into a muddy trap.

Will slowed the mare to a trot, but the enthusiastic chestnut pulled the cart with endless vigor, bouncing us along farm roads.

"I see it over there." Lucinda pointed over the edge of the carriage as a low-hanging branch whipped overhead. "It's disappeared beyond that barn."

A small rise hid a sharp right turn. Will tried to keep the calash on the road, but the wheels of the carriage slipped. The whole contraption leaned precariously to the left. I tried to hold on and lean into Lucinda, but it did no good. The carriage continued to overturn.

"Jump!" Will shouted. I leapt as hard as I could, but my skirt caught, twisting me before we splashed into a watery ditch to the side of the road. I struggled under the carriage, but couldn't pull myself up. I could barely keep my mouth above the water. I tried to breathe but the muddy dreck filled my mouth.

I tried to push my way out, but my hands sank into the soft mud of the ditch. I couldn't lift my head. I panicked, afraid I'd taken my last breath.

Strong hands grasped me under the arms and yanked. I choked as my head burst above the water, but my skirts were caught beneath the wreck.

"Hold on," Will urged as he kept my head up. I clung to his wet sleeve as he came around to the front of me and pulled. I kicked at the wreckage, struggling to get free. I felt my skirts ripping along the seam at my knee as Will pulled.

Whatever I was caught on broke loose, and Will tumbled backward, pulling me on top of him. I felt the heat of his body through the cold water, even as he lifted me up so I could grab onto the roots overhanging the edge of the bank. I scrambled up the bank, with the long loop of the ripped hem of my skirt and petticoat slogging about my feet.

"Are you harmed?" Will was beside me in a moment as I coughed and sputtered. "Were you crushed?"

He gripped my exposed knee right where the ribbon from the bottom ruffle of my drawers tied. The wet cotton of my thin stockings clung to my skin, becoming transparent.

My heart beat heavy in my chest as I stared at his hands clasped about my knee. They felt so warm and strong, and I could feel the firm pressure of his touch deep within me.

His eyes met mine, and I could have sworn I became part of the puddle. "Does this hurt?" he asked. His voice deepened, yet sounded softer than I'd ever heard it.

"No," I answered, though I hardly made a sound. I couldn't stop looking at his hands.

They slid down my exposed stocking, smoothing over the leather of my boot. His thumb brushed over the long line of buttons closing the leather in a curving seam along the inside of my ankle. His large hands clasped around my foot. I became aware of how delicate and shapely my ankle looked wrapped in the sleek black leather and resting in the strength of his hands. My heart stopped and I couldn't find my breath.

"How about this?" His eyes burned into mine.

I kicked out, overcome, unable to stand his touch any longer.

"I'm fine." In truth, I felt I was slowly dying, but I couldn't tell him that. I pulled my feet closer to the ruined hem of the dress, feeling the loss of his touch. "Nothing is broken." Even as I said it, I wasn't sure if it was the truth. My feet were fine. The rest of me was in question. "Where's Lucinda?"

I turned around to see Lucinda pulling her mare up.

Thank the dear Lord the creature was unharmed and Lucinda was well.

The carriage lay on its side, half submerged in the mud of the ditch. "I suppose this means we're walking," I grumbled.

Will shook his head in disbelief. "Can you stand?"

I nodded as I got to my feet. "I can't go very far with this dress, though." I gritted my teeth and clenched the hem. Yanking on the seam, I pulled the rest of the tattered fabric off, shortening my skirt to just past my knees, then did the same for the soggy petticoat.

"Thank heaven no one will see me like this," I mused as

I looked up. Will's eyes were fixed on my shapely boots. He blinked and swallowed as if he had a lump in his throat.

I felt hot so suddenly that I had to fight the urge to unbutton my collar.

He looked away, turning his attention to the horse. "Is she sound?" he asked Lucinda, who had managed to escape the mess with a muddy skirt, but her crinoline as full, fashionable, and modest as ever.

"She's fine." Lucinda handed the horse's reins to Will, who immediately ran his hands down each of the mare's legs just as he had mine. A tickle climbed up my back. "Meg, are you injured?" Lucinda called.

I crossed the road. My hands were shaking, and I felt choked from the murky water. My dress clung to my body, soaked through, but I was alive.

"My skirt suffered the worst of it," I answered.

How was I supposed to walk knowing Will could see my feet? Hell, how was I supposed to walk when I could still feel his hand upon my knee?

"I believe the raven landed near that barn. It isn't far at all," Lucinda said as I fell into step beside her. She smoothed a hand over her wildly mussed hair and pulled the wrecked bonnet from her head, then picked up the satchel containing the book and what little food we had hastily packed before leaving the toy shop. Thankfully, it was dry.

"Lovely shoes," she whispered in a conspiratorial manner. "Such a pity we have to hide them all the time, don't you think?" In spite of the misery we found ourselves in, I laughed.

CHAPTER THIRTEEN

THE RAVEN HAD PERCHED ON A ROTTING THATCHED roof. As we drew closer, I realized the crumbling heap of stone it topped had been a sheep barn. Now it was hardly more than four rough piles of mortared rocks with molding sticks clinging to the top.

The raven cawed over and over, a beacon of sound in the otherwise peaceful countryside.

With my sopping dress still dripping on my shoes, I shivered as I passed into the shadow of the barn and turned the latch of the large arched door. Gaps had opened up between the weathered slats, but I couldn't see anything through them.

"Careful, that roof could come down any moment," Will

warned as we pushed the door open. A flock of sparrows took wing in a flurry of motion and noise. I recoiled, ducking my head, and they darted out of a hole in the roof with swift precision.

"Look at that." Will's voice was filled with awe. I drew my gaze down the shaft of sunlight streaking through the open roof. Particles of dust glittered and swirled in the sun, then came to rest on the elegantly bowed heads of two metal horses.

"Gracious," I whispered. The sight drew me forward. The horses were just like the illustrations in the book, and yet to see them real before me took my breath away.

Silver plates formed their bodies, making them look like armored horses from the days when knights jousted for a lady fair. Each line, each seam in the plates was a graceful work of art. Instead of legs, they stood on large wheels with woven spokes that looked like shining frost on perfect spiderwebs. Every detail, from the soft curl of brass that made their long eyelashes to their wire manes tied neatly into little knots along the crests of their necks, was exquisite.

Behind them waited a coach that looked like something from the court of King Louis XIV, only each ornament was a small piston or gear so artfully created I had a hard time believing they were functional and not purely for the pleasure of the eye.

Lucinda let out a girlish squeal. "I haven't seen this since I was a child! Come."

She grabbed me by the arm and pulled me to the coach. With complete abandon, she threw open the door and climbed in with no mind of her crinoline. The wide hoops of her skirt nearly tipped up in a very unladylike manner. We tumbled in, landing in a pool of damp skirts.

The interior overwhelmed me, and I found I couldn't speak, only gaze with amazement. A rich velvet bench lined the back of the coach. Along the front, a single velvet-topped stool perched before a variety of knobs, levers, and wheels beneath the large window. Between my muddy dress and my habit of unintentionally dismantling things, I didn't want to touch anything.

Will stepped up on the footboard. The whole thing shifted under his weight as he hung on to the frame and marveled at the interior. There was a wonder in his eyes I hadn't seen since the key first opened in his hand. "How does a man make such a thing?"

Lucinda beamed. "It's beautiful, isn't it?"

"Never in my life could I have dreamed of this," I admitted. "How does it work?"

A thoughtful expression creased Lucinda's brow. "We have to find the right tumbler. Open the doors to give us more light," she ordered.

Will jumped off the footboard and pulled open the barn doors. Sunlight streaked in, shining on the magnificent horses.

"Meg, look." Lucinda pointed to the flower medallion in the center of the levers and wheels. "You have the key."

I smiled as I lifted the key from around my neck. Lucinda slid the medallion to the side and I fitted the blossom in place. I pressed the button and the song filled the interior of the coach. Lucinda tried to hum along, but she was horridly discordant, and got lost only two phrases in. I knew how it should sound. I knew what to do as the panel opened just beneath the medallion.

A piece of paper and a thick wheel that looked a bit like the tumbler in a music box fell out of the panel. Lucinda barely caught them as the song coming from my key stopped. I played the next phrase.

A great crank emerged just beneath the window. It settled into place with a grinding noise and a single loud *thunk*.

Lucinda unfolded the paper and began to read. The paper fluttered in her hand like a dry leaf in a hard autumn wind. She dropped the tumbler. "What is it?" I asked, moving closer to try to see over her shoulder.

"It's from Simon," she whispered.

Will returned and pulled himself into the coach even as Lucinda fell to a seat on the bench. She handed the letter to me, then pressed her unsteady hands in a steeple and touched them to her lips.

"'Dear Henry,'" I read, for Will's sake.

I looked to Lucinda. It was a letter to my grandfather? She nodded and circled her hand to indicate I should continue. I brought my gaze back to the letter, but my hand was trembling now too.

"'It is as you feared. So long as the heart of Rathford's atrocity is intact, he can re-create the pieces we've made, and so destroying them is useless. We must undo the heart of the machine to truly render it powerless.

"'Someone must convince him to forsake this mad obsession for reason. The only advantage we have is the lock guarding the machine. We've sabotaged it to give us time until we can convince Rathford to abandon this folly and relinquish the heart. Charles and I have alerted the others. We were unable to reach the machine, but we've broken apart the pieces of the plate lock and hidden them within our Amusements. The only single man who could open them all is you. Rathford's efforts will be futile until he sees reason and abandons his terrible ambitions.

"'You are the only one we all trust. The tumbler will lead you to my piece of the puzzle. Stay safe, for if you perish, we will have no chance to truly undo what has been done.

"'If you are reading this, I am likely no longer alive. I hope that you're able to finally end this. Good luck. Please give Lucinda all my love. Keep her safe for me. —Simon.'"

By the end of the letter I could hardly speak. Lucinda was biting her lip, her eyes shining.

I looked at Will, not knowing what to do next. He lifted the tumbler from the floor and turned it over in his hands.

Lucinda took a deep breath. She lifted her chin. "What do we do?"

"Go forward," I decided. "If your Simon gave his life to destroy this thing, we have to find a way to do it."

She nodded, her expression hardening with her resolve.

"Will?" I waited for his protest. I could hear him in my mind. *'Tis dangerous. You'll get yourself kilt.* Perhaps the accent in my mind was a modest exaggeration.

Will nodded as the muscle in his jaw tightened. "Let's see where it leads."

I stood with my mouth agape.

Finally I regained my composure. "Lucinda, can you work this thing?" My query broke her out of the shock from Pricket's letter.

"Yes, of course." She took the tumbler from Will and fitted it into a half tube of brass, then lowered a metal arm so it nestled into a groove on one end. She reached out and struggled to turn the crank.

Will stepped in and took over the job, winding the coach until a loud clicking echoed through the barn. He was so strong. I had to admit, it was a relief to have him with us.

"Get the raven," Lucinda ordered. "And tie Daisy to the back."

Will and I climbed out as Lucinda spun two of the control wheels. The mechanical horses tossed their heads, their perfectly round onyx eyes shining as they blinked. They pushed their noses forward, and the wheels beneath them began to turn. I thought I might go behind to give them a push, but it wasn't needed. They rolled forward with confidence. The sunlight reached through the fine sheen of dust and glimmered on their silver haunches as they exited the barn.

After following the coach out, I unwound Daisy's reins

from the fence and walked her to the back. Will scaled the stone wall of the barn with catlike grace, scrambled over the rotting thatch, then plucked the now silent raven off the roof. Any moment he could fall through. I tied Daisy's reins to the coach then winced as I watched him slip back down the thatch, jump on top of the wall, then down to the ground. Honestly, he was worried about *my* ankles?

"What?" he asked as he passed me and stepped on the footboard with the raven tucked under his arm.

Boys.

I grabbed my skirt out of habit, then realized I didn't need to lift it as I climbed in. Lucinda sat on the stool, her hands on the wheels. I fought the urge to start flipping levers and wheels just to see what they would do. Knowing me, I'd irrevocably jam the gears with my fiddling.

"Where do we go?" I asked, focusing on the task at hand. Lucinda pushed a lever forward and the silver horses began to roll, turning northwest on the country lane.

"I don't know, but the coach does," Lucinda said. "It was made for the Duke of Chadwick, who often found himself hopelessly lost because he had such a terrible memory for places. Part of the challenge was to create a conveyance that could remember where it had been. The tumbler is a recording of every turn the coach last made. When you turn it around, it retraces its steps."

"Remarkable," Will muttered. "So the lever controls the speed?"

Lucinda nodded. "Yes, and this wheel controls direction, but we won't need that just yet. It really was brilliant."

"It *is* brilliant." I felt a swelling in my chest, a strange sense of pride. The coach was more fantastic than anything I had ever believed to be real, yet it was real. My family was a part of it.

"They should patent this." Will sat on the velvet bench, looking at bit like a pauper sitting on the throne of a king. "People would pay good money not to swim through horse—"

"Will," I warned. "There are ladies present."

Lucinda laughed. "Would you like to drive?"

Will didn't even nod. He simply swooped onto the stool the moment Lucinda rose. He took the controls as if he'd invented them. I found myself compelled by the look of utter concentration on his face.

For the first time since falling into the ditch, I felt warmth radiating through me from deep within. I was very glad Will was with us.

"Meg?"

I shook my head, startled, then looked at Lucinda.

"Perhaps you should sit down," she suggested as she reached into the satchel and produced a loaf of bread and a lump of cheese. "You seem out of sorts."

I joined her on the bench then tried to pull my ripped skirt over my knees, but it wouldn't cover the bottom frill of my drawers. At least my stockings had dried some, making them less transparent, but I still felt exposed.

Will glanced over his shoulder then quickly turned his eyes back to the road. Was he looking at me? Why?

I crossed my ankles, but couldn't stop the flush of heat that burned in my cheeks. I was hardly one to command the attention of a man, especially sitting next to the gilded beauty Lucinda possessed. Will couldn't possibly fancy me, so why did he watch me so intently?

I'll admit, I had noticed he was handsome when I first met him. At the time, it might have only been my shock at seeing someone my own age. Even Lucinda had said he was handsome, and she was only a few years his senior. Whatever it was that plagued me, it was more than his looks. It didn't come from his dark eyes or reluctant smile. It came from someplace deeper than that.

Did I fancy him?

No, it was only a passing interest.

I looked out the window, afraid my thoughts would somehow show on my face and betray this feeling to him. No matter how much I felt a longing to remain near him, something about Will and this sudden adventure left me ill at ease, but no matter how deeply I pondered the matter, I couldn't put my finger on what had me out of sorts.

We rolled along the quiet country roads north of London. The silver horses never once veered from the center of the road in spite of several turns along the narrow lanes. Patches of light shone through the clouds, creating a quilt of bright and deep greens accented by clusters of budding woods.

At one point we passed a farmer carting milk, and he nearly drove his poor mule off the road in his amazement. I wondered what he'd say to his friends at the tavern that night, and how fiercely they'd laugh at his story.

After several hours, the coach finally rolled to a stop at the bottom of a small hill in the middle of a large open field.

At first I wondered if the horses had wound down, but we'd reached the end of the tumbler, and the mechanical horses still tossed their heads.

"Do you know where we are?" I asked Lucinda as we

stepped out onto the grass. Daisy had already dropped her head and grazed contentedly by the side of the coach.

"I haven't the faintest," Lucinda admitted.

I trudged up the hill, hoping for a better view of the countryside. Perhaps there was something we had to see. Will came after me, marching up the hill with long strides.

Lucinda followed, losing the battle between her long skirts and the nearly knee-high grasses.

"Meg, look at this," Will shouted from the crest of the hill.

A block of gray stone like a pagan altar lay before us. In the center, someone had embedded the flower medallion.

CHAPTER FOURTEEN

THE LARGE RECTANGULAR ROCK REMINDED ME OF Pricket's gravestone. There had to be another clue hidden inside.

"Wait," Will said as he watched Lucinda still struggling up the hill. He headed back toward her, and I found myself annoyed by it. I didn't know what had possessed me to believe for a moment that Will might be attracted to me.

Lucinda would have reached us in her own time without his wrapping his arm around her waist and steadying her hand. Besides, if I could gather the next clue, or perhaps another tumbler hidden in the rock, I could save her the effort of stumbling the rest of the way, and requiring

Will's assistance to walk. Honestly, did she have to lean on him so?

Perhaps it would be better if I could just finish this. I took the key and fitted it, then lowered my ear to it so I could hear the tune. The delicate notes got lost on the breeze and I had to struggle to hear the portion of the song. I finally recognized it, and listened for the final phrase.

Spurred on by impatience, I twisted the key slightly in an effort to make the song go faster. If I could open the stone quickly, Will would arrive to see me triumphant. The key was all I had. It was the only thing that made me special.

The song finished, and I thought through the next phrase of the music, preparing myself to play it on the keys that were sure to reveal themselves.

But no, instead of keys, a tiny dial rose out of the ring surrounding the medallion.

Panic set in. I didn't know what to do with the dial and I had to get the stone open. Surely Lucinda would arrive and know exactly how it functioned, and I didn't want to hear the derision in Will's voice as he argued that I should have waited. I couldn't stand the humiliation.

As I inspected the dial, my mind worked furiously on how it might function. Along the outside, there were twelve pegs, long and short. They had to represent the octave. Assuming the one at the twelve o'clock position represented middle C, I tried to piece out mathematically the notes floating through my head.

It took me far too long, but to my great relief, as I turned the dial to align my chosen pegs with the mark on the outer ring, the rest of the song began to play. My heart raced. It was tricky and unnatural turning the dial, and I didn't want to make a mistake.

Finally, I turned the dial to the last note.

Watching the rock, I waited for it to unfold the way the gravestone had. A *boom* shook the ground.

What was that?

The shaking grew in intensity until I could no longer stand. I tumbled backward onto the grass. The stone slowly sank into the earth, and my heart sank with it. I leapt forward to retrieve the key just in time before it disappeared into a gaping hole.

"Meg, what happened?" Will shouted.

"I don't know!" I called, turning back to the dark hole where the stone had been. Black and endless, the deep maw of the hole opened wider. I only had the courage to peek in the deep cavity before fear forced me to scramble along the ground in retreat.

The ground rumbled and shook so violently, it pitched me toward the hole. With my chin nearly on the edge of the chasm, I clenched the grass, pushing myself back. A pained cry rang over the hill. Lucinda.

Turning away from the hole, I tried to stand and run to find the others, but I only managed three steps before the quake threw me to the ground once more.

Great mounds of earth rose around me then slid to the side as enormous pillars of what seemed to be rusted iron sprouted from the dirt like massive oak trunks.

I covered my ears. The terrible din of rattling metal and grinding gears deafened me. I rolled away from the great towers as they rose higher, driven by huge gears turning slowly along their sides.

Surrounded by the pillars of iron, I hunched down and tried to protect my head from the bits of dirt and rock raining down from the iron. I had no place to run. I couldn't see Will or Lucinda. At any moment I feared the pillars would tumble and crush me.

The ground stopped shaking as the pillars reached their full height. They must have been more than twenty feet tall. I struggled to my feet and ran toward the largest gap between them. Just as I neared it, the top half of the pillar tipped.

I screamed. The top of the pillar crashed down onto the one next to it, creating a cascade of falling iron in a wave around me. *Boom, boom, boom,* the pillars slammed onto the posts, until finally the last one dropped. The force of the sound pushed the breath from my body.

I fought to regain my breath as my ears rang with the noise. To my amazement, I found myself within an iron ring of monoliths, a metal re-creation of a pagan altar from long ago. *Stonehenge.*

Slots opened in the bottom of each horizontal beam of iron. Slowly, like spiders descending on delicate webs, large crystal lenses dropped between the pillars, suspended from copper wires.

I tried to swallow the dry lump in my throat as a whir-ring began behind me. I turned to see an enormous crystal emerge from the ground where the stone altar had been. Set like a jewel in a lofty crown, it rose on brass legs driven by steadily turning gears that looked as if they crawled up the brass spindles of their own accord.

When the crystal had reached its peak, stillness returned to the countryside.

I took three long, slow breaths, waiting for something else to come crashing down. Nothing.

"Will!" I screeched.

"Over here," he called.

I grabbed my skirts and ran as fast as I could down the hill. Will had Lucinda in his arms. He glared at me as I skidded and slid down the slope to him. Why was he holding her?

"You couldn't wait," he snapped. He turned from me, Lucinda gripping his neck as he carried her down the hill. She was biting her lip in pain.

"What happened?" I stumbled trying to keep up with him.

"You nearly killed us." Will reached the coach. He managed to open the door on his own and place Lucinda inside.

"I'm sorry," I said. "I didn't know that would happen."

Will turned on the footboard and the heat of his anger could have burned me. I felt shamed, and a strange desperation to restore whatever had just broken.

"Blast it, Meg," he growled. "You don't think things through. That's your problem."

"Will," Lucinda interjected with a tone that reminded me of a governess one would not wish to cross. "I only twisted an ankle." Lucinda fought with her crinoline to reach her injured foot, then gave up and propped it up on the bench.

"You could have broken your neck," Will insisted, then he turned his ire back on me. "And you could have been crushed." His voice changed as he said it, sharpening with a hard edge.

"Enough," Lucinda said. The reprimand snapped through the coach. "We have to put it aside for now. I will be fine, and Meg is unharmed. We don't have much time before we lose the light and those pillars sink."

I peeked around Will's crossed arms to see Lucinda on the bench. She looked exasperated as she lifted the satchel onto her lap.

"I'm sorry," I said. "I didn't expect there to be danger."

Lucinda pulled the book out from the leather sack. "Then you have just learned the first rule of Amusements. Expect the unexpected, especially danger." She flipped through the pages of the book, until she found what she was looking for. She turned the book so we could see it.

I slid into the door, and Will reluctantly let me past.

"Here." Lucinda pointed to a diagram. "It seems we've unearthed Gearhenge. According to Simon's notes, there's a trigger that reacts to light just below the crystal lens in the center of the structure. If you align the outer lenses, you can focus enough light to open a stairwell into the chamber below."

"What are we after?" It seemed unlikely I'd know it if I saw it.

"I haven't the faintest, but you're clever," she said. I could see the determination in her face, and I didn't want to let her down. I felt awful about her foot. I truly did. "I trust you'll find what we need."

I nodded.

As I jumped down from the coach and climbed back up the hill, it seemed Will intended to make me feel even worse. He wouldn't even look at me.

It wasn't my fault. It's not as if I could have suspected giant iron pillars would rise out of the ground. I'd apologized. Yet his shoulders remained stiff as he trudged back up the hill.

"Will?" I implored.

We reached the gap that served as an entrance into the circle. "Don't." He inspected the tear-shaped crystal at the center. "I don't want to hear it."

"Why are you here?" I asked. I crossed my arms as I studied him. "At every turn you complain about how you don't really want to do this, so why do you bother?"

He turned to look at me, really look at me. He stalked forward with his mouth pinched in a hard line until he crowded into my space. I tilted my chin in defiance, unwilling to take a step back. While my heart seemed ready to fly into my throat, I held steady.

"I am here to watch out for you." He inched closer, until his head was too close to mine. I couldn't bear it, so I took a step back.

"You could have fooled me," I mumbled, looking down to my exposed boots.

He didn't say anything for a long moment. I didn't need to look at his face to feel the anger there. He snapped his cap off his head and put it in his coat pocket.

"The problem, Meg, is that you only ever think of yourself." His words were low, earnest in a way that made me feel a deep shame for every failing I had ever had.

My heart went from my throat straight to my shoes. Will turned away from me, tramping over to the first iron archway. His words played over and over in my mind.

Reaching above his head, he was just able to tip the bottom edge of the glass lens until a flare of light hit the crystal in the center.

"You find me selfish?" I followed after him as he walked casually to the next arch and tipped the second lens until the crystal glowed brighter.

He let his arms drop to his sides. "Aye, I do."

I didn't know what to say. What could I say? Never in my life had I been accused of such a thing. I wanted to retort, but something stopped me. I had a feeling nothing I could ever say would change his opinion, and by arguing, I'd only dig my grave deeper.

Will made quick work of the lenses, and I had to leave him to it, as I couldn't reach them on my own. I needed him. Over and over, he could do the things I couldn't. I hated it.

If he didn't wish to be here, then he was a fool for staying. And if I was selfish, it was only due to the fact that I felt so much of this mystery rested on my shoulders.

As he tipped the final lens, the crystal in the center glowed like a captive star.

The whirring started again and the earth around the center crystal began sinking. The hole opened wider as chunks of grass segmented into neat squares and dropped down. It looked as if the hole was slowly eating the earth, creating an entrance for the top of a stair while the crystal seemed to float above it, suspended by iron. I backed up, afraid that the opening would take the ground beneath my feet as well. Finally the whirring stopped, and I cautiously stepped to the edge of the hole.

Metal plates hung from a framework of vertical bars creating a floating spiral stair. I cautiously tested them out as I descended only a few steps into a great vacuous room. It seemed the whole of the hill was hollow, and the area beneath it a remarkable dome, like the top of some great cathedral sunken beneath the ground.

Losing my courage, I came back up and found Will. "Are you coming?"

He shook his head even as he closed the gap between us and joined me on the stair. We climbed down in silence, partly because of my nerves, as the steps swayed and the cables holding them trembled. I also didn't know what else to say. As we turned through the circles of steps and bars, drawing closer and closer to the deep center of the dome, one question was in the forefront of my mind. "What do you want of me?" I whispered.

Will sighed as we reached the floor of the cavernous room. "Think," he said. "Stop and think."

I hung my head as I hopped off the final step and looked around. Instead of dirt, the interior of the dome shone with polished black stone that glittered with tiny crystals embedded in the rock. It took me a moment to realize the crystals were a map of the stars. I could trace the constellations.

"What is this place?" I whispered as I gazed around. The cascade of light from the crystal lens above spilled down, showering a mirrored globe in the center of the structure. It reflected a blanket of glittering light throughout the room. The speckled light seemed to dance, bouncing off mirrors that ringed the outer edge of the dome.

The light played everywhere yet nowhere at once, creating a million pinpoints of light and making the crystals shine more brilliantly than their nightly counterparts. Standing at the center of it made me feel as if I'd been set adrift in a sea of enchanted starlight.

"We haven't long before we lose the sun," Will stated. Did he even see where we were? It was amazing. The coach seemed a toy wagon compared to this.

Reluctantly, I dragged my gaze from the crystal stars. I turned around, then started, jumping backward in shock. A man was slumped against the wall, his head hanging. I couldn't see his face, only a dapper hat and dusty coat.

"Is he dead?" I gasped, as Will stepped in front of me. He crept closer to the man.

"No, it's not a man at all. It's a machine." He took my hand and led me forward, but my fright had hardly abated. "Look."

I peeked around him. The man's skin was indeed brass, jointed so he looked a bit like a golden suit of armor in a hat and well-cut coat. He held a ten-inch square plate in each hand, their faces covered with interlocking gears.

"Those must be parts of the lock from Pricket's letter," I whispered. "He said they had broken it apart and hid it within the Amusements."

Will reached out to take one, but he couldn't pull it from the automaton's hands. "He won't let go."

I eased forward. Along the lapel of his coat, just above his heart, I spotted the flower medallion.

I fitted the key into the automaton with a growing sense of trepidation. Never again would I take an Amusement for granted. As I pressed the button, I took a step back. The man trembled, lifted his head, then blinked open dark eyes and looked at me.

I took a second step back and felt Will's hand, strong and reassuring on my shoulder. The golden man opened his mouth and began to sing.

The notes of grandfather's song rang out, sung by a voice eerily similar to my Papa's, but it wasn't the melody. It was as if the clockwork man sang a second part, similar, but not the same. At first it confused me. I started to hum, following the rhythm. To my amazement, the notes blended seamlessly.

It was the harmony.

I joined him, singing the melody as loudly and clearly as

I could. Our voices merged, ringing through the hall until the cords holding the stairs resonated, adding a peculiar harmonic to our song. I felt as if I were singing with Papa. My emotion swelled and nearly choked me, but I continued to sing.

As the notes soared through the room, the fingers of the clockwork man's hands slowly opened. Will took the first plate, then the second.

The automaton smiled, then his eyes closed and his head drooped down to his chest once more. I marveled at the wonder of the mechanical man, feeling a sense of loss now that I could only hear the echo of his voice in the chamber.

"Come on, Meg," Will urged.

I hesitated, not wanting to leave the amazing clockwork man in the dark.

"Meg." Will's voice dropped and I knew I had to leave. He was right. I shouldn't endanger him by lingering. I pressed a kiss to my fingertips and touched the clockwork man's flower medallion then dashed after Will up the hanging stairs.

CHAPTER FIFTEEN

HALFWAY UP THE STAIRS, THE LIGHT DIMMED. I FELT A tremble in the strands holding the stairs aloft. Will's foot slipped, and he gripped the thick cords as the whole stair swayed ominously.

"Hurry!" I clambered up behind him. The stairs shook, then slowly began to rise. I clung to the spindles, praying I wouldn't fall to my death. I tried not to look down as we struggled toward the circle of sky above us.

We burst from the stair and tumbled across the grass.

"Hold on," I warned as Will threw an arm over my back and ducked his head. The lenses retreated back into the iron beams, then the tops of the metal arches rose up once more into towering pillars.

The ground shook with violent force as the pillars receded back under the hill. The patches of earth and grass replaced themselves, and the stone altar rose back out of the ground.

All fell quiet again, though I could have sworn the ground continued to move. Realizing it was the trembling of my own body, I lifted my head and looked around. Except for the rumpled-looking grasses, there was no sign that the great iron arches had ever existed.

Will offered me a hand. His expression held no lingering anger, but I couldn't believe he had either forgiven or forgotten the harsh criticism he had inflicted upon me.

I placed my hand in his and he steadied me until I found my feet. The sensation of the ground moving only intensified. His gaze drifted over me, dark and mysterious as it had always been. I didn't like being on unsteady ground.

I walked away from him and picked the plates up from where he had left them in the grass, then I carried them back down the hill without a word. I reached the coach to find Lucinda sitting on the floor, swimming in a pile of tumblers.

She glanced at the plates in my hands. "What did you find?"

"They look like they might be parts of the lock Simon mentioned in his letter," I said as I handed them to her.

"I never dealt closely with locks," she said. "I wish there were someone who could tell us more."

"What are all these?" I asked as I tried to find room for my toes amidst the tumblers.

"His Grace recorded tumblers for all the recent Amusements. I found them under the bench."

I gathered a few of the bumpy cylinders and inspected them. On one side would be various estates throughout the countryside, but the other side had been marked the same on each tumbler.

Chadwick Hall.

"What is Chadwick Hall?" I asked as Will climbed up on the footboard.

"It's His Grace's country estate." Lucinda seemed concerned. "I was hoping there'd be one that could take us back to London."

Without a regular carriage of any sort, we'd either have to drive the coach to London ourselves, or trust our feet. Considering we were miles from the nearest habitable shack, I felt inclined to stay near the coach.

"If we head southeast we'll find London." Will pushed

past me into the coach and took a seat on the driver's stool. "Or we can turn the original tumbler back around."

"But we can't exactly tour the streets of London in this," I reminded him with a wave of my hand. "Whoever intends to murder me might find it conspicuous."

Will crossed his arms and scowled. "What do you suggest then?"

"Is the duke trustworthy?" I asked, helping Lucinda onto the bench. I lifted her injured ankle onto the velvet and took a seat on the floor beside her. "He had to be in on the conspiracy to hide the pieces of the lock, or he wouldn't have hidden his coach."

She shook her head. "I don't know. I don't know whom to trust. I haven't heard anything about the duke since Simon's death. He might be in hiding like the others, but even if the hall is abandoned, I know a way in." She sat straighter.

I looked through the tumblers until I found the one marked for Gearhenge and Chadwick Hall. I held it out to Will, but he seemed skeptical.

"Once we are at Chadwick Hall, the tumblers will be able to take us anywhere we need to go." I don't know why I felt I had to justify the decision to call upon the duke, but I needed him to know I was thinking this through and not acting rashly.

"We haven't been traveling quickly. We could have been easily followed," he reminded me. "Especially if the farmer we passed starts telling stories."

"It's a risk we'll have to take," I said. I felt a creeping apprehension grip my neck and shoulders. "There's no other way."

Will looked me deeply in the eye, then at the tumbler.

"How convenient. I suppose it's decided then." Will didn't bother to hide the edge of bitterness in his voice as he held out his hand. I placed the tumbler in it. He took a moment to examine it carefully before fitting the cylinder in the controls and lowering the arm.

He wound the coach, then started us off again. Relief poured through me as we rumbled along, the motion soothing after the turmoil of the afternoon. I didn't know what to do about Will, or how to regain his trust. I found myself wondering if I had ever earned it to begin with.

"Tell me all about the Amusement," Lucinda whispered, pulling me away from my darker thoughts. In the fading light she examined one of the plates we had retrieved. "Was it amazing?"

I told her about the crystals and the stair, the lights shining in the center of the hill and the clockwork man we had found there. She hung on every word.

"I wish I could have seen it." Lucinda sighed, looking out the window at the hills as if any one of them could be hiding a cavern of stars. "It must have been breathtaking."

"Yes," I admitted. "It was."

She drew her lips into a thin line as she watched the sun splash color over the clouds in the west.

The light died, and Will lit a lamp in the corner. The firelight caught in his dark hair and made his slightly tanned skin glow. He nodded to Lucinda, then caught me staring. Embarrassed, I focused on my dirty and torn fingernails as he took his seat.

My unease returned. "I didn't mean for you to be hurt," I said without looking up at Lucinda. I didn't want to see the terrible inequality between us. Lucinda was my better in every way. I couldn't help how I felt about her and Will, but I did feel sorry that she had been injured.

Lucinda smiled and placed a hand on my arm, the clean edges of her nails glowing like tiny moons. "I know. Someday we can come here again, and you can show me the chamber beneath the hill. We can bring a picnic."

"And wax for our ears," I added, reminding myself that she had only ever offered me kindness and that I should return it.

Lucinda laughed, then her expression became very serious. "Thank you, Meg."

Her words surprised me since I had done nothing to deserve them. "You're thanking me for injuring your ankle, destroying your carriage, and ruining your dress?" If she had any idea of the ugly thoughts in my mind, she would curse me for a year.

She offered me a wistful smile that seemed to show more in her eyes than on her lips. "Thank you for finding me. I think about Simon and our . . ." She paused, her voice catching. "Our life together, every minute of every day. I still have not stopped thinking about him, but today what I thought more than anything was that he would have loved this. It has made me remember him fondly."

I squeezed her hand then let my head rest against the wall of the coach. In that moment, I wanted Lucinda as a friend. I had to find a way to push my jealousy aside. Exhausted, I drifted off, my dreams filled with swirling speckles of light and a man made of shining brass.

"Meg, wake up."

My shoulder shook and my eyes snapped open. Will's coat covered my chest and lap, while Lucinda slept curled on her side on the velvet bench like a princess from a fairy tale.

"What's going on?" I asked, rubbing the sleep from my eyes. My hands lingered on the coat as I pulled it off me. The cold night air rushed in, and I suddenly wished to burrow under the warmth of the coat and remain there all night. The dim light of the small lamp in the coach cast the world beyond the windows in inky black.

"We've stopped." Will pulled a knife from his boot. Light flickered along the blade.

"Heaven's mercy, what do you intend to do with that?" I scooted back against the side of the coach.

"There're no lights. I don't think anyone's here, but we have to be careful." He took the pistol out as well, considered it against the knife, and returned his knife to his boot. Will opened the door and stepped down onto the footboard.

I was beginning to think perhaps Will was a bit too careful. It was one thing to be prepared, but such a show of force might not endear us to the duke. Still, I shrugged off his coat and climbed out of the coach.

My body ached, especially my back and legs. I had to fight the urge to hunch. My boot hit groomed stone. We were on some sort of drive. If only the moon were a bit fuller. We needed the light. The lamp inside the coach was fixed to the wall, and it did little to help us outside.

I could see the shadows of trees and a large building just ahead of us, but it didn't hold a candle to the monstrosity looming to the left. An enormous estate that reeked of generations of wealth and entitlement squatted like a fat old king on the throne of the rise.

We must have been near the stables, which were impressive enough. Five or six storefronts from Oxford Street could have fit across the length of them.

Good gracious, I'd never seen such wealth.

"How could an estate like this be empty?" I muttered, following Will toward the stables. It didn't seem possible. A house that size required the effort of hundreds to maintain it.

"That's what I'm worried about." Will held his pistol at the ready. "There has to be a caretaker."

Our boots crunched as we walked in silence. Everything seemed so still.

A shot rang out. I screamed, falling to the ground, as Will crouched in front of me. How had the murderer reached this place before us?

"Whoever's out there," a man's voice rang out, "it would be in your best interest to abandon any thought of looting the house. It might be a bit harmful for your health." I stared at a floating light coming toward us.

Will pushed his arm in front of me, perhaps under the assumption his limb could protect me from the man strolling up the path looking as if he were ready to engage in a duel and knew he would win.

I held on to Will's shoulder, peeking over his arm as the man ambled closer. He had wild hair that stuck out at odd angles in a short shaggy mop above his impressive sideburns. Over his eyes he wore a pair of glowing goggles, even as he carried an impossibly long rifle that sprouted tubes and gears along one side.

Dressed in a long brown coat that ended at the tops of his buckled boots, and a shirt open at the collar, he seemed from another world entirely.

Placing the stock of the rifle on the ground, he cocked his head and gave us a lopsided grin. Only then did I realize he couldn't have been much older than us.

"So, should I kill you, or not?"

"I'd prefer not," I stated, rising to stand. He was an Amusementist. He had to be. "We're friends of Lucinda Pricket. She's hurt. We need a place to rest. We had no place else to turn."

"Lucinda?" Her name fell from his lips like a prayer. He fumbled the gun and it accidentally went off in a shower of red sparks. He winced. "Where is she?"

"In the coach." I pointed behind us, and while I couldn't see the man's eyes, his posture went rigid, as if he'd just seen a ghost.

He ran toward it, and I moved to follow. Will grabbed my arm. "What are you for?" he scolded. "He could be the murderer."

"Does he look like a murderer to you?" I yanked my arm from him and hurried toward the coach. Will fell into step beside me.

"He has a gun." Will lengthened his stride.

"So do you," I reminded him.

I beat Will to the coach door, only to see the man kneeling beside Lucinda. He had her hand in his as she woke.

"Oliver?" she whispered. A smile played at her lips, but her expression appeared sad somehow. "What are you doing here?"

"I might ask you the same thing, Luli." His touch slid along her arm until he drew both her delicate hands into his.

She looked away, her eyes darting toward me, the light, anything but him. "I thought you were in America." She pulled her hands from his and straightened her skirt.

"I've returned." Oliver leaned back. "Who are your friends?"

Lucinda glanced at me. "Miss Whitlock, allow me to introduce you to the Marquess of Brairton."

I took a step back. "My lord." I bowed my head, but he folded me in a sudden embrace. Startled, I didn't know how to respond, other than to push against the soft leather of his coat.

"My God!" he exclaimed, holding me at arm's length. "Sweet little Margaret? I thought you were dead. Thank the dear Lord you survived." He patted me on the shoulders. "I haven't seen you since you were a baby, and I was a scruffy little tramp with skinned knees. You've grown quite well."

"I go by Meg, my lord," I clarified, stepping back from him as Will moved closer behind me. "This is William MacDonald."

"Are you one of Argus's boys from the Foundry?" he asked, genuinely pleased.

"No," Will answered with a puzzled look. "I'm just a tinker."

"He's a friend, Lord Brairton." The moment I said it, I felt my heart swell. Somehow whatever was between us, it felt more than simple friendship. He had saved my life not once but twice. A tingle shivered up my exposed calves.

"Unfortunately, it's Duke of Chadwick now. But please, call me Oliver. If I hear anyone say 'Your Grace,' I can't be held accountable for my actions." He ran a hand through his hair, making it stand up further. Only the glowing goggles perched high on his forehead kept it at bay.

Lucinda leaned forward. "You've inherited? What happened to your father?" There was no mistaking the shock in her face.

"It's too much to explain here." His rich voice dropped. "Come. We have much to discuss inside."

CHAPTER SIXTEEN

I HADN'T SEEN VERY MANY DUKES, BUT I FELT CERTAIN the majority of the House of Lords did not look like this one.

"Where were you injured?" he asked Lucinda, lifting his hand as if he were about to place it to the side of her face. He paused, then let his fingers fall away from so intimate a caress.

She gave her head a little shake. "Really, I took a silly tumble down a hill and turned my ankle. I'm quite fine."

Lucinda stood to prove she was sound. At the same moment Will put his weight on the footboard and the coach shifted. Lucinda winced. Her ankle gave, and she fell, right into the duke's arms.

"I see you're still stubborn." Without another word, he handed his gun to Will and swept Lucinda off her feet. She squealed and clung to his neck.

"Oliver! Put me down this instant." She hit him on the shoulder with enough force that he had to catch his balance. He glanced over at me and raised one eyebrow in question.

"We were at Gearhenge," I confessed. "We didn't anticipate the way the hill would shake."

"You raised that thing?" His voice pitched with awe as he edged to the door. Will and I moved to let the duke pass. "I thought Charles had locked it."

I followed the duke as Will guided the coach into the stable. Using my longest strides, I almost had to break into a run to keep up with him. "I had a key."

The duke stopped cold and turned to me. Lucinda brushed a wayward lock of hair off her forehead and wriggled. He didn't let her down. "A key, or *the* key?" he asked, as if the world hung on my answer.

Doubt flashed through my mind. Could I trust this duke? There was something about him, something open and guileless. It was very likely unwise to trust him, but in my heart, I knew it was the right thing to do.

"It's my grandfather's."

He visibly paled. "Then you're in grave danger."

Well, that much I knew. Will pulled the stable doors closed with a deep *boom*, and then jogged to my side. Together we followed the duke through a slightly overgrown formal garden, past a neat white kitchen gate, and down a set of servant's stairs in the back.

A low smoldering fire and single candle cast the majority of the enormous kitchen in shadow. Only the tiny glowing circle of light on a large but empty table welcomed us into the grand mansion.

The duke set Lucinda on the bench by the table then used the pump to wet a rag. "I apologize for the current state of my hospitality, but the entire household is in London with my mother. No one knows I'm here. I've made myself out to be the groundskeeper."

He knelt and reached for Lucinda's foot, but she shooed his hand away then took the rag from him before he could touch the hem of her skirt. She removed her boot, and modestly tied the cold rag on her swollen ankle.

"Why the deception?" I asked as Will settled on the bench opposite, near the cupboard. "Isn't your mother pleased that you've returned?"

"She doesn't know I'm here. No one does." The duke

hung his head as he took a small kettle off the fire. Whatever was brewing in the pot smelled potent and earthy.

Will gathered some cups from behind him. Oliver poured us all a good helping of the black liquid. I grimaced. Whatever was in the pot, it wasn't tea.

Oliver placed the kettle back over the fire, then returned to the table and nodded to me as if I should try it.

He took a long swig and closed his eyes, savoring it. Will sniffed his suspiciously. I delicately lifted the cup to my lips and took a sip.

Scorching liquid that tasted like burned wood poured over my tongue. I nearly spit it back out on the table.

Choking back my violent reaction to the bitter concoction, I did my best to look polite. Who would drink this?

Oliver finished his off with a quick swallow. "My mother believes my father died of natural causes."

I put the cup down and pushed it away from my person.

Lucinda looked stricken. "What happened?"

"My father was murdered," Oliver stated. My attention snapped to him. My heart ached so suddenly. I didn't wish to hear of another victim of this foul plot. Oliver placed his cup very carefully on the table, as if fighting the urge to throw it into the basin.

"How?" I asked. I felt for him, knowing the sickening feeling of having parents stolen from life too quickly.

"Poisoned." He rubbed his hair in the front then crossed his arms with a scowl.

He said it with such certainty. Still, poison was a difficult thing to prove. "How do you know it was poison, Your Gra—"

He held his hand out to stop me. "Oliver, please," he insisted. "My title was a trick of luck at birth. It's completely useless. We're all equals here."

Will snorted softly.

Frankly, there were more important things to discuss than the propriety of using one's title, so I returned to the question at hand. "How do you know it was poison?"

He shook his head. "All the rumors said he fell ill. But his dog . . ." He became more animated, moving closer to Lucinda. "His fat little pug, Percy, died that night as well." He placed a hand on Lucinda's shoulder and sat next to us on the bench. "He always gave that dog whatever he'd been eating, and I don't believe it was a coincidence."

"I remember that dog." Lucinda nearly overturned her cup, but the duke righted it.

"In our last correspondence, my father told me he feared for his life." He looked me in the eye. "Your father had asked for an audience with him. He wanted to destroy Rathford's machine and asked for my father's help in doing so."

His gaze drifted to the key hanging around my neck. I found my hand drawn to it.

"My father wrote that it was best to leave sleeping monsters in the dark. He turned George out. Less than a week later, your parents were murdered and my father was found dead."

"No." The cavernous room pressed in, the darkness blurring in a muddy tapestry of shadows. "That can't be possible," I said. "The fire was an accident."

"Father died six months ago, the same night as the fire. And as I said, I don't believe in coincidence." Oliver stood again and began to pace before the hearth.

No, it wasn't murder. I had woken that night and retreated to my father's workshop to read. I fell to sleep in my father's chair, leaving the lamp burning. The accident was my fault. I had been careless. When I woke, the fire raged. I couldn't breathe through the smoke. Blind and terrified, I'd been able to escape out the back into the garden then through the mews. My parents had not.

Will took my hand across the table and squeezed. The pressure drew my attention back to the present even as I felt the tears sting my eyes.

"I caused the fire," I admitted, though I didn't know why. It was as if I needed someone else's condemnation to make it real. "I was careless and left a lamp burning."

He paused next to me. "Your family was killed for that key, either to claim the key, or to destroy it. I haven't figured out which. The murderer is out there." Oliver gave me a warning pat. "And he is still willing to kill."

I couldn't believe the fire could have been set intentionally. But the most intense fire had burned in the front of the shop, not the back. Had it been my lamp, the first room to burn would have been my father's workshop, not the clock gallery.

My God.

Sympathy softened Oliver's expression. "You're very lucky to be alive."

Lucky? He thought I was lucky to have my parents murdered? To be forced to work in the household of the man who had likely killed them? What part of any of this was luck? I was beginning to believe I was cursed.

Someone wanted me dead, wanted us all dead.

I clenched my teeth and felt the press of Will's hand on mine.

I gathered my courage. Oliver needed to know the whole of it. "A man shot at me in London."

Oliver crossed his arms thoughtfully. "The key is the single most valuable thing an Amusementist has ever invented. It holds the power to bring to life any of the Amusements created in the modern era of our order."

And I was the only one who could use it.

"So, it isn't just Rathford who may want it," Will interjected.

Something twisted in the pit of my stomach.

Oliver nodded slowly. "That's true, there are many who would love to use that key."

I pushed back from the table. "But Rathford is the only one who needs it," I said.

"Then who is the murderer?" Lucinda asked. She locked her gaze with Oliver's.

"We don't know. That's the problem." Oliver poured himself another cup from the kettle. "Either the murderer wishes to unlock Rathford's machine, or the murderer is killing anyone capable of unlocking the machine to thwart the baron. If that is the case, it could be anyone."

I hated feeling frustrated, yet in that moment, I felt numb to anything else. "There are too many questions and we don't have the answers to any of them. How are we supposed to fight, when we don't know what we're fighting against?"

Oliver pinched his lips together. "Come with me."

CHAPTER SEVENTEEN

OLIVER OFFERED LUCINDA HIS HAND. SHE HESITATED
for only a moment then took it, and allowed him to help
her to her feet. With her arm tucked in his, she limped as
he led us up the stairs. In the main floor of the mansion, our
footsteps echoed down the long and empty halls. Oliver's
candle seemed to float, a bobbing anchor of light in the deep
darkness of the empty manor.

He turned the corner and entered a large room with a
high ceiling and tall arched windows. With care, he placed
the candle on a small table and pulled the thick velvet drapes,
ensuring they were completely shut. He lit a lamp and the
room revealed itself completely.

Heavy furniture rested under white sheets, giving the room a ghostly quality. In the corner, cobwebs had formed between the bust of a pompous-looking gentleman with a long roman nose and a globe so coated with dust I could no longer discern the continents. From floor to ceiling, enormous dark bookcases loomed over us, complete with rolling ladders to reach the highest shelves. Oliver began to climb, and I shuddered. I despised ladders.

Oliver pulled himself along the bookcase from his perch on the ladder, inspecting the spines of several volumes before meticulously tipping certain books forward. He then jumped straight to the ground, and walked to a small statue of a foxhound nestled in a corner of one of the shelves. With a single finger, he dusted the dog's head, then twisted it to the left. A loud *click* broke the silence, followed by a creaking sound.

One of the bookcases turned outward, revealing a secret passage. Will's eyes grew wide as he watched Oliver and Lucinda disappear through the narrow opening, taking the candle with them.

"You should have seen Rathford's," I whispered as I extinguished the lamp and followed Oliver's candlelight down the narrow passage.

Will came after me. I stopped in my tracks as I entered the small room at the end.

It was an ode to chaos incarnate.

A lamp burned unfettered in the corner, as there were no windows to reveal its light. Papers and armatures of brass and copper stood on an abundance of shelves. The odds and ends completely covered the surface of a small table in the corner. On the opposite side of the room a large round-bodied vessel bubbled as the contraption beneath it whirred. Cogs and pipes sprouted from it like whiskers on some disheveled beast. The lid jittered and Oliver clamped it down. I thought I smelled the unctuous odor of burned onions.

"Pardon the mess, I've been brewing—something." He reached up and pulled rolls of paper down from the shelf. Will tucked himself into the corner as Oliver cleared off the table with a swipe of his arm and spread out the plans. I marveled at the layers of drawings.

"What is this?" I flipped the top page up to peer at the one beneath.

"It's what I have gathered of the different plans for Rathford's machine, the ones I could access anyway." He pushed the curling edge of the pages down and studied them intently. "If the murderer is not Rathford, then it has to be one of the survivors who worked on the project. None of the other Amusementists knew anything about it. Rathford never brought these designs forward for the general assembly. Only someone involved would know what he was killing for."

"If no one else knew about it, why have all the Amusementists gone into hiding?" Will asked. "Those who didn't work on the machine wouldn't need to fear the murderer."

That was a good point. I turned to Oliver, who twisted the crank on the crazy kettle. It settled a bit.

"All meetings have been called off until further notice," he explained. "The leadership fear someone is targeting members of S.O.M.A. to destroy the Order. Such a thing happened once in our early history and the threat of it has lingered ever since. Even I believed such was the case until I received my father's letter and began digging into the murders. This is everything I've found since."

"What did Rathford invent?" I asked. "When I saw the plans in his workshop, it looked to me like some sort of conveyance."

"You saw Rathford's plans?" There was a hint of hope in Oliver's voice.

"Rathford offered me employment after the fire. I've been living as a maid in his house. I discovered his secret workshop, and then he turned me out."

"Brilliant," Oliver whispered. He rummaged through the contents of a drawer, then swept a new sheet of paper out over the others and handed me a drawing stick.

"Draw everything you can remember, even if it seemed insignificant," he ordered.

I did so gladly, thankful for the tutelage in drawing my mother had insisted upon. I had found drawing endless pictures of teacups and roses tedious, but my skill with detail served me well. I couldn't replicate the notes along the sketches, but when I was done, I had produced a fair replication of the plans I had glimpsed in the workshop.

"Could it be a weapon of some sort?" I asked.

Oliver shook his head. "I don't know." He lifted my drawing and inspected it. "I have never seen anything like this, and I have yet to study the pieces of the plans I have managed to gather. Creating weapons goes against the charter. Inventing one is grounds for the most severe punishment of the Order."

"Which is?" Will stepped closer and seated himself at the bench.

"Death." Oliver said as if it were nothing of consequence.

"Then what do you call the rifle?" Will asked. He straightened as Oliver met his challenge with an inscrutable stare.

"I didn't invent the rifle, I only modified it." Oliver waved his hand as if shooing away a meddlesome bee. "It's a world of difference."

Will crossed his arms. I glanced at him, and I could have sworn we shared a single thought. These Amusementists thought little of their own rules in spite of the consequences.

Lucinda took a step forward and peered at the plans. "The only way to find the murderer is to draw him to us. Once we know who is at fault for all this misery, the rest of the Order can help us stop him," she said. "But the murderer has been hiding for so long, and in spite of everything no one has managed to see his face. How do we force him to reveal himself?"

"We expose the machine," I said. My insides twisted with unease, but my heart beat stronger with sudden certainty. "If we unlock the machine, whoever the murderer is will reveal himself. If it is Rathford, he'll desire unlocking the machine so strongly, nothing will stop him from coming to us to try to use it, and if it is another Amusementist, then he will try to stop us from revealing it at all."

Will pushed to his feet, nearly knocking over a twisting contraption made of glass with eerie floating orbs within. It rocked back and forth behind him. "This is madness. You're suggesting we use ourselves as bait."

Oliver turned to Will. "She's right. From what I have gathered, Jean-Phillipe, Argus, Victor, Ludwig, Richard, and Alastair all worked on Rathford's machine, and they are still living. Charles, Henry, Simon, Thomas, Edgar, George, and my father are dead."

Lucinda seemed pensive. "Argus is in Scotland, and as master of the Foundry probably had little to do with hiding the machine, though he'd know what parts were made and how they fit together. Victor and Richard have supposedly been out of the country for some time, so they must be suspect. They could have easily remained hidden in England and carried out the murders. I haven't heard anything about Ludwig."

She huffed and let her gaze drift to the ceiling. "I'm thinking about this all wrong. If the men involved with the machine needed to hide the pieces to the lock quickly, they would have had to use those within their small group with Amusements on their land nearby. They wouldn't have had the time to traipse all over the country." Lucinda turned to a map near her elbow. "Charles had Gearhenge on his land. Henry fixed the locks. Your father set up the coach, and my Simon created the raven. The automaton was also probably his doing. So how did the others help?"

Oliver abandoned the plans and turned to the map. "The

only others with land nearby that have had an Amusement installed somewhere on their property are Thomas, Edgar, and Alastair. Since Thomas and Edgar are dead, it would be safer to begin searching there. I'm not sure I trust your father, Luli," Oliver confessed.

The use of Christian names had me befuddled. Wait, Lucinda's father? The only Alastair on the list of Amusementists was the Earl of Strompton.

"You're a lady?" I exclaimed.

She shook her head. "My father and I had a falling-out. I'm nothing but a toymaker's widow." She let out a heavy and resigned sigh. "My father certainly has his faults. But I can't believe he would stoop to murder."

The conversation stopped cold, leaving me feeling uncomfortably in the middle of a brewing war. I struggled for some means to head it off. "It seems to me the ones who were murdered would ask fewer questions. Perhaps it is best to start there. So, when do we leave?" I said.

They all turned to me. The pot jangled in the background as a coil rolled off the table and clanged against the floor.

Feeling uneasy, I placed a palm on the drawing of Rathford's machine to steady myself. "Whatever this is, we should destroy it, as my father, my grandfather, and Simon set out to do."

"I'm going with you," Will said. I let out a breath, thankful that I wouldn't have to face the next challenge alone.

Oliver shook his head, but his eyes gleamed in subtle amusement. It made me feel proud of myself for some inexplicable reason. "If anyone discovers I'm here, word will get back to the murderer. He could try to find us."

"We need more information," Lucinda said. "We can do little to dismantle this atrocity without first discovering the nature of the machine. I can ride Daisy back to Charles's manor and search for his plans. It would lead the murderer away from Meg."

"You're not going alone," Oliver insisted.

Lucinda looked to her feet, took a deep breath, then met the duke's eyes. "Then come with me."

Oliver drew himself up to his full height. He nodded. "Very well."

My heart swelled with sudden hope. We'd be able to find the machine and end this. I knew it.

Only then did the realization of what I was about to do weigh fully on my shoulders. We would only be able to end this so long as the murderer didn't end us first.

We had much to prepare.

CHAPTER EIGHTEEN

"WE SHOULD LEAVE EARLY IN THE MORNING," I SAID, "before the first light of dawn. It's best to travel when fewer people might see the coach."

"That would be wise," Oliver agreed. He led us back out of the passage and into the library. He shut the bookshelf then proceeded down the hall to the narrow servants' stairs.

We descended the steep treads and returned to the kitchen. Oliver helped Lucinda to the bench and handed her a new rag. "Lucinda and I can disguise ourselves with some of the clothing left about here then hitch her horse to one of the carts in the stable," he said.

Slowly Oliver lit the lamps in a neat labyrinth of clean

white halls and rooms. I could picture the whole area buzzing with prim servants in crisp uniforms, marching with military precision through their large, well-organized barracks. Only now it was silent, though not dead the way Rathford's house had felt. No, it was waiting.

Oliver showed Lucinda and me to a small room with modest white beds and a simple washstand.

"You can freshen up in the laundry," he said. "I've rigged a few things. If you leave your clothes in the tub, I can have them clean and dry by morning. There's a chest with some night rails and dressing gowns in the back. We shall make do."

Lucinda gave Oliver a quizzical look. "You've very much changed."

Oliver seemed to drift away for a moment, lost in a memory. "I spent a lot of time alone. I learned a few things." He let his hand slide over the soft leather of his sleeve as if soothing a deep wound there. "About what I'm really worth. What I really need."

His gaze locked on Lucinda with such intensity, even I felt it. Her lips dropped open, just the slightest bit, as if she wanted to say something, but instead she turned and escaped to the beds.

I felt a giggle deep in my chest, but I didn't dare let it out.

Whatever jealousy I'd felt for Lucinda had abated and turned into a deep curiosity about her past with Oliver.

Why did she scowl so?

Oliver offered me a conspiratorial wink, then disappeared down the hall. I shut the door behind me and leaned against it.

"What are you smiling about?" Lucinda grumbled as she opened the chest and explored the contents.

"He fancies you." I didn't mean for my voice to sound so gleeful, but I couldn't help it.

"I know." She pulled out a stack of neatly folded clothing and let the lid fall shut with a loud *crack*. "That's the problem."

"It's a problem to have a dashing young duke fall in love with you?"

Her eyes narrowed as she thrust a soft lump of clothing into my arms.

"Yes." She paused. "When it's Oliver."

"He's the boy from the picture, isn't he?" I couldn't help it. I had to know more.

She sighed. "Leave me be and go get cleaned up."

She gave me a friendly push out into the hall. I nearly bumped into Oliver, who was examining a small jar in his hands. "The laundry is that way. Lock the door and take your time. The water should be hot."

I entered the laundry expecting to find a pump, a low stove for boiling water, and hanging lines overhead. Instead I found a twisted maze of pipes. A large washtub sat in the corner beneath a lattice of tubes, while a barrel-like tub sputtered and churned in the corner. Hanging shirts spun around a machine, like the skirt of a twirling ballerina floating past a large cast iron stove.

The steam and heat felt both oppressive and soothing, while the churning, squeaking, and rattling of the crazy machines made me feel like a spectator of some peculiar circus.

I carefully removed my clothes and placed them in a basket in front of the waddling contraption. Retreating to the metal washtub, I looked for a pump handle. Finding it to the side, I pressed it in, only to scream like a banshee when warm water rained down on my head. I threw my hand out and knocked over a shallow pan with soap and a comb inside. It clanged against the stone floor.

How had Oliver managed this? He'd made it rain inside. Once recovered from my shock, I found myself delighted. I shook my head beneath the falling water, letting it seep through my muddy hair and wash away the filth from my adventures.

It was so much better than a bath.

A pounding knock sounded at the door. "Meg, are you harmed?" Will shouted.

I jumped again, trying to cover myself with my hands, but it did no good. *Please don't break down the door.*

"I'm fine!" I shrieked, worried all over again that my utter panic at the thought of having him walk in on me might actually cause him to walk in on me. "I was just startled by something," I called, trying for a calm I didn't feel. I understood he wished to protect me, but this was beyond the pale.

I rushed through my rain bath, washing the worst of the mud down the drain as quickly as possible.

"Is it a rat?" Will called.

"No!"

Good enough. If I wasn't clean, I'd have to make do. If he came through that door, I'd die on the spot. I pushed the pump handle until the water stopped, then leapt out of the tub and wrapped myself in the dressing gown. In my haste I accidentally kicked over a tin pail filled with little clamps. My damp hair soaked into the fabric on my back as I tried to right them.

"I heard something clatter." The handle on the door rattled as Will tested it from the other side. I curled my toes.

"Just go away," I demanded.

"Fine." I heard him stomp down the hall, and I hung my head. Why did everything turn into such an embarrassing disaster whenever I was around him? I couldn't help but think he was only doing all of this because I was so hopeless, he felt himself obligated to help.

I wanted to believe he cared for me.

But such thoughts were foolish. I wasn't a great beauty like Lucinda. I wasn't a girl a man would ever pine for. All I ever managed to do was end up in a state of disarray in front of an irritable tinker.

After properly donning the nightshirt, I wrapped the robe around me before combing out my hair and weaving it in my usual two braids. My exhaustion had caught up with me and all I wanted to do was sleep.

I found Lucinda staring into the small mirror on the washstand, absently rubbing her bottom lip with the tip of her finger. She looked flushed.

"Lucinda, is everything well?" I eased into the room and closed the door softly. She straightened as if startled then shook her head.

"Yes, yes I'm fine," she said.

"Beware of the contraption in there," I warned as she gathered her things for her bath. "The water rains on your head."

She chuckled and smiled at me. "I'll take great care then. Sleep well, Meg."

Try as I might, I couldn't settle to sleep. Even under the stairs, this house was clean and bright in a way Rathford's had never been. The odd chugging coming from the laundry soothed me. I was warm, dry, comfortable, yet I couldn't stop my mind. Lucinda returned and lay on her bed, and I felt as though we both lingered awake in the dark for what seemed like hours. Eventually she gave in to her fatigue. She even snored like a lady.

I couldn't find peace. I thought about my parents, and the secrets they'd kept from me. I thought about Lucinda and her reluctance to be near Oliver.

Mostly I thought about Will. How could I manage to bridge this gap between us? Could I? I didn't know how to give him whatever he wanted of me. I didn't even know what he wanted, *if* he wanted, or if perhaps this all was his own quest to find some sort of purpose beyond cleaning stables.

If only the Amusementists could invent a crystal ball to show the hearts of men.

Sleep must have claimed me at some point during the night, but I wasn't aware of it. I only knew when I woke it was early morning and I couldn't remain in bed any longer.

Six months of waking before the sun had worked its way into my bones. Figuring I could make myself useful, I headed to the kitchen to light the fires. I found my clothes neatly folded just outside our door. This was an amazing place, where a duke would see to the comfort of a maid.

Slipping them on, I was relieved that they were free of mud, but still troubled by my shortened skirt. At least it wouldn't be a hindrance as I tried to find the pieces to the lock.

I buttoned my boots quickly and kept a hand to the wall as a guide in the dark until I found the kitchens. There was a glow at the end of the hall, and voices.

"I don't know. Look at Lucinda." It was Oliver.

What about Lucinda? I paused and pressed closer to the wall.

"There's no accounting for the fickle nature of women."

I knew it was Lucinda's business, not mine, but I couldn't help myself. I peered around the corner and saw Oliver reclined precariously in a chair near the long table by the hearth. He wore fine shirtsleeves and a trim copper waistcoat with his collar loose. Wire spectacles perched on his nose as he kicked his boots up on the bench tucked under the table, while he balanced on the back two legs of his chair. "Heaven have mercy. Believe me when I say there's no rhyme nor reason to it."

"That still doesn't help me." Will stood across from him, also in his sleeves and unbuttoned waistcoat. His voice held an edge I hadn't heard before. His clothing looked tattered next to Oliver's, poor, but dashing nonetheless. He had his hair slicked back as if he, too, had had a go at the rain machine. I liked it that way.

I shouldn't have even acknowledged such thoughts. My parents would have been livid if they ever knew I thought such things about a stable boy. They had raised me for better.

"What are you going to do?" Oliver asked.

"I don't know. That's the bloody problem!" Will nearly shouted. I recoiled, shocked at his outburst. He ran his hands through his hair and winced. "I'm an orphaned tinker with nothing." He yanked at his cuff and the motion knocked a tin cup off the table.

He kicked it and continued. "No matter what I do, I've never been given my due. I've only ever been given obligations." The cup rolled under a stool. He took a deep breath. "It's fine to say position doesn't matter if your position is the highest. You can choose to give up your title if you wish, but I can't do the opposite."

He sighed and picked up the cup. "I'll never escape my circumstances. It's too late to be apprenticed. All I know is horses. I'm doomed to the stables until I die. What sort of life is that?"

Oliver placed his boots on the ground and leaned forward, resting his elbows on his knees. "Listen to me. The time is coming when only a man's wit, determination, and perseverance will matter. Mark my words. We shall no longer have barons of birth, but barons of industry. And wealth will come not from what a man can receive, but what he can achieve. There are places where a man can be free of his name. Stop thinking of yourself as a victim of your circumstance. That is where you start."

Will crossed his arms, but he didn't have an answer. I wasn't sure if there was an answer. Oliver made it sound so simple, but a man couldn't just become something other than what he was born for. It didn't work that way in England.

"Who knows?" Oliver continued. "One day the name MacDonald could be known the world over, while no one has ever heard of the house of Chadwick."

Will huffed, but then the corner of his mouth twisted up in a wry smile. "That seems unlikely."

"You have a gifted mind, Will." Oliver stood and clapped Will on the shoulder. "Have faith in that. You'd make a fine Amusementist." Oliver pulled something from his hand, and handed it to Will.

Will stared at it a long time before he slid it over his finger. He stood straighter, but it worried me. Oliver was right. Will could make something of himself, but it wouldn't happen here in England, where he'd never be anything more than a penniless groom and a tinker.

Suddenly the thought of him leaving to find his fortune disturbed me greatly.

"Thank you." I could see Will's heavy thoughts written on his face. "I've work to do." He headed up the steps and out the door. The door swung shut with a soft *thump*, leaving the kitchen quiet once more.

Oliver pulled down a canister and inspected the contents. "Meg, dear, lingering in doorways is rude."

I suppose I should have felt admonished. Before the fire, I never would have noticed Will. I would have looked the other way should I have seen him driving Rathford's cart down the street. Now the world felt turned on its ear. I couldn't think of anything past the dread that Will might leave to seek his fortune elsewhere.

"What were you talking about?" I tried to sound casual, like his answer didn't have the potential to break my heart.

"How much did you hear?" He tilted his head, considering me carefully.

"I didn't hear anything." I didn't hear nearly enough at any rate.

"Then what are you concerned over?" Oliver lifted his cup of tea in a halfhearted toast. "For what it's worth, he's a good lad." The duke brushed past me, strolling down the hall.

Will avoided me as we prepared to leave before dawn. He wouldn't even look at me when we sat down at the table to discuss the details of our journey.

Worry ate at me. I just wished I knew what he was thinking.

Oliver smiled at Lucinda as he sat, and she dropped her gaze to her hands. At least Oliver's intentions were easy to discern.

"Thomas would have hidden the plates in an Amusement at Tavingshall. He had several placed throughout his extensive gardens, but the centerpiece of the whole estate was his hedge maze. I'd look there first. It seems the natural choice for hiding something. He took great pride in that thing." Oliver rolled out a sketch of the mechanism for the lock to Rathford's machine.

From the look of the design, there were six plates like the ones we'd found in Gearhenge. One had to fit them together in a certain order or the mechanism wouldn't function. We only had two. We needed four more. Since two were in Gearhenge, Oliver seemed convinced the Amusementists had split them up evenly.

"Keep your eyes open for the medallion," Oliver continued. "I wish I could give you more, but I have no idea what Tom could have left for you to find, especially in the maze. He changed it depending on the season. It could be anything. Be careful. Some of the Amusements at Tavingshall were dangerous."

That didn't bode well. I was still shaken from Gearhenge.

"Take these," Oliver said, handing me his goggles. "They belonged to Charles. I haven't had much chance to study them, but the current setting will allow you to see in the dark, should it come to that." Then he handed the gun to Will with a nod. "I'll sneak out and check the woods. I can make sure no one is watching the road as you leave."

The thought of the murderer lurking outside sobered me.

Lucinda packed fine leather gloves with wide cuffs for both me and Will along with some nuts and dried meat from the pantry. "Are you sure you want to do this?" she asked. Her gaze slid to Will before returning to me.

"I'll be fine," I said, though the idea of being alone with Will unsettled me. By all respects, I was already ruined in the eyes of proper society. It was too late to project an outward show of respectability now. Still, I'd be alone with Will. "What of you?" I whispered as I leaned near her. As women, we were placing each other in a treacherous position. Neither of us had any sort of proper chaperone. We only had each other.

"Don't worry about me." She gave me a half smile, then a swift hug. I returned the embrace, feeling a true bond of sisterhood. "Remember the first rule of Amusements," she warned.

Expect the unexpected.

I took it to heart.

Oliver held out a mechanical bird, not as sophisticated as the raven, but similar. It looked like a stout silver dove.

"It's a homing pigeon," he explained. "Just wind the feet and release it if you get in trouble. It will fly back here. Lucinda and I will come for you as soon as we are able." He tucked it into a small sack along with some tools. The sack latched shut by two interlocking gears. He slid it onto a thick belt and handed it to me. I cinched it around my waist.

In the corner of my eye, I caught a reflection of myself in the dark glass of the window.

The girl who looked back at me appeared bold and daring.

I felt I didn't know her at all.

CHAPTER NINETEEN

"WE NEED TO TALK," I TOLD WILL AS HE SETTLED ONTO the stool and turned the crank to wind the coach. His hands stilled. He gave me an exasperated look.

Then he turned the crank again. "When a woman says those words, no good can ever come of it."

"You haven't said a word to me all morning." I handed him the tumbler marked Tavingshall on one end and Chadwick on the other.

I noticed the ring on his finger, marked with the seal of the Amusementists. "That's a lovely ring." I didn't know why Oliver had given it to him. It couldn't make Will an Amusementist. Simon's journal described a long apprenticeship process that lasted years. Maybe Oliver had just made Will an apprentice. Jealousy needled me.

"I'm not sure it fits." He twisted the ring on his finger in an absentminded way.

I tempered my envy. It could do me no good. I was only a girl. I couldn't join the Order if I wanted to. I'd always be on the periphery like Lucinda. But this could mean a new life for Will. I wanted that for him. I wanted to see him rise above his station. "I think it suits you."

He seemed to consider my words. I wanted to tell him that he suited me. I could try to cling to my former status, but it was of no use. If he thought he didn't have any prospects, well, I didn't either. In that way we were a strangely well-matched pair. We could make our way together. But he'd have to choose me. I didn't know what he felt, or even if he felt for me at all.

"I need to concentrate." He kept his back to me as he pushed the lever and started us forward down the long and twisting road to Tavingshall.

Concentrate? On what, exactly, pushing a lever?

Irritated, I crossed my arms and stared at the slowly breaking dawn. Will's silence at least gave me time to think. I'd had so few moments since leaving Rathford's house.

Rathford's house . . .

I felt cold and rubbed my arms to soothe them, but it did nothing to ease the ill feeling that came over me.

I could picture very clearly Rathford's workshop, and suddenly the globe and statue from Oliver's library came to mind. They had been coated in dust.

In Rathford's workshop, a fine sheen of dust lay over everything, save the spying machine. I may have noted it at the time, but didn't think about the implications of it. Rathford had been spying on the house, certainly, but why would a letter implicating him for murder simply be lying about right next to such a machine?

The letter was over three years old, and not the sort of thing one dragged out of dusty corners for a bit of pleasure reading.

My ill feeling increased, rising into my throat.

Rathford had wanted me to see that letter. He had wanted me to act upon it.

He had wanted me to use the key.

Dear God.

Rathford had set me up.

I looked at Will, seeing him in a new and horrifying light. "Why did you come after me?"

"What are you talking about?" He yanked a lever hard to the left.

"When Rathford sacked me." I stared at the back of his slightly curling hair as if somehow I could discern his expression. His shoulders bunched and the dread that plagued me rushed through my entire body until my vision blurred and my hands shook. "What made you come out after me?"

"Meg," he said in a dismissive way, as if this conversation were over. But I would have none of it. I had to have it out plain.

"Did Rathford send you to follow me?"

I waited for his answer, holding my breath. I needed to know if Will was on my side and my side alone, or if he had alternate motives for being with me.

Will turned slowly to face me, his eyes heavy with frustration, but in them I could see the truth.

"He did," I whispered. My breath left me in a sudden rush. I closed my eyes, unable to bear the terrible pressure suddenly weighing down upon my whole person.

When I dared open my eyes, the look on Will's face increased that pressure until I felt I would shatter. He appeared defeated. "The night you were sacked, Pratt came in with a note. She threw it at my feet then demanded I do right by you and marry you at the nearest churchyard." He leaned his elbows on his knees as he produced a crumpled bit of paper from his pocket.

Neat blocked letters had been written as clearly as possible, but there was no mistaking Rathford's mark in the corner.

Keep her alive.

The coach lurched. My hands shook as I dropped the paper to the floor. I hugged myself as Will came down from his seat and knelt before me.

"You're working for him." My voice barely escaped my constricting throat. "I trusted you and you're working for him."

I looked him in the eyes, even as mine burned.

His face twisted with regret. "I have one task. I told you before. I'm here to protect you." He seemed so sincere, but I felt crushed under the weight of this betrayal.

"He's the murderer, Will. He wants me to unlock the machine, and he wants you to help me do it. How could you?" I felt a tear slip and tumble down my cheek.

"He's not a murderer," Will said.

"By God, Will!"

"Dammit, Meg. Listen to me!" he shouted. "There's been a man prowling around the estate from the day you arrived. That's why Rathford gave me a pistol, to keep him at bay. He nearly caught up with you the night you were sacked, and he may still be out there. If you're looking for your murderer, you need look no further. I have been protecting you since before you knew I existed. Yes, I have answered to Rathford. He saved both our lives by taking us in."

"Why didn't you say anything before?" I cried.

Will dropped his head, his hand clenching. "It wasn't my place, and I didn't want you seeking out the bastard trying to kill you, looking for answers."

I shook my head. "How do you know he's not my grandfather trying to reach me? At every turn, Rathford has manipulated me, and he's manipulating you now like some mad puppet master." The words scratched out of my throat like the crunch of gravel beneath the wheels. "What are you to do once we find the machine? Do you aim to drag me back to him like the good little henchman you are?"

Will stalked back to the controls. I could feel his anger radiating off his stiff back. "You saw my only orders. Either you trust me, or you don't."

He had said that to me once before. I had made the decision to trust then, but I wasn't sure I could do it again.

What was I to do? I didn't know how to continue without knowing if the one person who had stood beside me, albeit reluctantly, from the beginning, was truly on my side.

We didn't say another word the rest of the carriage ride. I watched the sun rise, bloodred over the lingering shadows of dawn. Outside the window, the landscape darkened with the thick overhang of woods as the coach rolled to a stop. This was a country estate in the deepest sense of the word, and it seemed the wilds had attempted to pull the house back into their embrace.

I didn't want to look at Will, but as we lingered in front of the ghostly manor, I realized I had no choice but to try to find the lock. Knowing he was here on Rathford's orders didn't change anything. I still needed Will's help. "Is anyone here?"

He glanced around, looking more unsure than I had ever seen him. "I don't think so, but we have to be careful."

We jumped down from the footboard of the coach, and immediately I wanted to retreat back into it. Tavingshall had clearly been abandoned years ago. It wasn't usual for an estate to fall into such disrepair.

The small country retreat had been swallowed by ivy, and the lawns were overgrown, becoming meadows just beginning to regain the fresh green look of spring. A buck spotted us and crashed into the tangled woods beyond the house.

My heart broke for what must have once been an elegant house.

Will kept a tight hand on Oliver's rifle as we walked back to the gardens. I had to remind myself that he'd saved my life at least twice. I had to trust his word for now, but that trust was thin. As soon as we returned to Chadwick Hall, I had every intention of sending him on his way. I honestly didn't know how to feel about that decision. I wanted to feel strong and in control of everything, yet I found myself feeling hollow and so very alone as we reached the back of the house.

I had to focus on the matter at hand. The gardens were menacing in their squalor. Great topiaries that had once been shaped as whimsical animals had overgrown and died. Now their misshapen forms reminded me of monstrous beasts with grim skeletons of wire and dried branches.

Mildew blackened the garden statues, streaking down white marble faces as if the classic nymphs and muses shed an endless stream of dark tears.

We checked the house but all the doors were locked, the windows shuttered. We saw no signs of people at all. The gardens, too, were empty. I wondered who had inherited this place and why they would leave it in such disrepair.

A hedge, so thick and solid it seemed like a dense green

wall, rose before us. It reached so far in either direction that my eyes couldn't see the end of it as it gently curved toward the forests beyond. The entrance was little more than a gap the hedge sought to close with its stretching branches. *This* was a hedge maze? It was enormous. We could be lost within for days.

"Oliver was right. If I were going to hide something, I'd hide it in there," Will concluded. I didn't want to agree with his assessment, but I had no other choice. A labyrinth was the perfect place to hide something one did not wish found.

I stepped through the entrance to the maze and inspected the wall of hedge in front of me. "I wonder if we can push through."

Will stepped to my side. "Try it."

I eased away from him. Donning the leather gloves Lucinda had given me, I pushed my hand into the thick hedge until my cheek brushed against the scraping branches. My hand pressed against something solid and coarse.

Stone. It seemed the late Thomas had little patience for cheaters.

"The bushes are growing over a stone wall. We're going to have to find our way through." It didn't seem anything about this adventure would be easy.

"Well." Will looked one way, then the other. "Right or left?"

I shrugged, then turned to the right. Will followed, our boots scraping the weed-ridden bed of pebbles that served as the maze's floor.

With every step the tension between us grew. Each turn forced us together, reducing the world to narrow halls of greenery and dead ends. For hours, we wandered in painful silence. Eventually, the shadows from the western walls covered the path.

The shadow turned the air cool and worried me. I didn't want to be lost in the dark. Will stared at the tops of the shaggy hedge walls with determination.

"People honestly do this for fun?" he grumbled.

His words were flippant, but I agreed with his sentiment.

"It is a frivolous venture." I turned and walked backward, since it didn't matter what direction I faced. We were just as lost going forward as backward. "So long as one isn't attempting to thwart a murderer."

If his words had been an olive branch between us, I had just snapped it.

"At least if anyone is following us, he is unlikely to find us in here," Will quipped, but his eyes narrowed as he watched me.

"And we are unlikely to ever find our way out again." I sighed. My hand brushed the sack at my hip. What was I doing? Starting a fight wouldn't do any good. "Perhaps Oliver's goggles can help."

Pulling out the goggles, I inspected them. Oliver said they would help in the dark. I figured it was better to figure out how they worked before the darkness set in, or they would be useless. Constructed in an oddly elegant fashion, the goggles bore tiny levers along the brass casings that held the lenses.

I fit them to my eyes and peered through. At first, they only made things slightly blurry. Then I remembered Oliver's spectacles. Finding a knob between the two casings, I twisted it, and everything became clear again.

Will stepped in front of me and studied the outside of the goggles. "Do they work?"

"That depends, have you ever wished to have the perspective of a beetle?" I felt a bit like an insect with the goggles on my eyes.

"Here." Will shifted a small lever above my left eye. Suddenly the goggles hummed, tickling a bit on my nose. Everything lit up very bright in shades of green. What should have been shadow appeared eerily light.

"How strange, everything is green."

"We're in a hedge," Will grumbled. "That's not likely to help. Let's see what these do."

He flipped another lever and I looked around. It appeared as if I had my nose buried in the hedge of the dead end over thirty feet in front of me. "How remarkable." I stared down at a pebble, and could see every speckle, each stitch in the seam of my boot. "Try another one."

He set that one back and flipped another. This time everything around me appeared eerily blue, save Will, who glowed bright red. "How is this accomplished?"

"What do you see?" Will asked, but I had no answer for him. I handed them to him, and he peered through, though they didn't sit right across his nose. "I've never." He took them off and handed them back to me. "You wear them. Oliver gave them to you."

I put them back on and Will turned another lever for me.

"Will!" I squeaked. A glowing yellow line appeared beneath our feet. It went straight then turned sharply to the left.

"What is it?" He touched my cheeks, turning my face up to his.

"No, there's a thread at our feet." I pulled away and crouched, then dug into the pebbles, thankful for the leather gloves. The yellow line glowed brighter until I unearthed a metal cord buried only inches under the stones. "It's Ariadne's thread."

Will knelt beside me to inspect it. "What's Ariadne's thread?"

"Come on, I'll explain as we go." I told him the story of the prince Theseus who had to solve the labyrinth of King Minos on Crete to save his people from having to pay tribute to the king in blood. The king's daughter Ariadne fell in love with him and gave him a golden thread to help him find his way through the maze.

Will hung on my every word, and for a moment, I forgot our circumstance and remembered what it felt like to trust him as a friend.

We wound through the maze, right, right, left, straight, the golden thread leading us forward. The walls of the hedge all blended together, but I never took my eyes off the yellow thread. We followed it relentlessly, even when the turns seemed to defy logic. Suddenly we came to a gate.

It glowed so bright through the goggles, I had to lift them from my eyes. Will approached it cautiously. Like the plates we were trying to find, the door of the gate seemed made entirely of gears.

I eyed the gate warily. I'd learned one thing rather quickly. Gears were never an ornament for the Amusementists. If we pushed the door, the wheels would turn, and something in the maze would change.

Will tested the gate with a good deal of caution. "It's not locked." He opened it further and peered through. "I don't see anything on the other side."

"I guess we go on." I joined him at the gate even though part of me wanted to turn around and follow the thread out of the maze altogether. Reluctantly, I leaned my weight against the gate. The further it opened, the more difficult it was to move. The gears in the door turned as a sharp ticking punctuated the deep quiet of the maze. We slipped through, and watched as the gate eased shut behind us.

"I think we just wound something." A sinking feeling settled in my boots. I hadn't forgotten Lucinda's first rule of Amusements.

"We should go slowly," Will stated. I fitted the goggles over my eyes and continued along the thread's path, but now with trepidation.

The farther we wandered into the maze, the closer the hedges seemed to press around us. The untamed fingers reaching out from the feral hedge gripped at my clothing.

Spiders had spun webs across the path. Will knocked them down, but on occasion a wisp would cling to my cheek, and it was hard not to scream.

We passed through two more gates. At the third I hesitated.

I thought I'd heard something stomp the ground. "What was that?"

Will's expression was unreadable through the goggles. "There's nothing on this side."

"Are you certain?" Foreboding had me in an ugly grip. I didn't want to take another step forward.

"Come on, Meg." I followed him through the gate and we let it go. It swung shut with a *click*.

I thought I heard another *thump*. This time, Will must have heard it too, because he hesitated. Ahead of us the glowing thread led straight through a very narrow slot in the hedge.

I lifted the goggles and perched them in my hair. "Will?"

Something dark moved just on the other side of the slit. "Meg, is there something you'd like to tell me?"

A bellow, loud and monstrous, rang through the labyrinth, followed by the clang of metal striking metal.

My heart dropped into my shoes as I realized what it was. "I may have forgotten to mention the Minotaur."

CHAPTER TWENTY

MY LEGS FELT WEAK, AND I WASN'T SURE IF I HAD THE courage to take another step forward, but I managed until I reached the gap. In the center of a circle of hedge, a dark bronze beast with curling brass horns lifted his ringed nose to the sky. He snorted, pawing at the sand with his human-shaped foot.

Constructed like the automaton in Gearhenge, his body was a remarkable puzzle of sliding plates, geared joints, and sculpted metal, blackened and worn from neglect.

Only this creature terrified me.

Directly across the circle, the hedge had grown over the edges of another gate. That's where we had to go through.

The Minotaur swung his head, slashing his tarnished horns through the air. Along one wall of the hedge, a metal encasement housed a cutout of his body. Great gear pins jutted where the bull-man's shoulders would have rested.

"Look." Will pointed to the creature's back. "It's the plate."

The plate was fused to the creature's massive shoulders as if it were part of the beast's suit of armor.

"We have to find a way to wind down the beast." It was the only way we'd get the plate.

"We?" Will peered at me with one eyebrow raised.

"So, you're not going to join me?" I asked. Fine, I could figure out a way past that thing. It had no source of outside energy. Once it spent the energy we had given it by opening the gates, the beast would have to stop. I just had to keep it running and hope it wore down before I did.

"You're not going in there at all." Will leaned into the slit to get another look at the monster. "He can't fit through this gap. You're safe here."

He slipped his body into the opening. A sudden panic overcame me. I grabbed his sleeve, unwilling to let go. "No." For as much as I felt Will had deceived me, I couldn't stand the thought of seeing him harmed by that thing. "There has to be another way."

He placed his hand over mine. "I'm quick on my feet." He handed me the rifle as he slid into the beast's pen. I couldn't believe he was the one being rash.

"Will!" I screamed. I couldn't help it. As soon as he hit the sand within the Minotaur's circle, the beast turned its red stone eyes and focused on its prey. How did it see? It was just a machine.

It charged, roaring with the mechanical squeal of metal sliding over metal. The beast moved with the grace and fluidity of a real bull. I couldn't believe the speed of it. Will dodged to the left, hopping on his toes in the sand. He kept his feet moving as he raced to the other side of the arena.

He reached the gate and yanked on the latch. Nothing.

It was locked.

The Minotaur turned with surprising agility before it thundered toward Will again.

"Will, look out!" I shouted. Will dodged again, jumping and rolling right in front of the bull's feet. The Minotaur thrust its horns into the sand, catching Will's waistcoat and pinning it to the ground. I gasped, my heart thundering in my ears. Will shucked the sleeves and ran.

"This is not amusing!" he shouted as the Minotaur shook its head, stamped the ground, and charged again. It wasn't slowing. I needed to confuse it somehow, give Will time.

Gritting my teeth, I shoved myself through the gap. The Minotaur stared me down.

"Dammit, Meg!"

"Now's not the time, Will," I called, holding my hands out to my sides for balance. The Minotaur took a slow step toward me.

Will jumped, waving his arms. "Over here, you bloody bastard!" The beast turned its head. That's when I saw them, levers at the backs of his horns.

"His horns!" I shouted at Will. "Grab his horns."

"Grab them?" The monster charged Will again and he ran toward me. "I'm trying to stay away from them!"

We split just before the Minotaur reached us. The motion confused the beast for a second as if it couldn't decide whom to pursue.

It was tracking us somehow. I had an idea. I lifted the rifle, turned the crank in the stock, then aimed for the wall and fired.

The gun kicked into my shoulder, but a blast of red sparks shot out, just as it had when Oliver misfired it. The Minotaur's stone eyes followed the sparks, then it charged away from us, crashing into the wall.

"It's heat." I didn't know how to load the gun again. I'd

been lucky that it fired properly at all. "The beast is tracking our heat."

The great metal beast shook off the effects of the crash into the wall and stamped its foot. The force of it shook the ground.

It took one step forward, clanging as its foot hit the sand. Then another step. It shook its horns.

I took a slow step forward and grasped Will's waistcoat. The beast snorted. I looked it in its garnet eyes, then ran for the gap. The bull charged.

"Meg!" Will chased after us.

I barely fit through the gap as the bull crashed into the walls. He recovered too quickly and turned on Will, chasing him to the far side of the circle. I fumbled with the pouch at my hip. There had to be something I could use to . . .

My fingers tangled into a contraption with a round stone wheel that felt like, flint?

I pulled it out and squeezed the handles. The stone whirred, causing a rain of sparks to fly off the end. That was it!

I jumped back through the gap holding Will's waistcoat at arm's length.

"Over here, you brute!" I called, then lit the waistcoat on fire.

The beast charged and I threw the waistcoat on its head. It looped over one of his horns, covering his dark bronze face in a blaze of licking flame.

The beast thrashed blindly.

Will charged, leaping up the back of the monster and grabbing the bull by its horns. His hands slid over the levers and the beast crumbled into the sand. The Minotaur twitched as something in its chest let out a high-pitched whine. Then it fell still.

Will flung himself off the monster and crashed into me.

We tumbled backward until he rolled me atop him. He held me, his hand cupped over the back of my head as we lay there and just breathed. I could hear his heartbeat through his thin shirt as I stared at the neat stitches of one of the buttons I'd repaired.

"You were brilliant," he whispered. I lifted myself up and peered down on him. His fingertips skimmed along the top of my ear as he tucked a loose lock of hair behind it.

I didn't think my heart could beat faster, but it did.

I pushed away from him, not knowing what to do with my hands. Filled with nervous energy, I nearly tripped as I stepped to the side of the Minotaur and kicked sand over the remains of the burning waistcoat.

What was Will trying to accomplish? Did he think he

could make me forget about his treachery with flattery?

It wouldn't work. I didn't trust him or his intentions, not so long as he remained loyal to Rathford. I knelt by the fallen Minotaur and examined my prize.

The plate had been affixed hastily. I only had to turn four latches to pull it off the creature's back. We had one. The other plate still had to be hidden in the labyrinth somewhere. I felt weak in my knees. If this was only the first test, I dreaded the second.

Will stood before the gate, inspecting it.

As I joined him, he started spinning gears, slowly moving a tiny metal ball down through the gate by dropping it in certain gaps in the gears, then spinning the wheels to move the ball to a new part of the puzzle. In no time, he had it solved.

He pushed the gate open.

"You're clever," I commented, not quite sure if I intended it as a compliment.

He shrugged. "Not so very clever." He rubbed some sand from his hair. "You nearly killed me," he confessed. What did he mean? I'd saved his life. Now we were even. He looked at me. His scrutiny made me uncomfortable. "When you entered that ring . . . Don't ever do that again."

"Battle a clockwork beast from the pages of antiquity?

I'll do my best to avoid them from now on." I flipped a braid back over my shoulder. He had no authority over me.

"I'm serious, Meg." His voice softened. "Don't risk your life for mine."

We stood in the threshold of the gate, but I couldn't pass through until we had this out. "Such a loyal employee, obeying your master's orders."

He broke away from my gaze, staring at his hand on the gate. "You don't understand."

"I understand enough. So long as you are Rathford's man, you cannot be mine." I had not intended the words to come out the way they did. I had only meant to say if he was loyal to Rathford, he could not be loyal to me, but now that they were spoken, I couldn't unspeak them. My heart leapt into my throat as he watched me with silent intensity.

"I'm my own man, Meg." He didn't say another word as he passed through the gate.

His words seemed to hang in the air. I didn't know what to do. What had I just unwittingly confessed?

I followed him through the gate, stepping into another great hedge circle.

Will's hair fell over one eye. He stood resolute, and I saw power there. Conviction. Strength.

He stood before an enormous circular pit constructed of metal. It was easily as wide across as the length of the coach with the horses. A filigree grate covered the top. At one end, a waist-high lever and a large wheel were attached to a short platform.

Several feet behind him, a small glass building stood against the hedge wall. It looked like a miniature conservatory for plants with a patina copper roof and dusty glass panes held within artful curls of dark metal.

Will carefully pulled open the doors, revealing an enormous set of gilded wings.

CHAPTER TWENTY-ONE

"ICARUS WINGS," I BREATHED, STEPPING TOWARD THEM, pulled to their beauty. Each feather was a gorgeous work of art, an ivory canvas stretched in a golden frame. The feathers shone as the setting sun reached into the glass house. The edges of the wings glittered as if longing to reach closer to the glorious light. A leather harness held them to a frame against the back wall. The great wings were spread, waiting for flight.

I ran my fingers over the edge of one of the feathers. This was amazing.

"What is Icarus?" Will asked as he inspected the straps.

"Icarus was the son of the inventor who created the

labyrinth at Knossos. King Minos locked Icarus and his father in the maze, so they could never reveal the secrets contained inside, so Icarus's father invented wings for them to escape." I took a step back and turned to the pit with the grate covering the top of it.

"They flew?" Will stepped up beside me as I reached the platform attached to the pit. I nodded as I stepped up on it. Will seemed dubious as he tried to turn the wheel. It didn't budge.

"Meg, look," he said.

In the center of the wheel was the flower medallion.

I cautiously tried the key, but when I played the song, the earth didn't shake and no mechanical monsters erupted from the pit. The wheel simply came free, allowing Will to turn it slowly.

"I wonder what it does," I mumbled. The covered pit was too deep to reveal the bottom, but what little light filtered through the grate covering the top caught on the edges of something large. I didn't know what it was.

"So long as it doesn't release another Minotaur, I think we can manage." Will turned the wheel a little faster. My teeth clenched as part of me waited for Hydras, or something equally terrifying, to emerge from the pit. I could hear the low churning of gears below us, but nothing seemed to happen. At least the grate on top seemed sturdy and secure.

The breeze picked up. It caught the loose lock of hair that had pulled from my braid and lifted it. As I tucked it back behind my ear, I realized the wind was blowing up.

I leaned over the grate and held my hand above it. Sure enough, whatever was down beneath the filigree grate was generating a skyward draft.

"Will, spin it faster." I glanced back at the wings, wondering if they could actually fly.

As Will turned the wheel, the draft became stronger until it buffeted my hand with such power, I didn't have the strength to hold my arm within it.

Will halted the wheel and the wind died down. I met his eyes. He seemed to be thinking what I was thinking. "Were these bastards barking mad?" He jumped off the platform and rubbed the back of his neck.

Perhaps he wasn't thinking precisely what I was thinking. My thoughts had caught the wind and taken flight, just as I had done in so many of my dreams.

"Who hasn't wanted to fly?" Every time I watched a bird leap into the air and soar, I wanted to take the leap as well.

"Me. You fall you're dead." He smacked his hands

together in a rather gruesome gesture for emphasis. "Man was given feet to keep them on the ground. Now I have to—"

"I'm going to do it." I crossed my arms. He stopped in his tracks and his face paled.

"No."

"Will," I warned. He had just claimed he was not Rathford's man, and here he was, once again acting on his orders.

"I said no."

I marched over to the wings, tugging my gloves tighter and fitting the goggles back on my head. I dropped my belt. I didn't need the extra weight.

"Meg, you can't." Will grabbed my arm but I shook him off.

"You don't want to, and I do." This discussion was over.

"It's not . . ."

"If Rathford wants his precious machine, then this is the only way. I weigh less than you do, and you're stronger than I am. It only makes sense that I wear the wings and you turn the wheel down here. So obey your orders and help me find the next plate." The more I thought about it, the more it seemed certain.

"Meg." Will's voice dropped low. The muscle tightened in his jaw as his frustration forced his back straighter. He looked hard and unforgiving.

"Well?"

"I can't watch you fall." He grasped my arms. I nearly bit my tongue. His gaze lingered on my face. "You're so—" he whispered. "I can't watch you fall."

His words struck me with sudden force. There was pain and terror in his eyes as he gripped me. In that moment, I realized that this was about so much more than the wings or the lock. Rathford had nothing to do with this. I reached up and barely brushed the skin of his cheek before pulling my hand back. "Then don't let me fall."

My life was in his hands. I trusted him to keep me safe.

Will's touch slid down my arms. He brought my hands together and squeezed them. He clung to them just a second longer before he let go. I walked to the wings and lifted them, surprised by how light they were. It was both a relief and disconcerting. My excitement mingled with fear. One mistake and this could be deadly.

Sliding one shoulder into the harness, I felt Will lift the wings to help me into them. I had to buckle a web of leather straps across my chest and around my hips. Down my back, a metal spine helped support the wings. At the end of that support were two triangular sails that would form a tail of sorts. They had straps for my legs.

I didn't tie them just yet, afraid the spine of the wings would make it difficult to walk. I fitted my elbows through padded metal loops beneath the structure of the wings, and held on to the bars at the juncture where the long flight feathers met the framework.

The contraption was surprisingly flexible, with joints that moved with my body. When I held the wings out, they locked, giving me strength greater than my own to hold the wings steady.

I stretched and flexed my arms, amazed at how birdlike they'd become. I could move them, even fold them, as a natural bird would. I just hoped I could fly with as much grace and skill as one.

The walk to the grate seemed endless. With each step the pressure within me mounted. My heart beat in my ears. Will was right, this was insanity.

As I stepped up on the grate and looked down through the metal lace, my head spun. The void stretched below me and I felt I would fall. I nearly fainted.

"You don't have to do this." Will knelt and buckled the straps to my legs. I felt his hands on my knees, and a second wave of dizziness came over me.

"Yes," I murmured. "I do."

He rose slowly, standing before me with the sun behind him. In that moment, an aura of light shone around him, like he was the angel and I had merely stolen the wings.

"I'm not objecting because of Rathford. I haven't heard anything from him but the note I showed you. This has nothing to do with him." He paced away only two steps, then turned back. "I'm here for you. It's always been for you."

For a moment I could only breathe as his words melted away the fear and doubt in my heart.

"I don't want to see you hurt." His words were soft, like a prayer.

"Then help me fly."

He took my face in his hands and kissed me.

His warm lips caressed mine as I felt myself tumble and fall, then soar. All the doubt and uncertainty fled, leaving only my awareness of him.

He let go, gazing into my eyes with such intensity, I nearly couldn't breathe. Then he turned, ran to the wheel, and spun it with all his strength.

The wind rushed up from beneath me. I lifted the wings and launched into the sky. I gasped as I felt the wind, steady and powerful beneath me. The wings locked and it took surprisingly little effort to hold myself steady on the cushion of air.

255

He kissed me.

My heart had flown the moment his lips touched mine. He wanted me. He didn't long for Lucinda. He didn't care about Rathford. No, this was something more.

He needed me. I finally could see how much he needed me.

The rush of air pushed me higher, and the world fell away beneath me. I tipped the wings with barely a flick of my wrists and suddenly I shifted through the air this way, then that. I locked my wrists, holding on to the handles of the wings with all my strength as I felt a twisting and turning deep inside me.

The wings steadied and I again rested on the strong draft of air Will produced from the machine on the ground. I looked down to him. Dear Lord, he looked like a tin soldier standing there.

I was flying.

Who else in the history of man had seen such a sight? Never had the horizon seemed so large, or the world so small. It was an amazing view.

The wonder of it mixed with elation and terror as I gazed out over the labyrinth. Like a great quilt, its hedges stretched out over the land, a tapestry woven of gray paths and green walls. As I reached higher, I saw a larger picture emerge in the pattern of the maze—the three-petal flower. Beyond the labyrinth, the tangled woods looked like patches of green sticks amid great seas of waving grass and swaths of color from early blooming wildflowers.

I looked back down at the maze beneath me. The lock was somewhere within it, somewhere I could only reach with the wings. The fan was in a circle in the dead center of the maze, the Minotaur in a chamber just beyond. To my left, in the heart of the single petal that pointed north like a spade, there was a third circular chamber with no way in, save one. I could drop into it from the sky.

I tilted my wrist once more and the edge of the wing dipped, pulling me to the left. I stretched the wings, fighting to steady them as I glided toward the chamber. I heard Will shout from below, but I didn't have the luxury of taking my eyes off my goal. I slipped through the air, the leather straps tugging against my chest. I flapped the wings, aided by the gears at my back.

I didn't know how to land. As the circle rushed closer and closer, I tried to remember how songbirds alight on the sill.

I flapped the wings back to front, sweeping the air forward with all my strength as I dropped my legs. I started to fall. I screamed as I flapped in a panic. Something ripped. I prayed it wasn't the harness. I didn't have enough strength. I couldn't stay aloft.

I fell nearly fifteen feet straight down into the center of the circle. My boots hit first, and I crumpled, expecting to be crushed with pain, but the ground was soft. The landing jarred my knees and hips, but as I fell face-first with my wings outspread, the pillowlike surface cradled my fall.

Oh, thank heaven I was alive.

I pulled my arms out of the wings and struggled forward just enough to unstrap my knees and loosen the leather bindings. I wriggled out from beneath the wings then fought to stand. My boots sank into soft sand up to my ankles, and I felt a bit as if I were floating on water, though I wasn't sure if that was the effect of the ground, the flying, or the kiss.

Unless . . . I stamped my foot and the sand undulated in waves. I had somehow landed on solid water. Only the Amusementists could achieve such a thing.

My neck felt cold and I looked down only to find to my horror that the harness had ripped the top five buttons off my dress. The collar hung open exposing my throat nearly to the top edge of my bodice. I covered the bare skin with my hand. What a state.

"Meg!" Will shouted in the distance.

He'd found his way quickly through the maze. "I'm here!

I'm unharmed!" I yelled as loudly as I could. My ankles and knees hurt from the landing, but I could stand.

I peered around the unbroken hedge. How was I supposed to get out? Maybe this had been a mistake. I had the sinking feeling I'd just trapped myself.

I tried to push my hand over my hair and felt the goggles. I fixed them over my eyes and took a second look.

I didn't see Ariadne's thread, but something glowed yellow through the hedge on the far side of the circle. I wobbled over to it. As I reached into the hedge, my hand closed over a lever. I pulled it, and the sound of grinding stone made me jump.

Two doors opened on either side of the chamber as the sand seemed to firm beneath my feet. Something moved beneath the ground, lifting it until my boots no longer sank quite so badly.

Will appeared in the passageway, the panic clear in his face. He dropped the rifle, plate, and my belt, then ran straight into the chamber and swept me into his arms.

I felt as if I were flying and falling at the same time, and I didn't ever want it to stop.

"Don't you ever scare me like that again," he growled, then touched his forehead to mine. "Do you hear?"

"I think I'll keep my feet on the ground," I conceded as he

realized he was still holding me. He gingerly placed me back down then stepped away, looking a bit tentative.

I didn't know how to respond. Elated, embarrassed, and uncertain what I should do next, I tried to calm my overwrought mind. I just wanted to run, to find a safe place to breathe. Another little part of me wanted him to kiss me again.

"I think that's the way out." I pointed to the opposite door. "From the air, I saw a straight passage from this circle north to the outer edge of the maze. If we follow that path back around, it should take us to the beginning."

"Right." Will nodded without looking at me, then jogged back to retrieve our things. He picked up the gear plate we'd removed from the Minotaur. "Did you see the other plate?"

I shook my head as I donned my belt and tucked the Minotaur's plate in the satchel.

He reached out a hand, waiting for me.

I took it, connecting us with a simple touch.

We'd crossed the circle when Will noticed the slit in the stone of the door. It had been exposed when the door opened. There was something inside.

He reached in and removed the plate, then grinned.

Without a word, he held the plate out to me, an offering of trust.

Taking the plate, I felt warmth spread through me. He was on my side.

I glanced back at the wings crumpled in the sand. I couldn't leave them there.

"Help me set things right?" I implored, tucking the new plate in the satchel with the one we had obtained from the Minotaur.

"Always."

CHAPTER TWENTY-TWO

TOGETHER WE GATHERED THE WINGS AND FOLDED THEM enough to carry them back through the maze to their place within the glass enclosure. Will set the wings inside and shut the door carefully, so they would remain protected.

"I'm curious, why did the Greeks name the wings after the boy, and not the man who invented them?" he asked.

I flushed. "No reason."

He skewered me with a glare.

"Well." I searched for a way to explain without revealing that the wings were named for the boy because he came to a dramatic end while wearing them. "Let's just say poor Icarus served as the moral lesson in the story."

"He fell, didn't he?" Will crossed his arms.

"He was very rash." I smiled sweetly. "Shall we go?"

"Whatever the next Amusement is, promise me, it won't send you flying through the air again," Will said as he turned from the wings.

"Why not?" I asked. "The view was astounding."

He stepped toward me, pressing close to my body. I could feel his presence through every part of me, even though we did not touch. He traced a finger down the braid that lay across my shoulder, so near my neck.

"I've watched one person I loved die. I'll not do it again." His fingertips brushed up my neck, drawing me toward him.

My heart stuttered as a flurry of thought scrambled through my mind. Did he love me? Or was he only confessing his love for his father? For a brief moment I felt true horror as I realized he must have fully witnessed the murder of his father, but that thought faded as his lips inched closer to mine. I didn't wish to be mired in sadness anymore. I was alive, and so was he.

His first kiss had been a shock to every part of me. I tingled in anticipation, intending to savor every moment of this one.

Just as his lips met mine, he jerked his head up. I gasped as he shoved me behind him and pulled the pistol.

cuuute

I didn't have time to question before I caught sight of a dark figure stalking through the Minotaur's chamber. It wasn't mechanical, and somehow that terrified me more than any clockwork beast.

"Run." Will pushed, but I found my legs had gone weak. "Run, Meg!"

I grabbed my skirts and darted across the filigree over the giant wind machine. My footsteps echoed loudly in the pit below me as I dashed for the gate on the other side. I slid through it, knocking my shoulder on the edge.

Then I ran for my life, unable to look back, hoping Will was following close behind.

A shot rang out, but I couldn't tell if it was from Will or our pursuer. My legs burned as I raced through the maze, my mind focused on the path in front of me. I turned to the right, and stumbled forward, only to have a dead end loom ahead.

I screamed before I could help it. I'd made a wrong turn!

Twisting around, I saw Will appear at the crossroads. I nearly fainted with relief. "This way!" he shouted even as he pulled the lever on Oliver's rifle.

In two strides I was by his side, as he fired an ear-shattering blast behind us. I could see the door into the landing chamber for the wings.

As soon as I made it through, I grabbed Will and tugged him in, then grasped the lever and pulled it with all my strength. The door ground against the path as it shut with agonizing slowness.

The man turned the corner, and I thought I saw something glint like cold steel beneath the brim of his hat—a mask. He rushed forward with a guttural shout, but it was too late. The thick ivy-covered stone slammed shut.

My whole body shook, but I didn't have the luxury to recover. Will grabbed my hand and pulled me through the opposite door. We took the long straight path, running until we reached a final door that led out of the maze.

"Hurry," Will urged. "He might have marked his trail on the way in."

Will made straight for the coach, but a bit of movement in the shadows caught my eye. A large red bay was tied to a tree near the thicket. I veered toward it.

"Meg!" Will shouted, but I didn't heed him. I knew what I had to do.

I untied the reins of the horse and pulled the bridle from the beast's head, then I picked up a sharp switch and brought it soundly on the bay's rump.

He squealed then bolted toward the estate, racing across

the open grasses of the rolling hills. I swung the bridle upward, sending the straps of leather winging into the branches of a tree. It would buy us some time.

I hurried back to the coach just as Will finished furiously winding it. He turned the tumbler over and pushed the lever as far as it would allow.

The metal horses pushed their heads low, straining forward as their wheels gained traction, and we were off.

We careened at terrifying speed over the road. Will used all his strength and skill to maneuver the coach while I watched out the back for our pursuer.

Night fell, but Will didn't risk lighting a lantern. Instead I used the goggles to watch the road. Even though they cast everything in glowing green, at least I could see well enough to keep us from falling in another ditch. Will continued to wind and push the coach to the brink of disaster as the jarring ride shook my already battered body, but I didn't dare heed any discomfort. My terror kept me riveted to the darkness ahead of us.

We reached Chadwick Hall in the middle of the night. I didn't wait for the coach to stop completely before I jumped out and pulled the goggles from my eyes. My head pounded from the strain of wearing them so long. I let the door slam shut behind me as I jogged to the stable doors and pushed them open, throwing my weight against the reluctant wood.

The silver horses tossed their heads in what seemed to be appreciation, but that made no sense. The deep shadows of the empty stables swallowed them whole. It looked as if the amazing coach, and Will within it, had simply dissolved into nothingness.

I couldn't waste time out in the open worrying for Will. We were in trouble, and I had to warn Oliver and Lucinda. I hurried past the tiny hedges arranged in a pretty patterned knot of paths and knee-high bushes. After what I'd just seen, they seemed rather quaint. I opened the gate to the kitchen gardens and stepped down the stairs.

Digging through the sack at my hip, I felt for the key Oliver had given me, but couldn't find it. The cold grip of panic took hold. At the slightest sound, I turned, expecting the man in black to step out of the shadows.

My fingers brushed the key, and I grabbed it. *Finally*. I opened the lock and stumbled down the steps, tempted to lock the door behind me.

"Stop," Lucinda ordered. I halted midstep. "I don't want

to hear it again." She was talking to Oliver. I hurried into the kitchen.

Good heavens, she was transformed. Lucinda wore an antique empire-waist gown in pale dove gray with lilac trim and bows. She was breathtaking. Free, soft, and womanly, she glowed with beauty and life in a way she simply hadn't while oppressed by her mourning dress.

I stepped forward, keenly aware of how awkward I looked in my torn clothing with Oliver's goggles strapped to my head. I wasn't a lady. I never would be.

Lucinda turned away from Oliver with a scowl. When she saw me, her face lit up again.

"Meg! Thank heaven." She gave me a hug, and for a moment my worries eased. "Where's Will?"

"He's in the stables. We've been pursued."

The door opened, and Will entered the kitchen. Oliver placed his cup on the table with a *thud*. "Who followed you?"

"The same man that shot at Meg in London. I'm certain. He's wearing some sort of mask." Will snapped a lever on Oliver's rifle then leaned it against a barrel by the door.

"He must know we're here." Oliver rubbed the back of his neck.

"We have to leave as soon as possible," I agreed. "We lost

him in the center of the maze and I scared off his horse, but should he find the beast, it won't take him long to trace us back here."

"If he's riding on horseback, it will take him at least the night and a good portion of the morning to reach us," Oliver said. "We're safe for now, though we shouldn't linger."

"Did you find the plates?" Lucinda asked.

Will let out a heavy breath. "After the Minotaur nearly skewered us."

Oliver came out of his chair. "Tom brought the Knossos Amusements back out? Did you have to use the wings?"

Will shook his head. "Meg used them."

Lucinda gaped at me, horror-struck. "You didn't."

"I had to." I would have done it in any event, to be honest, though I was pleased I hadn't died. Flying was worth tearing the first few buttons off the top of my dress, especially now that I could appreciate it with my feet back on solid ground.

Oliver stepped beside me. "I commend you, Meg." He thumped a hand on my shoulder. He was proud of me. A fire in my heart roared to life. It felt good to have someone be proud of me again. "Not many men had the audacity to fly. I can count them on one hand." He held up only four of his fingers.

"Jean-Phillipe lost his nerve just before they turned the fan."

"Were you one?" I asked, the conspiratorial nature of our conversation eased my fear for the briefest moment.

Oliver grinned.

"Some boys I might have known were a bit foolhardy in their youth." He gave me a sly wink. "I promised someone I wouldn't."

Oh, he may have promised *someone* that he wouldn't, but he'd done the exact opposite. I'd wager my last penny on it. He put a finger to his lips and mouthed, "Don't tell Lucinda."

I smiled for the first time in ages. Lucinda huffed at him while he tried his best to look innocent.

"Now is not the time to be reminiscing about your misspent youth. We don't have much time." She shuffled us to the table. We sat, and the smell of roast rabbit brought out my hunger. She offered us some of the fire-cooked game and simple flat bread. "Tell us everything."

I tried to recount what had happened but found myself unable to start. I simply couldn't speak about it for fear I'd lay all my heart bare before the three of them. I didn't want Will to know how much he had affected me, and I didn't want the others to discern what happened between us.

I poked at a bit of roasted meat and shrugged.

Will came to my rescue. "We went into the maze, managed to turn the levers on the Minotaur's horns, then Meg used the wings to get us out. As we turned back to replace the wings, we ran into the man. I shot at him, but missed. Then we trapped him on the other side of the door to the place where Meg landed."

I turned to Lucinda. "What about you? Did you find the plans to Rathford's invention?"

She coughed, and her cheeks flushed. It seemed I wasn't the only one with a secret.

Oliver cut in. "We poured through all of my father's old records and correspondences." Oliver pushed the edge of his empty plate. "My father seemed to be in charge of the controls. Thanks to Lucinda, and her knack for hidden passageways, we discovered Charles's plans as well." Oliver twisted a ring on his finger engraved with his family crest. "Charles was a master at harnessing and redirecting energy."

"What does that mean?" I asked, though I wasn't sure I wished to know.

"If what I suspect is true, Rathford's machine had the potential to generate power on a scale I've never seen."

"And here I thought I'd seen everything," Will mumbled between bites of bread.

"Not by half." Lucinda delicately folded a bit of linen and placed it beside her plate. "Whatever this invention was, it had awesome power."

"Dangerous power," Oliver added. "Power equivalent to a massive lightning storm at the very least."

I speared another piece of meat but let my hand linger at the table. I found I couldn't eat. "But we still don't know what it did, or where it is."

"Ah, where it is, we might be able to answer." Oliver retreated from the kitchen. He returned carrying the two plates from Gearhenge the way one carries delicate china. "Look here." He placed one carefully on the table, then flipped the other and ran his hand over the smooth brass. "The back of the plate was coated with a thin seal. I was able to peel it off, and look what I found."

Swirling lines meandered over the surface in seemingly random paths. Some curved, some straight, they intersected in a nest of careful etchings that covered nearly the entire surface. Oliver held up one finger, then lifted the second plate. He inspected it, turned it. Turned it again, then placed it next to the first.

The lines flowed together through the edge, matching perfectly.

I inhaled and touched the key at my breast.

"It looks like a map," I mused.

Will took the satchel and pulled out the two plates we'd found in the labyrinth. Oliver held one up to the light, squinting through his spectacles, while Will ran his fingertips over the other. He found the edge of the coating and slowly peeled it off.

We crowded around. Will turned the plate over and over, a deep furrow etched in his forehead as his glance shifted from the plates on the table to the one in his hands.

Oliver approached the puzzle by trial and error. He picked the new plate up, set it down, picked it up again, working his way systematically around the outer edge of the two plates on the table.

"Mine goes here." Will aligned his plate beside the one closest to me. The lines fit perfectly. I smiled at him, but Oliver scowled. The placement of the plates in an L shape left him two extra sides to test.

After working around the entire shape, he found a match with Will's plate, turning the L on the table to a blocky zed. He ran his hand over what we had uncovered. "We're missing two of the corners."

We weren't merely missing the corners. The most crucial

element of any map was nowhere to be found. There was no compass rose to tell us which way was north.

It was impossible to make sense of these lines without some sort of orientation. There were no words, only tangled lines that may have been rivers or roads, or both. Speckled over the surface were small etchings of the three-petal flower, but none of the petals indicated which way was north. The compass rose had to be on one of the missing plates.

Unless it was somewhere else entirely.

A tingle raced down my arms.

When I'd first polished the key, I'd uncovered the etchings on either side of the silver casing. One side might just come in handy now.

Drawing the key from around my neck, I turned it over in my hand and inspected the starlike design on the smooth silver cover. Four long points like rays of sunlight reached toward the silver edge of the key. Four short arrows flared out from the spaces in between. One arrow reached longer than the others.

It had to be the north spire of a compass rose. I drew my finger over the fine etching, feeling the slight grooves so carefully cut into the metal. This had to be it. I believed in the key, in the cleverness of my grandfather. If I placed it on this plate, it would somehow show us the direction to go.

I laid the key on the plate nearest me and held my breath. It remained motionless.

No, it couldn't. This had to be it. I knew it the way I knew my grandfather was out there, waiting for me.

I nudged it with my finger, but nothing. I sighed.

"What are you thinking?" Oliver gathered close, the cuff of his shirt brushing the gleaming plates as his fingertips touched the edge of the key.

I didn't know what I'd expected. Half of me was waiting for the key to start spinning or to twitch. Sometimes I took for granted that the Amusements weren't magic.

I smoothed my hand over my hair and pulled one of my frazzled braids forward. "I thought perhaps somehow this design on the key could show us which way is north." I leaned my elbow on the table, finally feeling my exhaustion. I didn't want the journey to lead to a dead end.

If it did, I feared I'd never find my grandfather.

My heart stumbled.

Oliver squinted at the delicate pattern on the cover of the key. "Meg, you're brilliant." His fingers closed over the edge. "May I?"

I let go of the key, trusting it to Oliver. He gingerly slid the key over the plates, holding it between his thumb and first finger. As he reached the upper bend in the zed, the chain twitched.

Lucinda gasped. "My word."

I leaned forward on my palms. The chain clung to the plate as if by magic.

No, not magic, magnets!

Oliver placed the key in that spot and it snapped into a quick half turn, the magnets pulling it into perfect alignment in the blink of an eye. The longest arrow pointed toward me. The lamplight caught in Oliver's spectacles as his eyes met mine. "That must be north."

We all jostled to the side of the table so we could see the map from the right angle. Suddenly the lines made more sense.

"If this is a map of England, the shape is all wrong." Will leaned so close to the map his breath fogged a bit of it. He rubbed it clear then tapped part of the etching. "What is this gash?"

"It must be a bay for a river." Lucinda traced her finger over the curved line emanating from the lower right-hand plate. "The Trent looks a bit like that."

The lines pulled together into a picture I could understand. The land just to the north of the River Trent. "It's Yorkshire."

"Of course," Oliver exclaimed. "These straight lines must be the railways." He pushed his finger over them, almost as if it were a locomotive, stopping at each junction. "But if that's true, Leeds should be here. Yet there's no flower mark."

"Perhaps the flowers don't mark cities." Will furrowed his brow. "Most seem to be off the roads, but near rivers."

"Then what should they mark?" Oliver ran a hand over his head. "Bridges?"

"Castles," I breathed. "They mark the castles. Look, here would be Bolton and here Skipton. This one is probably Conisbrough. They must have hidden the machine in the ruins of some old castle."

Lucinda clapped her hands together as if she couldn't contain them, and I caught her excitement. I would have jumped if the bench had let me. Lucinda leaned over the map and inspected the flowers. "But which one is it?"

If the key showed us north, maybe it could reveal this as well. I flipped the key over, rubbing my thumb over the swirling lines and the Amusementists' symbol carefully etched on the small button in the center. The lines didn't seem to mimic any of the parts of the map. Just in case, I touched the key to each of the flower marks, turning it, trying to make it fit.

Nothing.

"The right mark could be on one of the last two plates."
I slipped the key back around my neck. We'd never find the
machine without the rest of the map.

Why did it have to be Yorkshire? Searching for a castle in
Yorkshire was like trying to find a sheep in Scotland.

"It looks as if we will have to head out to poor Edgar's."
Lucinda shook her head.

"Poor Edgar?" Oliver's eyebrow rose. "He's dead. I'm a bit
more concerned for us. We're going to need luck and wits if we
don't wish to join him." Oliver stood and placed one hand on
Will's shoulder and one on mine, as if he hadn't just warned us
of our impending doom. "Best get some sleep. We need to be
sharp in the morning when we head for Pellingbrook."

CHAPTER TWENTY-THREE

I FLOPPED INTO MY BED AND STARED AT THE CEILING, trying to sort out my thoughts. While my mind was reeling over what we'd discovered, Oliver's warning struck home. Whatever the Amusement at Pellingbrook was, it would be dangerous. Added to that, we had a murderer on our tail.

These Amusements were going to be the end of me.

As it stood I couldn't imagine any Amusement more exciting, or dangerous, than the last one.

Or than Will's kiss.

Lucinda seemed lost in thought as she brushed out her long red-gold curls. The small sphere of lamplight made the plain room seem even more secluded in the dark. I tried to think of a way to talk to her about Will, but didn't know how to broach the subject.

"Your dress was lovely. It suited you," I said, just to say something. And it had been lovely. Lucinda was too remarkable a woman to wear only black.

A modest smile touched her lips. "It belonged to Oliver's grandmother. We found some of her things while we searched for his father's letters. There might be a dress that would fit you," she suggested.

The gowns were probably exquisite, and whole, but considering my luck with my attire, I'd hate to ruin an antique dress that had once been worn by a duchess. Besides, no matter how well it would suit me, it would never truly fit me. That was the problem. I drew myself up, then rested my chin on my knees and hugged my shins.

"Why didn't you marry Oliver?" I asked, half to keep my mind from the feeling that danger was lingering just outside the walls.

Lucinda dropped the brush. She fumbled trying to pick it up then set it hastily on the washstand. "Did he tell you about that?"

"No." Not directly.

She shook her head. "Because it wasn't right to do so. I

had great affection for Oliver. I still . . ." Her gaze dropped to her hands. She gripped the blanket as her lips pinched tight, then she let out a weary sigh. "Simon won my heart. I chose him above all others, and I'll never regret it."

I didn't wish to pry, so I fell silent. Eventually she lifted her head and a curious expression crossed her face. "Why are you asking?"

"No reason." I felt my face flush. Even my ears burned.

Lucinda's eyes gleamed with that cat-in-the-cream expression she'd had back on the stair in her shop in London. "What happened between you and Will?"

"Nothing." I couldn't bring myself to say it.

Her expression hardened to something between shock and a scowl. "Dear Lord, Meg, did you tup him?"

"What?!" I nearly jumped out of the bed. "Gracious. No!" I was shocked a lady like Lucinda even knew such a word. "He kissed me." Suddenly it didn't seem like such a huge confession at all.

Lucinda let out a relieved chuckle as I yanked the blankets over myself, tempted to pull them all the way over my head. I wanted to die right there. How would I ever face her again? And why would she think I'd behaved like a strumpet?

"I'm sorry, Meg." Lucinda shook her head, but gave me a sisterly grin. "I should never have assumed such a thing. It was just your reaction—"

"I don't know what to do," I confessed. "I wish I knew his mind."

She nodded. "Will reminds me very much of my Simon. With men like that, it's best to have things out with them directly."

"What if he's sorry he kissed me?" I sank down into the bed, the knot near my heart growing tighter.

"He should be." Lucinda turned out the lamp. "It was an improper thing to do." Her covers rustled as she settled into bed. "But if he did it once, he's likely to do it again. Best be careful."

I felt a tingle skitter over my skin and I smiled at the thought.

The next morning I woke before dawn. Lucinda snored softly in her bed, so I dressed quickly and headed down the hall. The door to the men's bedroom stood ajar, and no one was about. I had volunteered to pack the chest Oliver had left in the kitchen, but the latch wouldn't budge.

I tried wrapping it in a rag, but still couldn't pry it loose.

Where was Will? According to our plan, he was supposed to check the coach for damage and wind it.

I trotted up the stairs that led outside and paused. I couldn't shake the feeling that the man trying to kill me was out there. I reminded myself that wasting time was our greatest danger and that there was no possible way for a living horse to travel as swiftly we had in the coach. I knew logically the man in black could not be out there, but my heart faltered with the prospect of finding myself face-to-face with a murderer.

I grabbed a paring knife and opened the door.

The gray light of dawn had barely breached the western sky as I opened the kitchen garden gate and stepped through. The wind had picked up and I glanced at the thickening clouds. A storm was coming. I raced to the stables, sliding into the dark building as the wind whistled through the door. It slammed shut.

Silence engulfed me.

"Will?" His name echoed in the massive building. "Will, are you here?"

My boots clicked on the stone floor.

Nothing.

Had he left? I couldn't find Lucinda's horse. The stable was completely empty except for the coach.

Will couldn't have gone. He wouldn't betray me and go back to Rathford. He just wouldn't.

I hurried out of the stables and ran back toward the kitchens, throwing open the garden gate.

"Good morning, Miss Whitlock," a man's voice greeted.

I was so startled I couldn't scream. Instead I tripped in my haste to turn around, nearly twisting my ankle.

Expecting to see the man in black holding a gun, I was shocked by the sight of a broad-chested older gentleman with fading blond hair and an artfully cut red beard. He dismounted from a sweaty red bay.

I could feel my pulse in my ears, my hands, everywhere. I stared at the horse as the man dismounted, trying to determine if it was the same one I had seen with the man in black. It was the same coloring, but bays were common. The horse looked tired, as if it had just run hard. I gripped the knife behind my back and studied his face. I'd seen him before. He'd come to our shop in London from time to time.

"I'm sorry to have startled you." He inclined his head, and his voice was melodic and soft, but my heart pounded like that of a rabbit in a snare. There was something about the timbre of his voice that was false, as if the gentleness of it were carefully crafted. "I am Lord Strompton. I believe we can help one another."

Strompton. I knew that name. Dear heavens, it was Lucinda's father.

"I beg your pardon, my lord." I ducked into a quick curtsy, putting on my best maid's face. "I believe you have me confused with someone else." When in trouble, admit nothing, deny everything. It had saved my skin countless times with Mrs. Pratt.

"Oh?" I heard the crunch of a boot on the drive and looked up. "What is your name, then?"

My name? Bloody hell. Something buzzed near my ear. "Bee." It came out too suddenly, and Strompton's eyes narrowed. "Bea, my lord. Bea Tavern . . ." Now I sounded like a lush. "Sham," I added. "Ton."

"Bea Tavernshamton?"

I lifted my chin. He'd never believe me if I didn't believe it. "That's right. I'm the new caretaker's daughter. We're staying here until His Grace returns from America."

I kept my voice from shaking, but my hands failed miserably. The wooden knife handle dug into my palm.

He smiled, but his stark blue eyes remained cool and focused. He glanced at the key hanging around my neck.

"Your clothing is in a rather sad state of repair, Miss Tavernshamton." He slid his hand over the fine leather reins of his horse and took a step forward. I pressed my backside into the garden gate.

"We have to make do until the new duke arrives," I lied. The story was coming easier. Whether or not he believed me, I had to keep his attention away from Oliver and Lucinda, or he'd demand to see them both. Lord Strompton had worked on Rathford's machine; therefore he was suspect. Owning a hard-ridden bay made him doubly so in my eyes. I felt a deep warning in my heart. Still, he hadn't shot at me. I supposed I should count my blessings.

"Well, Miss Tavernshamton." He smiled, but there was no amusement in his voice and no light in his eyes. He took another step forward. "If Mrs. Lucinda Pricket should come here in a silver coach that looks a bit like the one I believe I saw near here recently, please tell her it is past time to make amends. She's welcome at home. Surely my company and hospitality are better than hiding in an abandoned house."

I eased through the gate and shut it in front of me. The waist-high, white boards would hardly protect me, but at least I didn't have anything between me and the kitchen door.

"And should she have one Miss Margaret Whitlock with her, please tell her I want what she wants." His clear gaze bored into mine. My knees shook as I swallowed the hard lump in my throat. "The machine should never come to light. I will ensure it. That is all."

Gathering his reins, he mounted his horse. "I trust you'll give them my message."

He kicked his horse into a ruthless canter down the drive, and I watched him until he turned the bend in the road that led into the woods.

He knew.

Why was he toying with me? Whatever game he was playing, I didn't want any part of it. I just wanted to leave, immediately. He made my blood run cold.

With my legs unsteady, I ran into the kitchen. I nearly knocked Lucinda over in my haste to get inside and lock the door.

"Meg!" She caught me, even as I tripped on the step. "Meg, what happened?"

"Your father."

She leaned against the wall and looked as if she were about to faint. I pushed past her and planted my hands on the kitchen table to steady them.

"What did he say?" She watched the door with wide eyes. "Does he know I'm here?"

I nodded. "He saw the coach."

The floor vibrated, and I heard a rumbling beneath my feet. I jumped to the side as several stones in the floor lifted up, pulling away to open a gap, just the way the back of Rathford's fireplace had.

"Good gracious!" I took several steps back, not knowing how wide the hole would open. How many secret passages did this place have?

Oliver emerged. "Quiet, it's only us."

Will climbed out of the hole, his face tight with worry.

"Will!" I took his hands. He wrapped his arms around me as Oliver twisted an iron hook by the hearth until the stones patched back together into a normal floor.

"I'm here," Will murmured. We sat down on the bench and I leaned my head on his shoulder. I felt so good to have him beside me again. My heart finally began to settle.

"I thought you had gone," I confessed. "I couldn't find you in the stables or Lucinda's horse. Then Lord Strompton arrived."

"Oliver sent me to board the horse with a nearby miller he trusts." He touched my cheek. Relief swept over me. In this moment, he was here with me. It was enough.

Oliver looked at us as if we had lost our wits. "What did Alastair have to say?"

I sat up, pulling away from Will, though he held my hand. "I tried to convince him I was the new caretaker's daughter." If only it had worked. "I'm sure he didn't believe me. He saw the coach and knows Lucinda is staying here, but he believes the house is abandoned. I don't think he knows you're home, Oliver." I caught Lucinda's desperate gaze. "I think he left only to humor my lie and give me a chance to tell you he's coming for you."

Lucinda turned away from me, wringing her hands.

"I should have never left London." She paced. "I should have stayed at the shop, and never set foot outside."

"Stop," Oliver said. "By God, Luli. Stop this at once."

She halted her pacing but glared at him. "None of this would have happened. I could have remained in mourning in peace. Now I'm trapped here with you. And my father knows I'm here."

Oliver removed his spectacles and crossed his arms. "So what if he does? He doesn't own you, Luli."

"Doesn't he?" Lucinda shook a lock of hair out of her loose chignon. "What will happen when he finds me with you? He tried to force me to marry you once. He's not going to do it again. I will never marry again, Oliver. I can't. I won't."

Oliver's expression changed. He focused, the way one does before flushing a bird and taking aim. "I don't believe I've asked." He stalked forward. I feared both of them had forgotten Will and I were in the room. I didn't know what to say, so I huddled closer to Will.

"I'm going back to London." Lucinda lifted her chin even as she took a step back and put her hand out to stop the duke. "Retrieve Daisy at once. I've had enough of this. I'm going home."

Oliver reached out, but she pulled away from him.

"You're not going to run back and hide. I won't let you languish under a black veil, and London is not safe." He snatched her hand and pulled her closer. "You're alive, Luli. Simon would not want you to wither and die for him. He loved you too much."

Lucinda lifted her hand as if she were about to strike him. Oliver didn't flinch, he didn't retreat, and he didn't let go.

Glittering tears welled in Lucinda's eyes. "Don't you dare speak of him." The tears began to fall. "You have no idea what I have suffered."

Oliver wrapped his arms around her.

"I can't," she protested, even as he drew her in. "It hurt too much. I died. I died with them."

"You're alive," Oliver murmured. "Confound it, Luli, you're still alive."

He kissed her.

I couldn't seem to look away, even though my heart nearly beat out of my chest. I felt my own tears gather. I watched Oliver kiss her as if he needed her kiss to survive. His mouth slid over hers, hungry and searching. He pulled her tight against his body and held her as if he'd never let her go again.

Will hadn't kissed me like *that*. Our kiss was fit for Sunday by comparison.

I felt a squeeze on my hand. Will caught my eye. My breath hitched. He jerked his head toward the back hall. We made our exit, leaving Lucinda and Oliver to work out their own accord.

Will strode down the hall, then stopped close to me, looking as if he wanted to say something. Curse him, what was holding him back? I wanted to grab him and kiss him, let him know that he meant as much to me as Lucinda did to Oliver.

Only I couldn't bring myself to do it. I wanted to know he wanted me in that way.

My heart stopped. Will's gaze met mine. I took a step

closer to him. He placed his hands on my shoulders, then slid them down my arms and gathered my hands in his.

Why couldn't I just tell him?

Will, I love you.

Did I? Could I?

He took a deep breath. "We have to leave immediately. We have no more time to linger."

My disappointment felt as if it could crush me. Leave it to him to be sensible.

"I know," I mumbled. Unfortunately, sense had nothing to do with how I felt.

CHAPTER TWENTY-FOUR

WILL AND I GATHERED BLANKETS AND STACKED THEM IN the hall. We didn't know if we'd see another bed for some time. Then we raided the cellar, though there wasn't much to find there. Will gathered ammunition and a couple of pistols. Once we'd done all we could, I cautiously entered the kitchen, afraid to walk in on something revealing.

Oliver held Lucinda in his lap, her face bright red, puffy, and streaked with tears. He stroked her hair and murmured to her as she breathed shaking breaths with her head tucked on his shoulder. She looked weary and spent, as if she'd cried until she couldn't cry any more.

"Lucinda?" I wet a cloth and handed it to her, so she could clean her face. Oliver gave me a short nod of approval and helped lift her up.

What could I say to her? I had the feeling she'd just released her tears the way one purges a poison.

She sniffed, then pressed the damp cloth to her eyes. "Please forgive me," she choked out, her voice raw. "I didn't mean to make a scene."

"I understand," I offered. "But the danger has increased. We must leave."

"I hate him," she whispered against Oliver's shoulder. "I hate him and I wish he were dead."

I winced.

"Be that as it may," Oliver said, "we can't stay here. Are you ready for an adventure?"

She nodded, sniffed, then gave him a quick kiss on the cheek. "I can't very well go adventuring in this." She brushed her hand over her night rail and robe.

Oliver helped her to her feet, and she wandered off on shaky legs.

"Is she well?" I asked him.

He rubbed a hand over his face and replaced his spectacles. "I believe so. I learned long ago not to underestimate her."

He placed a strong hand on my shoulder and nodded to Will. "Come, show me what you've done."

Oliver helped us crack open the trunk. We stuffed it with the blankets, a frying pan, teakettle, ladle, small pot, and some tin cups.

We left the rest of the packing to Oliver, as he'd had experience wandering the woods and plains in America. We needed salt but no sugar, a knife but no spoons. I felt I was about to enter a world I'd never even glimpsed, having been too long trapped within the feminine realm of the kitchen. I trusted his experience, but I couldn't figure how we'd get by on so little.

Just as Oliver was packing the last of the trunk, a distant roll of thunder rumbled through the air followed by the steady thump of boots.

Lucinda descended the stairs into the kitchen.

I believe my eyes nearly fell out of my head.

She had abandoned her skirts in favor of a pair of short fall-front breeches that buttoned at her knees. The lace frill of her drawers ruffled beneath them, completely exposing her silk stockings and her trim boots. She wore a gentleman's shirt loose at the collar, though the fabric still rippled about her throat, and an antique chocolate tailcoat with two rows of buttons. She'd wrapped a long sash of red cloth around her waist, tying it at her hip, and piled her hair in a loose set of ties that let her curls fly in a wanton manner about her face.

It was scandalous.

Oliver gripped the edge of the table until his knuckles turned white.

Will flushed bright red to his hair and looked away, but Lucinda remained confident. My own ruined dress seemed the height of decorum by comparison.

"I've found crinolines to be a bit of a hindrance when dealing with Amusements." She shrugged, and I fought the urge to giggle. "Oliver's grandfather had a fine sense of style, don't you think?"

I took her arm. Her eyes were alight, and nothing made me happier. I had a feeling Simon would have approved. Thunder rumbled through the house. "The storm is nearly here." I smiled at the men, feeling a bit saucy. "Are you coming?"

Oliver rested his elbows on his knees. "I need to sit for a moment."

I grabbed one handle of the trunk and Will took the other. We carried it to the top of the steps, then Will made sure no one was near the house before we hauled it across the gardens and to the coach. My arms burned with the effort, but together we managed.

Once we had the trunk tucked against the far wall of the coach, Lucinda bounded up the footboard with deerlike grace. I recalled the first time we'd tried to enter the coach, falling on the floor in a tangle of skirts, and realized she might be on to something with the trousers.

Oliver joined us a minute later looking very unsettled. He eased onto the driver's seat. "Hold on." Oliver turned the crank. "We're going to have to push her hard."

The horses tossed their heads, and the coach squealed again in the way that almost sounded as if the horses had neighed. It surged forward out onto the drive.

Oliver drove the coach at a blistering pace. I watched the trees whip by.

"Whoever is after us won't be able to catch us on horseback." Oliver locked the speed and handed Will a gun. "If you see anything, shoot."

Will nodded.

We were taking a risk driving during the day, but it was a long way to Pellingbrook and Edgar's Amusement. The storm gathered overhead, thick clouds rolling along a cutting line in the sky.

Lucinda opened Simon's book and turned to an illustration of a ship and a giant sea monster. It had the body of a whale with a great long neck and club-like head, complete with a jaw full of pointed teeth.

"Don't tell me we have to face that thing," I exclaimed. The Minotaur was enough.

"I'm afraid so. The ship is moored on a private lake deep in Edgar's lands." Lucinda's eyes scanned the pages. "This Amusement was built when Oliver and I were very small, but it was the most amazing thing watching the monster rise out of the lake."

Oliver snorted. "The locals still haven't forgotten seeing MacTavish's working model rise out of the lake up near the Foundry. They will be talking about that for years."

"What is the use of creating a monster?" Will asked.

"At the time it was a contest to see which of the two Amusements could fight the longest without sinking," Oliver said. "The ship was fully automatic, and so was the monster. We were all able to watch from the safety of the shore. The monster won."

"Perfect," I muttered. "Let me guess, we're going to have to board the ship."

Oliver turned another crank, steering the coach around a bend in the road. "I'm fairly certain at least one of the plates will be on the ship, but if the other is on the monster, things might turn interesting." Oliver pushed our speed faster as we reached a long stretch of straight and well-packed road.

I leaned back on the velvet bench, my arm brushing Lucinda's. "I wish I could go back to a time before all this. I wish my biggest concern was conjugating German verbs and what to wear to tea with Mother."

Lucinda placed her hand on my knee. "Then we shouldn't have become friends, and I would still be in the shop in London under my veil. Look at us now." She leaned in and touched her shoulder to mine.

"You look ridiculous," I admitted. "But you have lovely shoes."

Lucinda laughed.

Oliver stole a glance at her, and my heart warmed.

Lucinda would make a wonderful duchess, should she finally come to her senses.

I turned my attention to Will. My heart skipped as I watched him stare out the back with his intense focus. He was brave, steady, and clever, but it was more than that. When I looked at him, I felt alive. ✳

Will glanced at me, his focus faltering just enough to catch me staring. My skin heated.

What would it take for him to feel the same way about me? Did he? I thought back on his confession, that he didn't want to see someone he loved hurt. I wanted to believe he loved me, but we had nothing more between us than one stolen kiss and a world of danger.

After racing along for what seemed an eternity, Oliver must have decided he'd gone well beyond the endurance of any living horse anyone may have used to follow us. He eased up on our speed, and the coach settled into a comfortable rocking rhythm.

My thoughts turned to Lucinda's father. He had offered to help, but then his words felt threatening. My suspicion of him grew with each passing moment.

I tried to remember the times he'd come into the shop. As part of S.O.M.A. he would have been friends with my parents. Yet, while he'd sought out a quiet word with my father from time to time, he never seemed any more personable than any other patron of the shop.

I didn't know what to think.

I had felt so certain Rathford was responsible for all these deaths, but now I was beginning to doubt. For the first time I understood that another may have as deep a motivation to kill.

The hours stretched on in the confines of the coach and

the air felt heavy with words left unspoken. Eventually the tension felt thick as bread pudding. I wanted to jump up and down and scream just so someone would say something.

Lucinda stared out the window, and I extracted myself from the bench, perching on the edge of the trunk so I could speak to Oliver.

I toyed with the key, unsure of how to say what was on my mind. I decided to just have it out. "Do you believe Lord Strompton could be involved in the murders?" I whispered.

His eyes flickered to Lucinda and back, as if he were carefully considering how to answer. "This is what I know," he began, his voice hushed as well. "Alastair is a man who craves control. I've found men with such a proclivity can be dangerous if they perceive they might lose what they value most."

"What happened with you and Lucinda?" I asked. I knew it was none of my business, but I didn't like guessing at what had happened, and I didn't feel Lucinda would confide in me at the present.

Oliver let out a weary sigh. He responded louder. "I was young and foolish. Luli was my best friend. She was just coming out into society, and I was horribly jealous. I couldn't imagine myself marrying anyone else, so I went to her father and asked for her hand."

"Isn't that what you're supposed to do?" I asked. I stole a glance at Lucinda. She looked away with a scowl.

Oliver grimaced. "Let's just say I was a bit rash. At some point I probably should have told Lucinda I loved her or showed some sign that I wished to court her. I caught Simon giving her a toy mouse as a gift, and I lost my temper."

He sighed, and I allowed him to continue, though he hushed his voice again. "I knew she was falling for Simon, so I thought I would win her with the one advantage I had. My name. Alas, her father, wishing to unite our families since our birth to increase his political power in the Order, brought her into his study, informed her the wedding would be that spring, that she'd wear his mother's dress, and he expected a male heir before the New Year."

How horrible. No wonder she'd tried to escape.

Oliver lifted one shoulder in a resigned shrug. "Lucinda blamed me, said I took her heart for granted. She claimed I was just like her father, an arrogant tyrant. Then she told me she hated me and married my best friend. That's pretty much that."

I felt for Oliver. Such a rejection must have cut deep, but in all honesty, he had been a bit of an ass. Still, his story revealed Lord Strompton was indeed a ruthless man, even with his own daughter's heart.

"What about Lord Rathford? Do you believe he could commit murder?" I asked.

"I don't know," Oliver said. "But I do know your grandfather once trusted him deeply, at least until he discovered the purpose of the machine. Henry did everything in his power to convince Rathford to relinquish the heart of the machine."

Oliver slowly turned the crank, giving the coach more power. "During that time, Rathford was on a verbal warpath, threatening everyone. But no one actually died until the thing was safely locked. Soon after, Thomas died, followed by Charles's hunting accident." He paused, lowering his gaze to the lever in his hand. "Then Henry supposedly went into the river, and after that, Simon was shot like a dog in the street."

Oliver spun one of the controls and the horses picked up speed. "When your father revealed he had found Henry's key, and my father revealed that he knew the whereabouts of the coach, they both ended up dead."

Oliver didn't say any more. He pulled the coach off the main road and drove it across an enormous open field.

Thunder rumbled as the coach rolled under a thick canopy of trees.

The coach lumbered to a stop, perched on the edge of a high sheer cliff overlooking a deep indigo lake, the water lingering undisturbed beneath a threatening sky.

CHAPTER TWENTY-FIVE

OLIVER AIDED LUCINDA AS WILL AND I STEPPED OUT OF the coach. A cold wind stung my cheeks. I rubbed my arms, imagining how much colder it would be out on the lake. I wandered toward the edge of the cliff to get a better look. It was a straight drop to the water, as if God had taken a great knife and sliced off half the hill the way one would a cake. Shaken by the dizzying drop, I backed away into the thick grove of oaks sheltering the coach.

I held the key at my chest while using my other hand to hold back the loose strands of hair pulling from my braids in the wind. It rustled through the budding branches. "I don't see a ship."

Of course, I hadn't seen Gearhenge either and it had been right beneath my feet.

"Meg, Will, this way. Quickly," Oliver ordered. Lucinda was already turning a bend in a path between the twisted trees. They must have been some of the last medieval remnants of what once was the southeastern edge of Sherwood Forest before farmers, roads, and railways cut it apart. We followed through blankets of wild bluebells on the verge of bloom, trembling in the sweeping wind.

Oliver stopped and turned a slow circle in the center of the copse. Each enormous trunk had been weathered and worn into muscular curls of wood and bark. The trees huddled together like a coven of witches at some pagan ritual with their bony arms and knotted fingers reaching over our heads.

Oliver ran his hands over the bark of the nearest tree. "Now where was it?" He thumped his fist on a curl of wood before moving on to the next lumpy trunk. "Lucinda, do you know?"

"My father worked on the island with the Leviathan team." Lucinda picked a tree to our right, patting and pressing the bark.

"What are we looking for?" I asked, thumping on the tree nearest me.

"There's a secret latch in the bark of one of the trees. It should respond to pressure," Oliver answered.

I patted and thumped every odd lump, but didn't find anything more unusual than a chattering squirrel's stash of acorns. In my haste, I stubbed my toe on a root and fell forward, my hands landing hard against the trunk.

Clunk! Something very untreelike echoed from within.

I jumped back as Will trotted over. "I think I've found it," I called. A series of sharp *tick*s rattled through the air. A crack opened where the bark split and curled over a small archway formed by the tree's bark. The inner section of the bark split with a loud *snap* and opened inward, revealing a narrow hollow pocket inside the tree.

Will peered in, then let out a low whistle and tossed in a rock. It disappeared into the darkness, clicking a couple of times before falling silent. "That is a long drop," he commented. I took a step back. There was something about deep wells and holes that always unsettled me. If you fall, there's no way out.

"Do you see the ladder? It's the only way into the chamber beneath the hill." Oliver cocked his head as he reached my side. "Hopefully it hasn't fallen into terrible disrepair. Meg, do you still have the goggles?"

I reached into the pouch and retrieved them, though my fingers trembled. We'd have to climb down a ladder? I didn't care for this one bit.

Oliver fixed the goggles over his eyes, with his wild hair curling just above them. He turned a lever and they hummed as the outer edges glowed with green light. The black lenses seemed to swirl, as if they held restless smoke within them.

He dug his fingers into a groove in the bark, then leaned in and peered down the hole. "The ladder seems solid enough. It doesn't look as if there are any missing rungs at any rate. I'll go first just in case. Take care on the way down."

Oliver lowered himself into the hole and began his descent into the pitch. Lucinda followed next. Planting her hands on the loamy earth, she stepped down the rungs, catching the half-buried top rung and lowering herself into the deep.

"Let me go," Will said. I nodded, not wanting to admit this frightened me far worse than flying. I pulled on the leather gloves Lucinda had given me, terrified my palms would get clammy and I'd slip.

Will sank into the hole in the tree, steadily moving downward through the earth as if he feared nothing. I looked over my shoulder at the path and silently wished I could just stay amongst the bluebells.

I bit my lip and turned so I could crawl backward onto that first rung. My foot dangled in the air. I couldn't see where to step. Clinging to the base of the tree, I braced myself against the trunk and slid lower until my toe found the rung.

My stomach twisted. Digging my fingers into the groove in the dirt at the top rung, I leaned back. My weight shifted over the hole, and I felt the nothingness, the deep empty void beneath me, as if it was a living thing with its mouth open wide ready to swallow me whole.

Nothing held me to the ladder but the strength of my hands. One slip and I'd fall. I simply didn't have faith in my ability to hold on.

I eased down, reaching below with my toe. It found the next rung. Gripping the ladder, I lowered myself, finding the next rung and the next, clinging to the iron bars as tightly as I could. Cold damp air wafted up from the chasm, raising gooseflesh on my arms as I clung to the icy steel and listened to the clanging of footfalls on ladder rungs below.

Oliver's voice echoed from below. "Meg, if you are in, feel to the right for a lever. It will shut the door."

He wanted me to let go? Had he lost his mind? Then one hand, just five fingers, would stand between me and certain death.

My heart thundered and it took all my effort to pull my hand open and reach for the lever. Without a double grip on the rung, all sense of security fled. I felt as if at any moment I'd tip backward and fall into the blackness. I yanked the lever down and then grasped the rung again, holding so tightly I felt the ache of it in my palms.

The door above my head closed with a rattling *boom*, plunging us into darkness. Bits of pebble and dirt from the edge of the door tumbled down, down, down. The soft clicks echoed off the cold metal walls of the shaft, then nothing, nothing but the damp smell of earth, rust, and stagnant water.

Bloody hell.

I edged lower, reaching for the next rung with my foot. I felt the bar and I put some weight on it.

My foot slipped.

I gasped. My hands locked as I pulled my body as securely as I could against the ladder. I couldn't move. I couldn't let go. I tried to breathe in, but my chest constricted. My arms felt as solid as strawberry jam. I wouldn't be able to hang on forever.

I was going to fall.

"Meg?" Will's voice reached up to me. It brought with it a dizzy wave of warmth. He was just below me. I fought to take in a real breath. It came a bit easier.

"I can't move." My voice shook as I said it. I couldn't open my eyes. What good would it do if I did? We were in a narrow shaft within the earth. Surely this was what it felt like to descend into the grave.

Or fall to hell itself.

"Just take a step down. I'm right below you," he said, his voice ringing loudly in the closed space.

I wanted to. I tried. Every time I shifted to take a step, my body shook with such terrible tremors that I felt I would pull the rungs from the wall. I couldn't make my foot lift, no matter how much I willed it to.

"I can't." My voice sounded like a broken sob, and my shame burned me.

"Don't move. I'm coming up."

Move? I twisted my wrists, holding on to the rung with all my strength as I felt it vibrate. What was he about? How could he come up?

I felt him then, his hands reaching the rungs on either side of my legs. His body brushed upward, sliding along the backs of my thighs as he pulled himself up behind me. A shock like lightning caught fire within me.

His arms closed in beside mine, his hands sliding over my hands as I felt the heat and pressure of his body sheltering me from the terrible dark. I could feel his touch in every part of me as his thighs cradled mine and his feet found purchase on the same rung I stood on. His breath curled against my neck just below my ear as he squeezed my hand.

"I've got you," he murmured. "I won't let you fall. One rung at a time. We'll do this together."

A wave of dizziness swept through me. I felt as if I were falling, but his steady hand closed over mine. "One rung at a time," he said again, his hot whisper kissing my ear. "I need you to let go."

My body shook as I felt a hot tear slide over my cheek. I forced myself to take a deep breath and pulled my hand open. I could feel the heat of Will's palm through my glove as he leaned in tighter, sheltering me from my fear and the dark. He guided our hands lower, until my fingers touched hard steel.

I clenched the new rung as his hand slid around my waist and he eased me downward.

"Now the foot." His calm assurance couldn't ease my panic enough to allow me to lift my foot on my own, as I felt him lower his body, urging me to follow. With my leg pressed against his, he led us down, guiding my toe to the next rung.

I exhaled, my breath leaving my body in a shaking rush.

"Good." I felt his lips brush my neck. "One at a time. Just one at a time."

Hand, foot, hand, foot, we fell into a rhythm as his body slid against mine with each slow step downward. Surrounded by his heat and strength, I could no longer focus on the dark or the terrible height of the ladder. The world became no greater than the steady circle of his arms and the heavy pulse of my heart beating so loudly it seemed to echo through the chamber.

My arms and legs ached with effort, and my insides fluttered with such power I thought for a moment I might float back up to the tree. It seemed we'd been climbing for hours. Overwhelmed and undone, I could no longer form a thought in my head.

Finally I heard Oliver and Lucinda shuffling below.

"You did it, Meg," Will said, his voice deep and hoarse. "It's not far now. I'll help you down."

His body slid down mine, then fell away, leaving me cool and breathless. My heart wouldn't stop pounding beneath my breast. I gritted my teeth, determined to do these last few steps on my own.

Will's hands slid over my hips and clasped me about the waist as if his arms belonged there.

I let go of the ladder, and turned, wrapping my arms

around his strong neck instead. He lifted me down as the rush of dizzy elation stole the strength from my legs. I didn't think I could stand. I'd been so overwhelmed by my fear.

"Thank you," I whispered, shaking.

"You're welcome." He held me, his lips nearly touching mine.

I couldn't stand, couldn't breathe. Surely my feet were not touching the ground, for I could not feel it. Only aware of his closeness, his touch, I waited. My anticipation twisted through my shaken body as I longed for him to kiss me.

The hiss of an oil lamp broke the silence, and my eyes stung with the sudden stab of light. One by one, a procession of lights flared to life, illuminating the chamber.

Wincing, I scrambled away from Will. I blinked, only to see a very smug-looking Lucinda and Oliver staring at us.

Oliver was still wearing the goggles, and grinning like a cat in a room full of canaries. "Afraid of heights, Meg?"

"No." I scowled at him, rubbing my skirt to try to ease the shaking in my hands and weak feeling in my knees. Will was doing his best to look innocent, but it wasn't working. "Only ladders."

"I guess you won't be the one scaling the rigging, then," he stated as a matter of course.

I was about to say something else to the smirking inventor, but I lost my words as I stared into the deep chamber before us. The hill where we had stood above the lake was merely a shell. Now we were within a great carved cavern, closed off to all daylight by enormous doors that must have formed the sheer cliff face on the outside.

I gazed in wonder at the ship moored in a wide canal. Its sturdy hull had been patched together with plates of brass and iron. A row of small doors for the cannons had been fitted with interlocking gears. There were also three large brass ports, great circles with teeth, just above the waterline. No ship I'd ever seen had looked anything like this.

Three surprisingly short masts jutted up from the decks, and the lamplight glittered on the enormous wheels set next to them.

"Would you look at that?" Will took a couple of steps closer to the ship as Lucinda lit another lamp.

"Mare-ee-ment," he said, sounding out the ship's name. "No wonder it didn't defeat the monster. It's hardly a name that would strike fear into the heart of the beast."

My eyes took in the shining letters along the side of the ship.

Merriment.

It seemed the perfect name to me.

Lucinda lifted the lamp off the wall and followed Oliver to the gangplank. "They patched her up. I didn't think anything would ever repair the hole the Leviathan smashed in the side."

"Is she still seaworthy?" Will asked.

"She doesn't have to be, least not any more than what is required to stay afloat," Lucinda said.

"Isn't that the most important part?" I questioned.

She let out a huff. "Simon wrote several pages on the construction of the ship. The ship is chained to a carriage on a rail beneath the water. Once the carriage starts down the track, it will pull the ship to the right location, then keep the ship from drifting too far away from the monster during the battle."

Drifting away from the monster sounded like a fine idea to me. Being stuck on a track meant there was no way out of the fight should the battle turn against us.

Will seemed as skeptical as I. "That doesn't mean she can't sink," he whispered to me.

As we walked over the gangplank, the light from Lucinda's lantern reflected off the smooth black water beneath us, turning it to shining glass. With the lowered masts and the patched hull, I imagined myself stepping onto the deck of a ghost ship.

Lifeless automatons slumped in the shadows. They had

all been fitted with the ornate blue coats of the navy. Their faces were smooth blank plates. As I passed one, my own visage reflected back at me from the mechanical man's empty face and I shivered.

We climbed over large pipes and rails running across the surface of the deck, a framework of brass connected directly to the automatons' legs. They must serve as rails for the crew to move about the deck. Large cogs emerged from slots in the deck, connecting the levers and wheels above to whatever was hidden below. We reached a door leading into the cabins beneath the higher deck in the back of the ship.

I pushed the door open, and it yielded with an ominous creak. We entered what appeared to be the captain's study with a large desk, and a harpsichord facing the windows in the back.

The Amusementists had an eye for detail, it seemed. From the thick velvet draperies to the hand-blown glass of the lamps, the cabin looked as if some grand naval commander had charted the course of his ship in this room for years. Framed woodcuts depicted ships locked in battle with giant tentacled beasts. Cobwebs hung from the arms of the lamps and the carved molding, subtly shifting with the power of our awed breath.

"It's the captain." Oliver's voice stabbed through me, even though he'd said nothing extraordinary. It had merely broken the silence. That was enough to set me on edge.

An automaton stood at the desk, looking stately in a dusty bicorn and dark blue coat with buttoned-back white lapels and gold braid. He reminded me a bit of Napoleon. He even had the emperor's stature. His blank face, though completely smooth, somehow seemed to scowl at the charts strewn out before him.

"Look." Will rubbed his hand over the captain's chart.

The words "Play it" had been scrawled in a rough hand across the surface of the map.

CHAPTER TWENTY-SIX

THERE WAS ONLY ONE THING I COULD PLAY, AND ONLY one place to play it. I crossed the plush Turkish carpet with a great deal of apprehension. I'd only ever performed on the pianoforte, never the harpsichord. Although the two instruments looked similar in shape, they couldn't have been more different.

For one, the harpsichord's keys were black with the half steps white. A delicate mosaic of blue and green tiles surrounded the double-level keyboard. Beneath the lid, a hand-painted image of a ship lost on a stormy sea loomed over the taut strings, and inlays of pale wood swirled like growing vines in the dark red cabinet.

But more than that, the entire instrument had been fitted

with wheels, cogs, tiny pistons, and brass shafts, so beneath the strings, the entire inside of the cabinet looked like the crowded inner workings of a pocket watch.

Please don't let me forget.

The thought of missing a single note terrified me. I had no idea what the consequences of a mistake might be. I only knew one thing. I had to play my grandfather's song.

The key could not help me now.

I pulled off my leather gloves and placed my hands on the smooth ebony keys, leaving dark smudges in the fine coat of dust. I let my grandfather's song play through my mind.

Once again I could see him in our sitting room, laughing as I stood on his toes and we danced.

I wanted to be with him again so badly.

I pressed the first note, then the others followed in steady rhythm as if each note followed the beat of my heart.

The harpsichord plucked the tinny-sounding strings and filled the ship with high, metallic notes. The cogs and wheels were set in motion, spinning shafts below the instrument that disappeared through the floor. The ship, or perhaps it was the cavern itself, rumbled and shook.

I continued to play, refusing to break my concentration on the song.

Light spilled in through the dusty windows along the back of the room. The rumbling increased, the ship swaying against its ties.

"Keep going, Meg," Oliver urged.

Something struck the ship. I started, and Oliver ran out the door. I turned to watch him go.

"Don't worry about him. You can do this," Will encouraged, taking a place by my side.

I gritted my teeth and played. Out of the corner of my eye, I watched humongous stone blocks slowly lowering on huge chains along the back of the cavern as a narrow shaft of light grew, much the way the light used to stream in when I pulled back the heavy curtains in Rathford's study. I stared at the counterweights, now bathed in light, with awe, watching them drop with a grace that belied their enormous mass. Only those counterweights had the power to wind the ship and open the massive doors in the cliff face. Only I had the power to lower them.

My fingers stumbled and the ship shuddered. The sound of groaning metal filled the cavern. I had to keep going. I took a deep breath and focused on the music with everything I had. It was all that mattered.

The song flowed through me as I played. It was a part of

me. I didn't need the key around my neck. I was the key.

Hitting the notes with greater fervor, I made the harpsichord sing merrily as the world outside seemed to shake to pieces.

As I reached the end of the song, the stones hit the floor of the cavern with a crushing *boom*.

"Meg, come look," Will said. I pushed off the bench and joined him at the captain's desk.

The automaton had come to life, perusing his charts with a slightly jerking motion of his head. His tall bicorn slid on his smooth head as he looked this way and that. Then his hand, nearly as golden as the braids at his cuff, rolled the chart to the side and reached under the desk. Will glanced at me and grinned almost as if he enjoyed this. How far we'd come.

"You seem amused," I teased.

"This one doesn't have horns."

Click. Gears rattled as the center of the desk rose straight up on brass legs.

Beneath it, the light caught the edge of the fifth plate.

Will gave me an impressed nod. "Well done."

I reached into the secret compartment and my fingers closed around the plate. A part of me couldn't believe it had been that simple, but then, it wouldn't have been a simple task for anyone else. It would have been impossible. I tucked the plate into the satchel and savored my moment of victory.

A gust of wind blew the door to the captain's quarters open. The rush of air straight off the cold lake waters cut through my clothes, and I rubbed my arms.

Will pulled the coat off the captain's back then held it out for me.

I slid my arms into the sleeves, pulling my braids forward so they wouldn't catch on the epaulets. Will helped settle the comforting weight of the fine wool and linen on my shoulders then dusted off the back.

"He's not going to need it," Will commented as he looked at the naked brass torso of the captain. "And it suits you better."

I ran my hand over the lovely ivory panels held back by brass buttons in the front. It made me feel important.

Will gazed into my eyes. It made me feel important to him. "What now, captain?" He gave me a mock salute.

I smiled. "It's time to set sail."

We hurried out of the captain's quarters. "We found the fifth plate!" I called to Oliver and Lucinda.

"Best be off then before this storm closes in." Oliver tugged on a waist-high lever, forcing it down. The lever gave suddenly with a resonant *clunk* that nearly pulled him over.

A brass shaft detached from the side of the ship and receded slowly back into the stone bank of the canal. "Help me with these others." Oliver shoved back his cuffs and pulled on another.

Lucinda tried a lever, but it took my efforts combined with hers to release the shaft. Working around the deck, we managed to detach them all. Finally, the ship was free.

The deck rose and sank in a disconcerting motion. I found I had to steady myself by holding on to the rail. For the first time I could really see the interior of the cavern. I felt as if I'd stepped inside the innards of a gargantuan locomotive. The complex gear works reached up both cavern walls, as brass girders supported pipes arching over the ceiling of the cave.

The cliff doors had slid open, revealing the lake beyond. Wind-swept water rushed into the short canal, lapping at the hull of the ship. The sounds of wind and water surrounded us as I marveled at the mechanism that engulfed both walls of the cavern.

The gears seemed to be the size of houses. How did men make such things?

This was too big for me.

"Who's going to sail this thing?" I asked Oliver. I had never been on a ship, much less driven one, if that was even the proper term.

"Well, you, of course," Oliver said as if it were obvious.

"What?" I couldn't steer the ship. Clearly he had lost all sense completely. "I'm a girl. The closest I've come to sailing a ship is floating a saucer in a tub full of water."

Oliver waved his hand as if shooing a fly. "This ship has been sitting in this cave for years now. The gears are going to give us trouble. You'll need me down below manning the cannons."

"You?" Lucinda interrupted. "Your aim is terrible. You couldn't hit the lake. I'll man the cannons." She crossed her arms. "And if I can be the gunner, you can be the captain, Meg."

Oliver cocked his head and glared at her. "In any case, if gears or levers are caught, Lucinda and I know how to work the automatons below."

"What about Will?" My voice pitched higher. "I can keep lookout while he's steering up on the high deck."

"It's called the poop deck." Oliver tested one of the levers we'd just used to detach the winding shaft.

Poop deck? Surely he was jesting.

"I can do it." Will straightened, looking a bit like a brawny sea captain.

"We need your strength on the main deck," Oliver reasoned. "The automatons down here raise the sails and spin the wheels that drive the carriage below us. If they aren't working, you've got to crank the gears or we won't be able to move. You've got an eye for how these things work."

"But . . ." I didn't know if I could do this.

Oliver clapped his hands on my arms. "If you can fly, you can sail."

I suddenly regretted telling him anything about the Icarus wings.

He led me to the steep stairs that rose to the poop deck. Oh heavens, he was going to make me do this. "Just hold the wheel steady. The chain will keep you tethered to the track."

Yes, a track that would lead us straight into battle with no chance of retreat. I drew the captain's coat close around me. Was I expected to go down with the ship? Damnation, if something went wrong, we'd all drown.

"How do we win?" I asked.

"Simple. The creature has a target at the base of his throat. We only need one good shot at it," Oliver explained.

"You mean like that target?" My voice cracked as I pointed to the large medallion fixed to the main mast.

Oliver shrugged. "Well, yes, that . . . if the Leviathan hits that, a hatch opens up below and the ship goes under."

I felt the blood drain from my face.

Oliver lifted a hatch in the deck, revealing a narrow set of stairs. "All you have to do is find a way to get us in line for the shot, and keep us from sinking." Oliver jumped down the first two steps, holding his hand out for Lucinda. He thumped the deck twice with his fist. "Good luck!"

Good luck. Honestly? That's all he had to say? "Go right ahead, Meg, sail the ship. Oh, and don't drown us," I muttered.

Will snorted as he unwound one of the ropes from a cleat on the rail. "At least we don't have to grab the sea monster by the horns."

"This isn't over yet," I warned. "I just hope Lucinda's a good shot, because that's the only thing that's going to save us from a long swim." I helped Will with the rest of the ropes, and then we climbed up the steep stair to the poop deck.

An automaton waited with his hands on the wheel. "Why can't we just let him drive?" I tapped his smooth blank face then pulled on the lapels of my new coat.

"He didn't do such a good job the first time, remember?" Will studied the brass man, then pulled down two levers in his calves, detaching him from the deck. I helped him drag the automaton to the railing. He slumped against it as if he'd just been demoted.

"Then *you* steer the ship," I said. "I'll make sure the automatons are working."

Will clasped his hands on my shoulders and leveled me with an intensely intimate stare. "What is the matter?"

My words caught in my throat. I looked down at the deck, unable to say a thing.

"Meg, you've jumped headlong into every Amusement we've encountered, with no care for anything, even your life. Why are you balking now?" He lifted my chin, forcing me to face the scrutiny of his gaze.

How could I explain? I didn't want to fail. I didn't want Oliver to feel I was a disappointment, or Lucinda to think I wasn't daring.

More than anything, I didn't want to let Will down. With the coach, all I'd had to do was release the raven. Gearhenge was an accident. And at the labyrinth, I'd faced the Minotaur to save him. I hardly knew what I was doing, and he was the one who defeated it, not me.

Steering a ship took skill. Skill I didn't have.

"I don't know what to do. What if I get us all killed?"

Will cupped my cheek in his hand. "You won't. I know you won't. Just hold the wheel steady. I'll raise the sails and keep the crew in line. We should pray Lucinda is a good shot for good measure, because she's right. Oliver is terrible."

I chuckled, then covered his hand with my own.

"I'm with you." He brushed a quick kiss on my cheek then led me to the wheel.

Those simple words did more to bolster my spirit than anything else could. He was with me. I knew he held affection for me. Was it enough? I wasn't sure, but in that moment, it was what I needed.

I grabbed hold of the wheel.

Will pulled a waist-high lever in the deck, and with a jerk and another low groan of turning gears, the ship sailed forward.

The wooden pegs of the wheel pressed into my hands as the ship sailed through the massive cavern doors. The waves lapped against the false cliff front, echoing in the chamber before we cleared the cavern and the wind buffeted me.

Taking a step back, I braced myself and held tightly to the wheel as I felt the first drops of rain against my cheek.

The automatons had come to life. About half of them jerked in metallic spasms, as the others turned various cranks on the deck, like tiny figures in a strange but beautiful music box.

Will hurried over the deck, repairing the automatons, occasionally kicking them back into motion. Then he wrenched at the cranks, loosening the stiff machinery, helping to power the various wheels with his own strength. Slowly the masts rose, reaching to the sky until they towered over us.

The brass crew pulled ropes and secured the lines as enormous square sails, beaten and tattered, unfurled from the risen masts. Will yelled to them. He'd taken naturally to his new role as quartermaster of the most bizarre crew to ever sail.

The last light of the sun caught in the ripped linen, before the clouds drowned it in a darkly storming sky.

Wind caught in the sails, billowing them out and pulling the ship forward at remarkable speed.

"All guns at the ready!" I shouted, imitating something I thought I'd read in some seafaring adventure I could no longer remember.

I didn't even know if Lucinda or Oliver could hear me.

The wheel pushed against my grip, and it took all my strength to fight the pull of it and keep the ship steady.

Distant thunder rumbled, and I looked to the masts. A shredded flag with the seal of the Amusementists whipped forward in the wind. I prayed the lightning wouldn't strike the metal mast.

My heart dropped, but there was no turning back now. The water ahead churned near the small island at the center of the lake.

Lightning was the least of our problems.

CHAPTER TWENTY-SEVEN

WILL LEANED NEAR THE RAIL, TYING OFF ONE OF THE ropes. I watched the first rolling wave rush toward us. The water foamed, churning like a giant cauldron over too much heat. He could be thrown from the deck.

"Will!" I pointed toward the roiling water.

He grabbed the rigging just in time as the ship was buffeted by the first of the waves.

The deck swayed and I pulled the wheel, trying to turn broadside to the disturbance. It took all my strength, my grip nearly slipping off the handles.

The sky opened up, rain falling in sheets, slicking my hair to my face and spilling into my eyes.

The automatons continued turning their cranks as if nothing of consequence were happening at all. No wonder they'd lost the first time. Clearly they were not taking this threat seriously.

Will hung on to one of the taut ropes as he shouted down the hatch. I couldn't hear him over the wind, but I was glad he could be a set of eyes for Oliver and Lucinda below.

We were going to need them.

"Get ready to fire!" I shouted, but I could barely hear my own voice. The sails snapped and my arms ached, but I held the ship steady as she swooped to the left.

The Leviathan burst from the water, sending a crashing wave into the open cannon bays. Its long snakelike neck whipped above us a good thirty feet in the air. Long strings of lake grasses and scum clung to the articulated joints.

Heaven have mercy.

My horror nearly seized me as the beast's enormous flipper slapped the water with a *crack*. Water sprayed from the violent splash. I could hardly see the medallion at its throat as it swung its huge head. A shining silver frill unfurled around its face as it arched like a cobra about to strike.

Its slanted eyes fixed on me as it opened its mouth, filled with jagged teeth. With the weeds hanging from it, I didn't see a machine. I saw a great dragon come to life from under the dark waters. An unholy scream of grinding metal erupted from the monster, then it lunged.

"Fire!" I shouted as loud as I could, holding the ship broadside to the creature. Will echoed the war cry. I braced myself for the explosion, but none came.

The monster ducked its head and slammed it into the ship. It missed the mast, but crashed its metal skull like a great battering ram into the deck. The deck splintered, sending Will leaping for safety behind the main mast.

Three of the automatons flew over the cracked rail. They landed like brass cannonballs in the water, spurting great plumes into the air as they met their watery end.

I turned the wheel, trying to pull the ship away from the metal beast. We just had to retreat to a safe distance. A few more feet and we'd be out of range of its neck. The sails caught the wind and the ship surged forward. My heart swelled with hope.

Then the ship slammed against the tether, rolling precariously as I fought for my footing and turned the wheel to keep the ship from capsizing. I brought it back around to the monster. I had no other choice.

Will lay prostrate, sliding across the wet deck as the creature curled its neck and opened its gaping jaw.

No sound came from my mouth, but I felt a scream within me like the wail of a banshee as the beast lunged for Will.

I closed my eyes, unable to look as the bone-crushing blow shattered the deck. The scream escaped, the panicked wail bursting from me as my eyes flew open. All I could see were arms and legs hanging from the creature's mouth.

No. Please, dear Lord, not Will.

It felt as if the monster had just gripped my heart in its terrible teeth and ripped it from my chest. Time slowed in that moment. I didn't hear the rush of the wind, or the wail of the grinding metal, nor could I feel the rain on my face. He was gone.

The monster released the body, and all I saw was a limp form as it dropped into the dark water.

My hands slipped from the wheel.

Dear God. No.

"Will!" I screeched, my voice ripping from me in my terror and rage.

"I'm here!" he called.

Oh, thank the Lord. I looked up just as he launched himself over one of the large gears on the deck.

He's alive.

I sent a quick prayer of thanks even as the monster lifted

its head to the sky and roared. The beast had taken one of the automatons.

Will hurdled the steps two at a time as he climbed to me. "I saw the plate. It's in the mouth!" he shouted, as sheets of water spilled from the sky, drenching us. I wanted to throw myself into his arms—then his words reached my consciousness.

In its mouth?! How in the name of all things holy were we supposed to get it there?

No matter what, we had to stop the thing before one of us was killed. "We've only got one shot. Tell Oliver to get those blasted cannons working!" I held on and used all my weight to pull the ship back around to give the others a chance.

Will leapt onto the main deck as it tipped precariously toward the water through the turn. I pulled her straight as the beast rose beside us. "Fire!" he bellowed, lifting a piece of splintered wood and wielding it like a saber.

Boom, boom, boom, boom.

Four of the cannons fired in quick succession, the arc of each ball sailing closer to the monster's neck. It reeled back snapping its jaws.

Boom! The fifth shot hit it square in the center of the medallion.

I let out a whoop of victory, and the wheel nearly spun out of my hands. We did it!

The great Leviathan tossed its ghastly head from side to side, as it slapped the surface of the lake with its enormous flippers. Sheets of water splashed over the deck, then sluiced through the rails.

We were safe. It would sink.

And take the plate with it.

No.

The Leviathan began to go down, the water around the huge brass body bubbling as it descended. Its head thrashed from side to side as it wailed, the discordant squeal slicing through the rumble of the storm.

"Will! The plate," I shouted. He grabbed a coil of rope and tried to throw it around the beast's head. The rope sailed through the air, but landed lifelessly on the water just as the monster submerged.

Please, no.

I clambered down the steep steps, slipping on the wet wood, and leaped down onto the deck. Will climbed over a fallen automaton to reach me.

He took my hands then pulled me into his body as the rain poured from the sky. "Are Oliver and Lucinda hurt?"

Lucinda climbed up to the deck, pressing her palm to a cut on her forehead. "We're fine, just a little scraped up. Where is the plate?"

"It's gone." We had been through all of that for nothing. Oliver climbed up the steps. His spectacles had cracked.

Our shoulders sagged as the rain poured down on our miserable little crew. What could we do now? We couldn't swim down and pry the thing's jaws open.

Oliver let out a heavy breath.

"We have to pray the location of the castle is on the one we have." I felt completely defeated.

"Come," Oliver said. "Let's turn this ship around and find shelter before the storm gets worse." He offered me a comforting pat on the shoulder, grabbing one of the epaulets and giving it a little shake. It didn't do any good.

We'd bested the monster. But we had still failed.

I knew the castle wouldn't be on the plate we had. We'd never find it. Our path would end here.

And so would any hope of finding my grandfather.

Water dripped into my eyes and off the end of my nose as I hung my head. In that moment, all I wanted was to feel warm, dry, and safe again.

Will released me, and I let him as I made my way back

toward the ship's wheel. Over my shoulder, I caught a glimpse of him at the rail.

"Meg?" The warning in his voice made my heart stop. I turned and gazed out over the water.

The surface was churning once more.

Oh no.

"Brace yourselves!" I threw myself toward a large gear wheel and hung on to the spokes as the monster burst from the surface once more.

Lucinda screamed as its head reared up then whipped toward the ship. The long neck cracked against the main mast in a clash of metal on metal.

The deck rolled as the monster screeched its grinding howl. I hunched my shoulders, but couldn't protect my ears from the painful cacophony as I held fast to the gear with all my strength.

"Oliver!" Lucinda shouted as I watched him topple over the side and into the turbulent water. Lucinda threw herself at the rail, but the deck pitched again.

She clung to it as the monster smashed its head down on the deck again. The loud snap of splintering wood assaulted my ears.

Will grabbed the rope and managed to throw it overboard

as one of the flippers connected with the iron patch on the side of the ship.

It struck with such force, it shook me from my feet. I scratched at the slick deck, trying to pull myself away from the monster.

Why had it returned?

How were we supposed to defeat this atrocity? It didn't make any sense. There had to be a way for my grandfather to collect the plate on his own. He couldn't steer the ship, man the cannons, and retrieve the plate from the beast's mouth. It was impossible.

There had to be another solution, something we hadn't thought of.

Play it.

I heard my grandfather's voice within my mind as clearly as I had ever heard it.

Clawing across the deck, I pulled myself into the captain's quarters.

The bench of the harpsichord had toppled over and landed on a swath of broken glass. I grabbed it, shook it once, set it right, and threw myself at the keys.

Please, Lord, let this be the answer.

I played the first of the notes.

The great metal beast squealed again, then moaned. I closed my eyes and played, pounding out each of the notes as hard as I could, though the tin sound of the plucked strings could not get any louder. Will shouted in pain, and my heart stopped.

"Please," I whispered. The ship pitched and rolled, but I played. My life depended on it. The lives of my friends depended on it. The stark reality of our situation shook me, the tremble reaching my hands, but I still played.

A clap of thunder punctuated the song like a great drum in some terrible orchestra.

Yet, I held the stage. This was my song. I believed in the power of it.

As I reached the final phrase, the low groan of gears reverberated through the ship.

Then all fell silent as the last note hung in the air like a man at the gallows.

I lifted my hands from the keys. Stillness. Rain dripped off the jagged shards of broken glass in the windows.

With my whole body shaking, I eased away from the harpsichord and steadied myself against the captain's desk, then stepped out of the quarters.

The deck swayed with the wind-tossed water, but to my amazement, the Leviathan floated on the surface of the lake, its head resting against the rail like an obedient puppy with its hard metal jaw agape.

A soaked Oliver knelt beside Will, who had a bloody gash on his thigh. Lucinda ripped a bit of her red sash to tie it off.

"What happened?"

"Caught on a piece of the broken rail," Will explained. "I'm fine."

Still, I felt sick with worry as I climbed over the shattered deck.

Oliver gave Will a hand up. "That, my dear Meg, was inspired." He shook his head in amazement. "You truly are Henry's granddaughter."

Standing there, in the cold rain on the deck of a half-wrecked ship on a windswept lake, I felt such an infusion of warmth spread through me, I could have been burned by it. I closed my eyes, savoring the moment as I turned my face up to the steady rain.

A warm hand clasped mine.

I opened my eyes only to fall into the heat of Will's gaze. He said nothing, but a flood of emotion coursed through me. If I had died in that moment, I wouldn't have noticed, because heaven couldn't have been any more wonderful than the feeling in my heart.

We did it.

"I fear I love you, Will," I whispered.

Whatever glow I felt had surrounded me, it seemed to encompass him as well.

He brushed a kiss across my lips, pressed another sweetly to my cheek, then whispered in my ear. "You light a fire in me. One I'm not sure I can fight."

A deep thrum beat through my body as all awareness of the world slipped away. In that moment, only Will and I existed in the falling rain.

He gathered my hands, brought them to his lips, and pressed a reverent kiss to my knuckles. "What will I do with you?"

He said the words softly, reverently. My heart answered a million possibilities, and they all filled me with hope and wonder. I loved him. I knew in that moment, I'd never again need wings to fly.

CHAPTER TWENTY-EIGHT

WILL HELD MY HAND FOR THE FIRST FEW STEPS AS I approached the mechanical beast. Gaining confidence with him beside me, I let my hand slide from his. The deck creaked under my feet as I approached the monster. I half expected it to rise and lunge forward in a sudden attack, as if its tranquillity were nothing but a ruse to lull me into complacency. I touched the cold metal of its snout, but it remained motionless.

Up close, I could appreciate the hideous beauty of the metal beast. Except for the row of sharp silver teeth in its enormous jaw, it almost looked harmless with its eyes closed. Yet the weight of the head resting on the rail caused the ship to list toward it. The splintered wood and ripped brass gears around me spoke to the machine's violent nature.

I glanced back at Will before I edged down to the mouth. I had to lean my head inside the jaw to detach the plate and lift it out. Lake water dripped on the back of my neck from the creature's teeth, and I had never felt anything more unnerving in all my life. Choking on the damp scent of lake water and thick grease, I grasped the plate, slipping as I stumbled backward on the slick deck. Will caught me and kept his arms around me as the jaw slowly closed.

The Leviathan seemed to smile as a low but resonant clunking sounded from within the beast's throat. Like a strange purr, it reverberated through the metal creature. The monster's head slipped from the rail, returning to its home beneath the lake.

I clutched the plate to my chest. Lucinda hugged me tight, and Oliver crossed his arms with pride. We were in a state, soaked to the bone and bleeding, every last one of us.

"Oliver, can you take us back?" I'd had enough of steering the ship. My arms ached, but my heart felt light.

He gave me a sharp salute. "Aye, aye, Captain."

The tether clanked as the ship limped home after the

vicious battle. Oliver guided the ship the way a surgeon eases a wounded soldier back in his bed.

I sat on a broken crate, too exhausted to stand. Will stood by me, not saying a word, just offering his steady comfort.

The climb back up the ladder didn't seem as daunting as the climb down, in spite of my aching muscles. It seemed a small thing in comparison to what we'd just faced.

Once we were safely back in the coach, it was Lucinda who voiced my primary concern as she pulled out the blankets from the trunk. "Where do we go now?"

"That's up to the map." I nodded to Oliver as he lifted the plates. I gathered the final two, holding them like precious tomes.

"Wherever we're going, I hope it's dry." Will pinched the transparent shirt clinging to his chest and pulled the sopping fabric from his skin. I could see the definition of every muscle of his torso. I suddenly felt much warmer.

Oliver laid out the four plates we had, leaving the last two to me. I crouched in front of the trunk, feeling the press of the others as I lifted the first plate and peeled off the coating, revealing the swirling etchings beneath.

Judging by the lines, it had to be the lower left piece of the puzzle. I turned it once, twice, then laid it reverently next to its brothers. It detailed most of Lancashire.

I touched my key, barely looking at the etching because I already knew they wouldn't match that plate. The back of the key had impressed itself upon my mind. The lines curved too much, reminding me of hills and twisting brooks.

The last plate had to be the one.

I removed the coating and didn't have to turn it at all. It fell into place, and I had the overwhelming sense that everything was about to come together.

My gaze wandered over the twisting lines of North Yorkshire. Somewhere between a pair of streams, the lines felt familiar.

I lifted the key from around my neck, and couldn't help feeling the pull of some ordained future as I placed it on a lonely flower symbol etched into the northeast section of the map.

I gave it a half turn.

All the lines came together seamlessly, matching the button on the back with the etched seal beneath.

"Those are the moors," Lucinda whispered.

The high Yorkshire moors were barren hills of brush and heather. When they bloomed in summer, they were lovely, but in the winter and early spring, they were a treacherous maze covered in mist, with little shelter.

Oliver let out a slow breath. "We'll have no place to hide. The land is wide open and filled with bogs and hills. I don't know if we can even drive the coach into them."

"We have to try," I said. My gaze locked with Will's. "We have to destroy this thing, or none of us will ever be free to live out our lives."

Lucinda tucked the plates in the trunk then perched on the edge of it next to Oliver as he turned the crank. The silver horses strained against their ties as Oliver pushed the carriage forward.

There'd be no turning back now.

Will and I settled on the bench and wrapped ourselves in a blanket. I rested my head on his chest as he leaned back and stared out the window. With my hand over his heart, I felt the steady beat as the long road rumbled beneath us.

We found shelter late that night in an abandoned millhouse on the outskirts of a sleepy little village. Fortunately, there was enough of a roof to protect us from the storm. We were able to build a hot fire in what remained of the crumbling ovens, to dry our clothes.

All the next day we pushed on. Will and Oliver took turns winding the coach so we wouldn't have to slow our pace. On the rare occasions we did stop to rest, I continued to feel the relentless jostling of the coach even while standing still. Will didn't say much, and I felt the prickling of warning that something wasn't right. But I was exhausted, and overwrought. I didn't wish to imagine ghosts that didn't exist.

We continued endlessly over as many small farm roads as we could manage. Will took his turn at the controls, but said nothing.

After the entire length of the day had passed, flames of orange and pink painted the western sky as the desolate moors rose before us. Tufts of dried grass clung to the hostile soil in the winter-ravished tangles of dormant plant life that had yet to awaken to spring.

Shaggy gray sheep, heavy with their winter coats, dotted the landscape, blending into the subtle palette of the barren hills. It was lovely in a bleak and lonely way.

"We should stop for the night." Oliver rubbed the back of his neck and winced. "There's no way to safely navigate the moors in the dark. According to the map, we don't have far to go. We may be able to walk if our luck holds out."

"There's a cottage." I pointed out the window.

Will lifted his hand to his eyes as he peered to the west. "It looks abandoned."

The cottage was little more than a pile of stones with a

worn thatched roof and a long stone fence meandering to the north.

"Sounds heavenly," Lucinda sighed. She looked nearly as weary as I felt. Oliver pulled the coach around to the back of the house, though the hut did little to conceal it. The coach stood out like a gleaming gem in a bed of dusty pebbles.

The vast emptiness of the moor held our only hope of remaining unseen. We stretched our sore muscles as we investigated the cottage, but there was little to inspect other than the stone walls and a hearth. Not even spiders had decided to make a home here. At least the hard dirt floor was smooth, but I had a feeling we'd find little comfort. There wasn't even a chair.

"I'll look for something for a fire," Will offered, adjusting his cap.

"I'll go with you," I said. After all that time, cramped together with Oliver and Lucinda, I longed for a moment alone with him. I needed to know if something was wrong between us, or if it was only my insecurities plaguing me.

He shifted, as if he were about to protest, but Oliver cut in. "Good idea. Be careful out there."

Will clenched his jaw and strode out of the cottage. I hurried to follow him, nearly having to run to keep up with his long gait.

"Will, wait," I called, but he kept up his pace without looking back at me.

We walked deep into the moors, far away from the cabin and any chance that someone would overhear us. I tried to take his hand, but he pulled it away from me.

I grabbed him by the sleeve of his coat. "What is the matter with you?"

He slowed his pace, but still didn't look at me. I didn't let his reluctance hinder me from staring him down. I would have whatever thoughts were tumbling through his mind.

"We're supposed to be looking for wood." He bent and picked up a dried hollow stalk of some dead reed, then threw it back to the ground.

"Will?" I stopped and waited. How many times had I gone to him? I needed him to come to me just this once. "Is this because I said I love you?"

His face betrayed his guilt.

My heart sank. "Don't you love me?" My voice didn't sound my own. It was too soft, too uncertain.

He surged forward and took my face in his hands. He kissed me with a passion that burned brighter than the sun that painted the enormous sky overhead. I succumbed to the kiss, opening to him, wishing to let him in. His kiss filled me with sensation until I could do nothing but hold on.

My heart sang like a choir of angels beneath the blazing heavens, but the falling darkness of my doubt pulled me back.

Touching his forehead to mine, he didn't let go. "I love you, Meg. I have always loved you. I will always love you."

I closed my eyes, feeling the swell of hot tears. I couldn't let them fall.

"Then why?" I wrapped my arms around his neck, holding him close. "Why are you pushing me away?"

His eyes shone, deep and tormented as he ran his hands up the backs of my arms. I felt the touch through the captain's coat, and it lingered in my arms as he gently brought my hands down from around his neck.

I waited, though the slow burn of anger sparked in my heart. I couldn't think of anything he could say that would justify kissing me on one cheek, then slapping the other.

"I can't torment us this way." He pressed his lips together in a resolute line. "No matter how I feel, this isn't right."

CHAPTER TWENTY-NINE

"ISN'T RIGHT?" MY WORDS MANAGED TO ESCAPE MY throat even though I felt as if a noose were constricting my neck. How could he say such a thing? I'd never felt anything more right. I looked at him, I touched him, and I felt something greater than myself. As if my life were bonded to his so completely, I couldn't imagine my life without him in it.

I swallowed the tightness in my throat. "You sound as if you're waiting for Mrs. Pratt to scold us. We're not children." Children didn't have to face the things we had faced together. Children only heard about such things in daring stories before they fell to sleep, safe and warm in their beds.

Neither of us had been safe or warm in ages. We were

stronger for it. I wouldn't let him back away from us now. I swept my hand out over the empty moors. "There's no one here to judge us. Rathford is not standing between us. It is only you and only I."

He pulled his cap off and shoved it deep in his coat pocket. "And what are we supposed to do when this grand adventure is over?"

"We shall find our way." Isn't that what we had been doing? We had survived. We had made our way across all of England on our own. Surely we could find a way to be together.

"With what?" He held his hands out at his sides. "We have nothing. I have nothing. I haven't had any schooling. I have no family, no home, no money, no employment, no name. What could I possibly give you but my love?"

I felt the first tear slide down my cheek and brushed it away. "I don't care. It's enough for me."

"Love won't feed us." He turned away, walking toward the remains of a broken cart that was now nothing more than a lump of rotting wood and weeds.

No. All of that was of little consequence. The future wasn't written. My life had changed so completely in the course of a year. At this time last year I had loving parents and a home. I had a fine education and lessons in music and art. I was respected and admired within my class. Now I had nothing as well. I didn't know where the future would lead, but I knew I had to trust that I could make good things happen.

"After all we've done, you have so little faith in yourself? In us?" I strode to him, reaching for his arm and the tenuous connection we had shared. My hand was knocked away as he ripped a chunk of a board off the broken cart.

"Have you ever starved?" He slapped the board into the crook of his arm and pulled another. "Because I have. Can you imagine looking at your child after two days with no food and telling him there is no bread? Nothing! I've had nothing. I'm used to nothing. I have been poor my whole life, and that, my dear Meg, is never going to change. My father died in a ditch, beaten to death by men who laughed as they did it. His dead body was picked apart by dogs and buzzards, because he had nothing, and so he didn't matter enough for anyone to bury him."

Will let out a shaking breath. "Anyone but me, and I didn't have the strength. If Rathford hadn't taken me in that day, I would have died that night. No one would have ever known I existed."

My tears flowed freely. Will's eyes shined with the tears

he refused to let go. I wanted to hold him, soothe him, but there was nothing I could do to save him from this hurt.

He smacked another bit of wood into the bunch in the crook of his elbow. "I loved my father, and he loved me." His steady gaze bored through me. "Trust me, it wasn't enough."

"But Oliver and Lucinda . . ."

Will yanked at another board, cracking it in half. "Oliver and Lucinda aren't going to pay our way through life, nor should they. I won't live off their charity." His shoulders sagged as if his burden pressed on him. Then he walked back toward the cottage. "I have to stand on my own."

"That doesn't mean we can't be together." I felt a deep stabbing, a pounding that threatened to crush me. I loved him. My heart belonged with him. Even if what he said was sensible, in this moment, I knew it wasn't right.

He was all I wanted. We could find a path so long as we were together. A horse neighed from somewhere on the moors. Will lifted his head.

As the sound died on the bitter wind, he brought his gaze back down to me. Dropping the pieces of the cart by the door of the cottage, he focused on my face with such intent, my heart cried for him.

He trailed his fingertips over my cheek, brushing the

stinging tears. His lips parted, just slightly, as if he wanted to kiss me. I could see the strain in his eyes. "You tempt me," he whispered as I drew closer to him.

I needed to feel his arms around me, to know there was a chance for us.

He stepped back, turning the slight distance between us into a gaping crevasse.

"I would ruin you, Meg." He took another step. "You deserve more than I could ever give you."

He walked away from me out onto the empty moors, the setting sun turning him into nothing but a shadow.

My breath came in a choked sob. He was leaving. He wouldn't stay with me. I knew it now, and that knowledge tore my heart apart.

I felt it. Deep in my chest, something was tearing. I curled my hands together and pressed them there, trying to ward against the deep ache, but I couldn't stop it.

My heart was breaking.

Turning around, I looked for the others, tears streaming from my eyes. I didn't know where Oliver and Lucinda had spirited off to.

It didn't matter.

I was alone.

Every part of my body felt as if it were made of lead as I stumbled blindly around the back of the cottage. Through my tears I felt for the latch on the door of the coach and swung it open. It took all my strength to climb up, pull the door shut, and collapse on the velvet bench.

I cried. Deep crushing sobs racked me as I tried to let out the well of pain that had sprung forth from my shattered heart.

He loved me. It wasn't enough. He didn't love me enough, or perhaps it was too much. Of course I didn't want to starve, but there was no room for compromise, no way to make things better.

Was I supposed to sit and wait until he felt completely secure in his fortunes before I allowed myself to feel for him? That time had passed.

He was good. He felt like the other half of me, and now he had torn me asunder. For the second time, he had betrayed my trust. Nothing could ever feel worse than this.

When I felt I could cry no more, I pulled myself up and stared at my knees. It was dark. Smoke from the chimney curled in the air enough to tinge the cool night with the scent of burning wood and some sort of roasted bird.

Oliver must have set a snare.

Heaven knows he didn't shoot the poor thing.

Each thought wandered through my mind like a stick floating aimlessly down a twisting stream. I didn't want to face the others. I didn't want them to know I had been crying.

I huddled deeper into the captain's coat. Although it hurt, I had to face this. I had needed Will's help, but I had to continue alone, and I would do it. It would be miserable, but I would do it.

Biting my lip, I mustered my fortitude and opened the door to the coach. I didn't know how long I had been crying, only that the wind had died as the night stole the remaining warmth of day. I watched the ghostly mist rising on the moor and felt so completely alone.

It reminded me of a cruel and tragic story I had read of bitter love and the spirit of a heartbroken and abused woman lost on the moor. I felt a bit like her, lost and lovesick.

The mists seemed to call to me, inviting me to lose myself forever in their cold embrace.

A figure stepped out of them, the white tendrils of fog curling around his legs and face.

"Will?" My heart stuttered to life, then leapt as fear claimed me. The man didn't walk like Will. As he came closer, my gaze fixed on the pistol aimed at my heart.

"Good evening, Margaret." He had a raspy voice, as if he hadn't used it for years. A fine black coat covered his figure, while his creased face bore a heavy Hungarian mustache. A single shock of white streaked the front of his shaggy black hair.

Rathford.

I didn't know how I knew it exactly, but I did. He looked like a physical manifestation of his house, outwardly elegant, inwardly mad.

"Good evening, my lord." I lifted my chin, keeping calm. He wouldn't shoot me. He needed me. He always had.

"I would trouble you not to scream." He tilted his head, his eyes fixed on the key around my neck. "You see, I already ran into young William out on the moor."

Had Will given me away to Rathford? He wouldn't. No matter what he said, he wouldn't do that.

"Regrettably, William wasn't as cooperative with my plan as he should have been. I'm afraid I had to discipline him."

A new shot of fear sliced through me. Rathford's eyes gleamed. "If you do as I say, no one will be hurt. But should you disobey me, poor William might end his life as he began it: quite tragically."

My heart squeezed and I feared I would be ill. "What did you do to him?"

"Nothing that can't be undone if you do as you're told. Now go fetch the plates." He waved the triple barrel of his pistol toward the coach. "We're going for a walk, just you and I."

I swallowed the heavy lump in my throat. What choice did I have?

CHAPTER THIRTY

I BACKED INTO THE COACH AND LET THE DOOR SHUT behind me. For only a moment I considered setting off in the coach. It would do no good. I couldn't wind it or set it in motion without angering the baron and possibly hurting Will.

I opened the trunk, my mind racing through the possibilities. I had to alert Oliver and Lucinda. They were probably sitting by the fire in the little cottage, unaware of the peril I found myself in. But whatever I did, I had to do it quickly while under Rathford's scrutiny. I had to think like an Amusementist.

What did I have?

I opened the satchel slumped against the trunk and rifled through the contents. The pigeon, Simon's book, a lump of coal . . . There had to be more. I rummaged through the rest of the sack and the contents of the trunk.

I needed the others to know what happened. I had to leave some sort of message. The black dust of the bit of coal coated the tips of my fingers.

That was it!

My hands shook as I tore a blank page from Simon's book, then pulled the plates from the trunk. I hastily rubbed the etching from the plate that marked the castle to give Oliver and Lucinda a map. My fingers blackened with coal, I turned the nub and used it to scratch, "Rathford. Will's hurt on moor."

I rolled the page and folded it, grabbing the tiny silver dove from the sack. He rested his head on the gears of his breast with his soft gray wings pressed tightly against his body. I turned the bird over and tucked the note into the embroidered pocket sewn to the belly.

Twisting his feet, I wound the bird. His beady eyes blinked at me. I squeezed his tiny silver beak together hoping he wouldn't peep.

"It's up to you," I told the small mechanical bird as I

tucked him into the satchel, leaving the flap open. The heavy leather weighed him down, and I watched the lump move around inside the satchel, searching for a way out.

It didn't give me much time. I stacked the plates in my arm and held them against my heart. I had gone through so much to find them. I didn't want to let them go. But as soon as the bird worked free of the leather, he would fly around the interior of the coach, causing a racket.

I hoped it would be enough for Oliver and Lucinda to hear. At least they would see the pigeon if they bothered to look for me in the coach. With a fortifying breath, I opened the door and stepped out, then closed the door securely, trapping the pigeon inside.

Rathford held his gun on me, a potent reminder that he meant very real harm. The hand holding the gun shook as he held the other out to me. His hooded eyes remained fixed on the plates, the way a starving man ogles roast pig.

I was tired of his manipulative games. I had lived in fear of this man's scrutiny for months. I didn't want to play them any longer. "Will you put that away? We both know you aren't going to kill me. You can't, or you'll never unlock your machine."

I clung to the plates, but he held out a sack. He waved the

gun at it and I reluctantly slid each of the plates carefully into the coarse burlap, not wanting to damage the gears on their faces.

He smiled but I could barely see it under his heavy mustache.

"You always were a clever girl." He swept his hand out with a short bow. "After you, my dear."

We trudged through the soft mud as the mist and darkness swallowed us. I could see the shadowy line of one of the many rock walls that cut across the moors, but nothing else as the mist enclosed us in a chilling haze.

"I hope you know the way." One wrong turn, and we could end up wandering the moors forever.

"I've been here waiting for you for a long time." He flicked on a lamp, which did little more than light the ground just before our feet.

"So you knew I had the key." I could hear my frightened heart pounding in my ears, a steady drumbeat across the silent moors.

"Yes, but I didn't know if you could use it," Rathford admitted. This was my chance for answers, and if he was going to abduct me, I felt entitled to them. "No one else knows the song. And so, you are unique."

"You sent me out to find the plates, didn't you?" I needed to know it was true.

"Yes." The baron's mustache and his morose eyes gave him a heavy, serious expression. "And the plan worked quite well, though I didn't expect William to forsake gainful employment for your modest charms. I had hoped for more compliance from him on the moor." He rubbed his jaw. "But then, love makes a man do irrational things."

"Like murder?" I stopped and he did as well. I expected him to grab me, force me along, instead he blinked, his eyes so very much like a bloodhound's. I needed to know the truth. "Were you the one who set the fire that killed my parents?"

"No. I did not." He took a step closer to me. "I saved your life by taking you in. There was no one else who could have protected you from the one who wants you dead."

Dear Lord, Will could have been right all along. Somehow the thought didn't make me feel any safer in Rathford's presence. He could be lying.

But protect me? Rathford made my life miserable for six months, working me night and day until my bones ached. He didn't do it to protect me. He took me in for the key. He had just admitted it. He must have noticed defiance in my expression because he gave me a superior scowl and continued walking.

"I'm not a rash man. I only ever wanted to make things right." He turned to avoid a soggy patch of mud. The plates clanked together in the sack.

"If you didn't murder my parents, who did?"

"You should ask your grandfather." He lifted the lamp as we continued on.

I felt as if he had just struck me. Was he implying that my grandfather had killed them? That didn't make any sense. He was only toying with me as a cat does a mouse. "Do you know where he is?"

He chuckled. "Alas. I did, but I'm afraid he somehow escaped even my sight. That is no small feat, my dear."

"Where was he?" I demanded.

"As I said, I no longer know. So what I do know is irrelevant. I don't like to waste time." His eyes gleamed.

That was it. I wouldn't let him manipulate me any longer. I refused to ask any more questions. But it only infuriated me more when I realized that had been his aim.

We must have walked an hour, two? I couldn't know for certain, but my legs shook with fatigue. On the one hand, confirmation that my grandfather might indeed be alive lightened the burden on my heart and mind, but they were still weighed down by the knowledge that I was no closer to finding him than I had been when I first found his letter.

Rathford was taking me to unlock the machine. I knew I had to stop him.

I just didn't know how.

I didn't even know what the machine did; I only knew it was dangerous. Yet I didn't feel fear. My curiosity outweighed any fear. I had to keep my wits, but there was something in me that needed to know what could possibly cause so much pain and suffering.

The mists retreated as we climbed a hill, leaving the fog that lingered in the vales. It seemed so solid and thick as the moonlight shone down on it. I prayed Oliver and Lucinda were helping Will to me, before it was too late.

We reached the top of a plateau where the moonlight bathed the dried heather and round tufts of dead grass in silver. My breath swirled before my eyes.

At the crest of the hill, the ruins of a castle clung to the barren earth. The moon shone through what remained of the arched windows of the keep. The once mighty stronghold had become nothing more than crumbling walls reaching toward the heavens. Time was slowly destroying this old warrior standing in silent guard over the moors.

Something moved near a gap in the outer wall. I stifled a gasp as two enormous beasts walked toward us with a jerking gait. Their eyes glowed green, reminding me of Oliver's goggles. They must have been the size of small horses, easily five feet tall at the shoulder. As they drew closer, I realized what they were.

The lions from the gate had come to life before me.

We passed between the beasts, and I stared in awe and horror at the gears spinning in their shoulders and turning steadily in the centers of their chests. It was as if the outer shell of stiff brass had been stripped away, revealing their inner workings. There was a raw power in these creations and the same awareness that had been so unnerving in the Minotaur and the sea monster.

"Stay close, they do bite," Rathford warned, leading the way into the castle. The one nearest me turned his massive head. One bite from those metal jaws could crush a man's skull. I didn't want to think what it could do to me.

Shadows from the outer walls stretched over the uneven stones that had once been a paved courtyard of the keep. Now weeds and tufts of grass grew from between the buckled stonework.

"Welcome to Heverdon," Rathford said, winding through the maze of deteriorated walls and piles of fallen stone. It was hard for me to tell where we would have stood in the original building, but as we reached a long wide ramp leading down beneath the tallest section of remaining stone, I knew exactly where we were going.

The walls of the dungeon rose up around us as we walked down the ramp and passed beneath an archway with a heavy iron portcullis hanging like jagged teeth in a jaw of stone.

Cool, stale air that smelled of dust and mildew enveloped me as the light from Rathford's lamp cast our shadows on the walls. Behind us, the metal paws of the lions clanged against the stone.

I swallowed my fear, holding my key like a talisman as we passed by what looked to be old storerooms. The lamplight glinted off gears and tools, tucked into the various nooks. A bed of straw lay in the corner of one of the thick stone cells. Rathford had slept here, like a common prisoner.

The clatter of the lions halted behind me. If they had been alive, I would have felt their hot breath on the back of my neck. I didn't know what unnerved me more, the thought of them that close, or the fact that they didn't breathe.

Rathford lit a torch, the firelight blazing to life in the deep chamber. Flickering orange light played over an immense iron gate. Like the plates, the sides of the iron framework were made up of a tight web of cogs and wheels.

In the center, a large brass rectangle had been fixed to the iron bars. Rathford placed the lamp on the floor and pulled the plates from the sack.

With the grim austerity of a medieval monk, he placed the plates on the floor in a line, inspecting each of them. He chose one from the middle and fit it into the top left corner. It struck the lock with a bell-like tone, then the gears embedded in the face of the plate came whirring to life.

One by one, each in sequence, Rathford fitted the plates with an expert hand. With each new plate, the gears on the others shifted, some extending toward us on delicate pins. Others slid out, locking together with the plates around them.

If any plate had been placed out of order, the gears would have snapped and broken as they tried to fit together in unintended ways.

I never would have been able to open the door.

As the last plate fit into place, all the gears that had emerged from the plates eased back in, locking with the other whirling mechanisms.

A resonant hum filled the chamber, like the sound that

lingers after a grand chord is played on a pipe organ.

Counterweights sank down through the iron gears, bringing the entire gate to life with motion.

"I've waited so long," Rathford whispered. The light caught in his eye as the gate opened inward.

Iron lamps lit themselves, the sparks showering onto them from flint wheels spinning along the walls. A long ramp continued down to the floor of a large open room. Two stone pillars supported the arched roof, like a cathedral had been pressed into the ground.

At the far end, the machine waited.

The brass egg rested on elegantly curved arches of metal, an enormous framework of rings surrounding it in a loose sphere.

It was beautiful, more magnificent than anything I could have imagined when I had looked at the drawings.

"What is it?" Caught in the moment, no warnings came to mind. This elegant creation was a thing of marvelous invention, not destruction.

Rathford grinned. "That, my dear, is the key to time itself."

CHAPTER THIRTY-ONE

TIME? IT WASN'T POSSIBLE. DEAR LORD IN HEAVEN, NO man could make a machine that could control time.

Rathford patted one of the lions on its hard muzzle. "You see, Margaret, I've discovered time is like a fabric, woven with many loops. If you find the right thread, and have enough power to open the portal, it's possible to go back and reweave the tapestry."

My heart thundered to life as Rathford twisted a dial on each of the lions' chests. They bowed and walked up the ramp, exiting the dungeon with their tails twitching like cats on the hunt.

My resolve found new strength. There was no way he

could make me unlock that machine. No man should wield such power. I needed to escape, to find the others. "You have what you want. Let me go."

"Now, Meg." Rathford grabbed me by the arm. His grip tightened, holding my elbow in such a crushing way, I couldn't escape him. "I have been waiting for this moment for eighteen years. Don't you wish to see the glory of my greatest triumph?"

"No." I glared at him.

"Of all people, I thought you would." He shrugged. "No matter. Your grandfather made it clear he disabled my key. I'm afraid I still need your aid. I have some work to do. If you don't mind, I'll have you stay put until I need you."

I stumbled backward, jerking away from him, but I couldn't pull free. His iron grip caused an aching burn in my arm. I beat him with my fist. "Let me go!"

He pushed me hard, and the floor dropped out from beneath my feet.

I fell.

Screaming, I grabbed on as tightly as I could to Rathford's coat, but he shook me off. I landed hard on the stone floor of a dark, cramped little room.

My legs crumbled beneath me. The pain of hitting the

stone burned through my shins. I looked up as a heavy iron grate closed over the small opening above my head.

Rathford's face appeared above me, the only thing I could see in the pit I found myself in. "Enjoy the oubliette. The rats find it quite agreeable."

"Rathford!" I screeched, but he disappeared, leaving me alone in the dark. I felt the walls close in around me, as if I had just been lowered into my grave. Oubliettes were for the forgotten, tombs that kill their victims slowly through despair and neglect.

I couldn't let my panic take hold. I concentrated on my breathing. I wasn't forgotten. The others were out there. They would find me. I knew it. I just hoped it wouldn't be too late.

I stood, staring at the flickering torchlight through the square grate only four feet above my head. I reached for the squares of light, cut into neat rows and columns by the grate. I jumped to see if I could reach it, but it was no use. Blackness surrounded me. As the stale air choked me, I listened for the scuttle of rats.

Only the relentless *ping* of a hammer striking metal echoed in the chamber above. With my hands outstretched, I took a step forward. I didn't have to move far before my fingertips brushed the cold wall.

I felt the rough stone, testing every crack of the tiny prison. It didn't take long. The room was barely big enough to lie down in.

The only way out was up.

I was trapped.

Stepping into the checkered square of light shining through the grate, I hugged my arms and sank to the floor.

What was I going to do?

I had to stop Rathford. My grandfather, Simon, they all were right about the danger of the machine. This was a horror beyond my imagining, and now I was helpless. There was no way to determine how one small change in the fabric of time would affect all events thereafter. Rathford wasn't going to reweave the tapestry. He would unravel it. I could hear the slow grind of metal turning against metal. How long would it take Rathford to finish?

I wondered where the others were and if they had even found my note. The idea of Will alone and injured on the moors tormented me.

My throat tightened at the thought of losing Will forever.

This was all my fault. If I had never opened the key, none of this would have ever happened.

Rathford's machine would have remained buried forever.

What had I done?

As I stood in the tiny patch of light, the true torment of the oubliette overcame me. Time passed, marked only by the sounds of Rathford's hammer. Minutes? Hours? It could have been days, and I wouldn't have known.

I had to do something. I had to try to escape. Feeling the floor this time, I crawled around on my hands and knees. But there was nothing. My hands simply passed over hard smooth dirt. Escape seemed so close, if I could only reach it. But the oubliette had been designed to make escape impossible.

I thought about making a rope. I even tore more material off my tattered petticoat, but then realized that even if I could hook the rope up through the bars, as soon as I used it to climb, my own weight would prevent me from pushing the grate up.

There was no way out.

I sat alone for what seemed a lifetime, letting my dismal thoughts torture my battered mind. The only way I would ever escape would be if someone came for me.

I had to pray the others would find me.

If they didn't reach me in time, there was only one thing I could do. I shuddered. If Rathford forced me to use the key, I would have to play the wrong notes. I swallowed a hard lump in my throat as my insides twisted. I didn't know what would happen to the machine if I did. Likely it would explode, or something equally horrible would happen. Or Rathford would lose patience and shoot me for my subversion.

No matter what, I was going to die. I had no other choice.

Sitting in the square of light, I held my hand out and traced the shadowed cross on my palm with my finger. Over and over, I traced one line and then the next, chanting a prayer as I did so. It gave me something to think about other than my impending death.

The cross slid off my palm, leaving my hand bathed in light.

I inhaled, then squinted at the hatch. The grate had been removed and a hand reached down for me. Yet I could still hear the *ping* of Rathford's hammer.

Yes!

From my angle, I couldn't tell if it was Will or Oliver who reached down for me. I didn't care. It was a way out.

I leapt to my feet, stretching on the tips of my toes as I grasped at my salvation. Locking my grip around the wrist, I sent a prayer of thanks for the strong fingers that held tightly around mine.

My rescuer hauled me up in one swift jerk. I scrambled out of the hole onto my knees and looked up.

No!

"Alastair." I retreated an inch, nearly dropping back into the hole. The torchlight caught in the earl's pale hair and eyes. I could see that an obsession burned there. Obsession and rage.

"We meet again, Miss Tavernshamton." There was no amusement in his voice.

"How did you find me?" I whispered.

Dread crept into my heart. I slowly wiped my hand down my torn skirt.

"I knew all our paths would eventually meet here, so I've waited, keeping an eye on Rathford. It seems you didn't disappoint." He offered me his hand again, but I refused to touch it. There was something frightening about his eyes. I got to my feet.

The warning in my heart felt too stark and clear to ignore. I couldn't trust him.

Alastair held out his arm as he peered around the gate. "We don't have much time before the lions return. I'll distract Rathford. You need to sneak inside the machine, use your key to unlock it, and then shatter the lens inside. It's the only way to destroy the machine once and for all."

I nodded. Break the machine. I could do that. But would it destroy me in the process? I had the feeling that this man wouldn't care if my life were forfeit. Once again, I found I had no choice, and my only options all pointed toward a violent end.

"Wait until I have his attention. Keep out of the light." Alastair stood to his full height, straightened his lapels, then walked through the iron gate.

"Ulysses," he greeted Rathford. Alastair's breeding came out in his voice, which had an air of authority and command I had never heard before. I peeked around the edge of the gate, holding my breath in fear that even a soft sound might give me away.

In the distance I heard a clanking. I needed to move.

Rathford rose slowly, leaving his wrench in the machine. He wiped his hands on a smithy apron and faced Alastair. His sad eyes spoke volumes. Rathford looked as if he were staring at the reaper himself.

"I would like to say it's good to see you again, Alastair." Rathford's voice pitched lower as he fumbled with something in his pocket.

Alastair circled to the left, drawing Rathford's gaze and giving me the chance to sneak along the chamber to the right. I tiptoed as quickly and silently as I could, then ducked behind one of the thick stone columns supporting the chamber ceiling.

"It's been years," Alastair said. "You haven't changed a bit."

Rathford took a step back. Luckily for me, he hadn't taken his eyes off Alastair. "I wish I could say the same for you. When we met you were a decent man."

"What would make you think otherwise?" Alastair asked. I crept out from behind the column. The time machine was only twenty feet away. The door was open. I could get in, smash it, and be done with all of this.

"Because you've been trying to kill me, and I have no doubt you killed the others," Rathford stated.

I stopped in my tracks.

Alastair drew a modified pistol from his pocket and aimed it at Rathford's heart. "You were too persistent, Ulysses. The deaths of the others are on you."

He pulled the trigger, and I let out a shriek, but the pistol exploded as it misfired. Alastair swore, dropping the weapon. It clattered to the floor as he pulled his burned hand into his coat.

Rathford turned to me with wild eyes.

My foot caught on a stone and I stumbled, crashing to the floor. My scraped palms burned, but I didn't have a chance to recover before a heavy hand grabbed me by the neck. Rathford pulled me into his body, using me as a shield against Alastair.

"I should kill you now, Alastair," Rathford swore as Alastair rose, reclaiming his pistol even as he grinned a bit like a mad dog. "For months, I've lived as a hostage within my own house, watching your assassin prowling at my gates."

Alastair's eyes narrowed. "What are you talking about? I've hired no assassin." He raised the pistol. "I need no assassin."

We were going to die. Alastair would have no trouble shooting me to get to Rathford. This was the end. What could I do? Desperately, I looked around. Rathford backed us toward a column, until the lower tip of one of the torches nearly touched my ear. Yet Alastair hesitated.

"That's right. Kill her and all your carefully laid plans to secure your bid for control of the Order would be destroyed. I'm sure even now you're having visions of calling everyone back and announcing your victory." What did I have to do with any of this? I felt Rathford tremble even as the clatter of metal striking stone grew louder. The lions were coming.

"They already are destroyed. My eldest daughter took

care of that. I've nothing left to lose." Alastair's expression turned to steel.

I jerked my head to the side as hard as I could, knocking the torch off the wall and onto Rathford, then I grabbed his wrist with both my hands, turned, and bit it.

He screamed as a shot snapped against the stone just above my head. Rathford let go.

I ran.

Throwing myself at the machine, I just made it to the steps. Rathford was on my heels, but Alastair leaped on him, smashing them both into the floor.

"Go!" he shouted at me. I stumbled up the steps and under the arch formed by the rings around the time machine. I hated that our purposes were united, but someone had to destroy the machine.

Crawling inside, I shut the door.

The entire upper half of the machine was made up of open windows, so I could still see the chamber.

Rathford crashed his fist into Alastair's face. My heart cheered for a second. I wanted to see the bastard suffer.

Alastair threw a fist of his own, snapping Rathford's head back, just before the cavern filled with the roar of the clockwork lions.

Dear God. Chaos reigned around me.

The lions snapped and lunged at Alastair. One grabbed the tails of his coat and pulled him off of Rathford.

Rathford rose. With blood streaming through his mustache, he grabbed the pistol then aimed it right at me.

CHAPTER THIRTY-TWO

"MEG!" I TURNED AT THE SOUND OF WILL'S VOICE.

A shot rang out and I dropped to the floor as the round hit one of the metal rings surrounding the time machine.

A second shot filled the chamber with a bright flash of white light.

Thank you, Lord.

Will charged down the ramp, crashing into Rathford as Lucinda and Oliver took on the lions.

I had to stop this, before they got killed.

Within the inner chamber of the machine, I looked for a means to unlock it. It reminded me of the interior of the coach, except much more compact. Panels all along the lower edges of the windows were crowded with levers and knobs.

I found the flower medallion in the center of one of the panels to my left and quickly fitted the key.

The soft song was barely audible over the roaring lions and clashing metal. I closed my eyes and tried to block out everything else but the song. I had to get this right. Every second we remained in the chamber was another second in peril.

Alastair shouted Lucinda's name in panic. I looked up. Lucinda screamed as one of the lions leapt for her. Oliver fired, hitting the lion in the face. The lion stumbled, its momentum throwing it toward the column. Alastair pushed Lucinda. The lion crashed into the column, shaking the chamber and crushing Alastair beneath it. The time machine shuttered with the force of the impact. I lost my breath, horrified.

The song stopped.

No. I'd only heard some of the notes. Putting them together in my mind, I panicked as I realized the notes I'd heard could fit three different places in the song. Which was the right one?

Closing my eyes, I guessed, praying I had chosen correctly. If I didn't, it would give Rathford and his lions that much more time to kill us all. Or something horrible would happen, and my mistake would end this, for everyone.

I waited.

Nothing. Had I guessed wrong? What other phrase could it be?

The time machine hummed to life.

Thank you, mighty Lord!

Blue light glowed from the edges of the levers and gears as the floor shuddered. Like the key, a three-petal flower opened up at the apex of the conveyance. It was so beautiful. The light, I had never seen anything like it.

A crystal descended, much like the one at Gearhenge, only this one was smaller, about the size of a man's fist. It was covered in tiny metalwork, far finer than any of the smallest pieces my father had ever made.

He would have marveled at this. I could almost see his face smiling at such a thing.

The gears glittered as they spun.

Another shot rang out and I flinched as I heard this one whistle through the machine and smash into the stone wall on the other side.

Someone cried out in pain.

I had to hurry. Where was the lens?

I flipped the lever to my left. It looked identical to the one that started the wheels turning in the coach. The machine hummed, the vibration traveling up through the floor.

I heard a loud snap, then a web of light cascaded around the outer rings, as if someone had caught lightning and trapped it on the surface of a sphere. Tendrils of whip-like blue light reached out from the heart, writhing like captured lightning as they reached through the windows toward each of the people in the room. One then curled toward me.

"Meg!" Will shouted.

The heart, it was the crystal. That was the lens. I had to destroy it.

Clenching my fist around the heavy handle of the wrench, I started to swing at the crystal, but the tendril of light shocked me as it connected with my shoulder. Stunned, I watched as wide beams of white light projected from the heart out into the windows. Everything beyond the windows slowed, as if time itself were winding to a stop.

I lost my grip on the wrench and struggled not to drop it.

In each of the windows, I could see a scene playing out as if I were looking through a foggy glass, spying on a ghostlike world beyond. Alastair, in a back alley of London, raised a pistol and fired. Lucinda, in her black veil, clutched her stomach and cried by a fire. Oliver tended a gash in his arm near a stream in a vast wilderness. A young boy, broken with sadness and so skinny he looked on the verge of death, stared down at a bloody body.

My breath hitched. In another window, Rathford ran down the stairs. He cried out in agony as he gently lifted the lifeless head of the pregnant baroness from the shards of the vase that had tumbled down the stairs with her. My eyes filled with tears as I dared to look at the final window.

I saw myself asleep in my father's favorite chair as flames licked along the walls. I dropped my book.

Grabbing the wheel in front of the window that showed me in the fire, I spun it to the left. The images in the window changed, the flames moving backward, condensing together in a surreal ballet as the house around the image of me repaired itself.

I kept spinning the wheel. Time retreated faster. I walked backward up the stair, laid peacefully in my bed. My mother walked backward through the room then kissed me on the forehead as my father watched from the doorway.

I stopped the wheel.

It was the last moment I'd seen my parents alive.

I looked down on the controls. A simple lever stood

next to the wheel. My hand hovered over it as the humming around me reached a frenzied pitch.

I could go back.

I could save them.

My mother smiled at me, smoothing my hair. I loved her so much. My heart ripped open in that moment. I missed them. They were taken from me. I wanted them back.

My fingers slid around the lever.

If the fire had never happened, my life could be the way it was again. I could sit and embroider with my mother as my father read a book by the hearth. Mother could finally teach me her recipe for lemon biscuits. I could hear my father say he was proud of me.

"Meg!" Will's voice reached to me through the eerie silence. It sounded low, and muddled, as if I were hearing it through water.

I let out a breath, unable to take my hand from the lever.

If I pulled it, Will would never be in my life. I would never find Lucinda. She would still be in mourning.

Rathford would still have the machine, and Alastair would still kill to stop it.

My heart pounded with a slow, steady beat.

I looked over at the starving little boy in the other window. His eyes, they broke my heart.

Tears streamed down my face.

If Rathford ever went back to save his wife and baby, Will would die, because no one would have been there to save him.

I gripped the wrench.

Turning back to my parents, I let the tears stream down my face. My mother took my father's hands in hers. They looked so happy and at peace.

How could I do this?

They were alive, right there. I could bring them back.

I could have their love again.

Gasping, unable to breathe, I couldn't. No. I couldn't.

I had to.

"I'm sorry," I sobbed. "I love you so much, I'm so sorry."

I swung the wrench straight into the heart of the machine.

It shattered. The tendril of blue light snapped against my shoulder. Blue sparks and glass rained down on me as I covered my head and collapsed on the floor. My sobs racked me, even as another *boom* crashed through the machine.

The images within the window spun out of control, flashing bits and pieces of time. I watched the baroness turn at the top of the stair and fall.

Alastair kicked over the body of his son-in-law and watched him die.

The fire consumed the gallery of our store as a man's image reflected in the mirrored face of a large clock.

Wait!

I grabbed at the controls, trying to stop the spinning, but a sharp snap of electricity forced me back. The imaged faltered.

No.

"Meg! Get out of there!" Will shouted.

I pulled myself closer to the window. I just needed one more moment.

In a flash of light, I saw the man amidst the flames. He lifted his face and I gasped in horror. Half of his face was covered in a steel mask of ominously turning gears. A gold eye met mine, and I knew I stared into the face of the stranger who had destroyed my life, the man in black.

An explosion knocked me down, my head slamming against the controls of the machine.

The tendrils of blue light writhed through the interior as the images in the windows faded to darkness.

A high-pitched whine sliced through the air.

The door to the time machine crashed open.

"Will," I breathed.

He stood in the doorway. The whipping blue light glowed behind him. He reached out, and I took his hand.

He pulled me into his arms, and I clung tightly to him as we passed under the blue fire licking over the arch in the rings.

I felt the power of it snap over my skin as my hair clung to Will's cheek. Stones crashed around us. Lucinda huddled over her father, his body crushed beneath the broken lion. She stroked his hair as a trail of blood seeped from the corner of his mouth. He said something to her and she nodded even as she shook with tears. Oliver pulled her away. Alastair reached for her before his hand fell lifeless on the stone.

A chunk of stone smashed to the ground beside us.

The ceiling could collapse at any minute.

Peering over Will's shoulder, I watched in horror as stray whips of lightning snapped out from the rings of the machine. Oliver took Lucinda's hand and they ran up the ramp together. Rathford pulled himself up the steps with his arms. He fought his way into the center of the machine and closed the door.

Will placed my feet on the ground. "Run!"

We raced up the ramp, through the iron gate, past the storerooms, and up the final ramp. The portcullis loomed overhead, backlit by the new light of dawn.

My lungs burned. I could taste blood in my mouth as I clung to Will's hand and ran with all my strength. A high-pitched whistle, like steam being let from a vent, split the air.

Will pulled us behind a section of thick stone wall then covered me, wrapping his arms over his head as he sheltered me with his body.

An explosion rocked the earth beneath us, far more powerful than thunder or cannon fire.

I gripped Will's shirt, tearing the seam.

Fragments of stone showered the empty moor. Then all was quiet.

My body began to shake. I couldn't control it.

"I've got you." Will kissed the top of my head. He stroked my hair and pressed my cheek to his heart. "I've got you."

I lifted my face to his. Reaching up, I ran my palm over the rough skin of his cheek. Drawing his face to mine, I kissed him.

He crushed me in his embrace as he kissed me back. We were lost in a moment that was only ours; the rest of the world simply didn't matter. We lingered in the kiss, savoring the bitter victory for only a moment, a moment with the power to mark my heart forever.

When we finally broke the kiss, Will held me as I cried.

CHAPTER THIRTY-THREE

I CRIED UNTIL I SIMPLY COULDN'T MOVE, COULDN'T think anymore. I felt sick with guilt even as I tried to reason with myself. The past was still the past, and our future was unknown once more.

It felt as if the world had changed. Will held me. Softly, so softly at first I barely heard it, he began to sing.

The music reached into me and wound itself around my heart. I remembered it from that day in Rathford's carriage house when he had tended Old Nick and I'd brought him the tart. It felt as if a hundred years had passed since then. As I listened to the sweet flowing melody rumble through his chest, the pain of what I'd just witnessed eased. Will stroked my hair and offered me the simplest comfort he could.

What love I felt for him must have swelled like an unstoppable tide in that moment. I let him hold me, let him sing, until the heavy burden of our situation settled on my shoulders once more. I blinked my burning eyes and looked out at the ruins. "Where are the others?" My voice cracked as I said it.

Will pulled me to my feet. That's when I noticed the bleeding cut at his hairline. None of us remained unscathed. "Let's find them."

We discovered Lucinda tending to Oliver, setting his arm in a sling she had fashioned from the red sash. She looked as stricken as I felt.

"He saved your life," Oliver was saying, brushing a tear from her cheek. "Whatever loyalty you have for him as your father, don't feel guilty for it." Oliver lifted her chin with the side of his finger.

"He asked me to forgive him, but . . . how can I?" She swallowed. "How can I?" She wiped her tears then noticed us. "Meg! Thank the dear Lord you are unharmed." She rushed to us, pulling me into a hug, then embracing Will as well.

"Lucinda," I began. I didn't know what to say.

A tear slid down her cheek. "It's over. Let's go home."

I didn't feel like speaking on the way back. For a long time, it seemed as if none of us did. We rode the coach in silence, Lucinda driving, Oliver nursing his broken arm, and Will holding me as if I were precious.

We spent a quiet night in a pasture under the stars, and our conversation was nothing more than a functional sentence here or there.

The next day, the need to make some sort of greater sense of what had happened overcame us, and we recounted our parts in the story for the benefit of the others.

Rathford had confronted Will on the moors. Will had tried to act as if he were loyal to Rathford, but Rathford saw through the ruse. Rathford used some sort of gas explosion to knock Will out. When he came around he ran back to the cottage. Oliver and Lucinda had assumed the worst of our behavior and were leaving us to our ruinous devices. They were livid with themselves when they discovered what had really happened.

They found the valiant little mechanical pigeon flailing in the coach. I could still see his wing marks scarring the once pristine paint and wood.

I told them about Alastair and how he had pulled me from the oubliette. I didn't tell anyone what I had seen in the time machine. It wasn't right. Some of the secrets I had witnessed,

I would take to the grave, though I was terribly curious about Oliver's wound in the wilderness and how he had received it.

I couldn't bring myself to speak about my parents, or the choice I had faced. The wound was too raw. I mourned their deaths a second time, far more deeply than the first.

The terrible weight of my guilt burdened my heart.

My parents were gone. They had died in a fire months ago. I couldn't change that, not without destroying everyone around me.

I would feel the pain of their loss until the day I joined them, but it was time to move on. I was alive.

I had my life before me. With Rathford and Alastair defeated, my grandfather could return.

There was only one thing that would continue to haunt me. I told Oliver about the man with the steel face. He seemed both shocked and appalled by my revelation, but didn't know his identity. He mentioned that long ago, before any of us was born, there had been an Amusementist with an interest in developing new limbs for soldiers who came home injured from war, but he had never heard of a man with a false face.

It would have to wait, but I was patient, and I knew I wouldn't be fully safe until I found my parents' murderer and watched him hang.

CHAPTER THIRTY-FOUR

BACK IN LONDON, I SAT WITH LUCINDA IN FRONT OF THE hearth at the toy shop. She sipped her tea as I opened a formal invitation.

"Her Grace the dowager Duchess of Chadwick has invited me to a dinner party to celebrate the return of her prodigal son. I wonder how I came to be on her list of acquaintances." I felt a deep warmth in my chest as Lucinda chuckled while trying to sip her tea.

"You have some fine friends, Miss Whitlock. I'd wager she choked on a biscuit when she found a Scottish tinker on the guest list," she quipped. It was my turn to chuckle. Lucinda tucked her chin. "I have a favor to ask."

I reached over and placed my hand on hers. "Anything."

"Now that my father . . ." Her voice faltered, but she took a deep breath and continued. "I feel I should return home for a time. Between my mother and everything she has to deal with, and Oliver—"

"Has he proposed?" I nearly squealed. Lucinda silenced me with a look.

"As I was saying." She folded a serviette and placed it on the table. "This shop means so much to me. I want you to look after it."

My heart stopped entirely. "Me?"

"I will pay you a salary plus a percent commission, and I wish to hire one of my old nurse maids to be your house-keeper and chaperone. I've recently discovered my father left her with very little when she was of no more use to him. I wish to make it up to her." Lucinda looked at me hopefully. I felt my eyes begin to water. "I know it is an enormous responsibility."

"Yes." I hugged her as tightly as I could. "Oh, yes. And thank you. It's an honor. I promise, I'll make this shop a wonder."

She patted my back. "I know you will."

On Wednesday night, after a grand dinner of everything other than beef stew, complete with treacle tart for dessert, I found myself in the library of the Duke of Chadwick's enormous London town house, idly polishing the glass of an unlit lamp.

One of the female foot soldiers in the army of Chadwick servants caught me cleaning the lamp and gently took my cloth away. A young, blustery girl with ample cheeks, she blushed as she looked to her feet. "Pardon me, miss. You shouldn't be doing that."

I blinked at her, surprised. She blushed further. "You're not a maid, you know." She bustled out of the room.

I clenched my hands in my lovely dove-gray skirts, with black braid and lavender trim. My dress was properly modest with a genuine crinoline, and Lucinda's new lady's maid had tied matching lavender ribbons in my fashionably styled hair.

Will entered. He looked spectacular in a silver waistcoat and finely cut trousers. The two of us certainly didn't look as if we didn't have a penny to our names.

"You look lovely," he said, walking toward me as if he had a purpose.

My heart fluttered. We hadn't had much of an opportunity to be alone since our return to London. Oliver had hired him as a courier, and he had been busy. It was as if the freedom we had known had disappeared, crushed by the expectations of society.

"I thought you said you didn't wish to live off the charity of others," I teased. A courier's salary wouldn't have bought a waistcoat like that. He looked regal.

"I don't want to live off it, but I figure Oliver owes us this much for all the trouble he put us to." Will shrugged, tugging on the edge of his coat.

I laughed.

"That's a fine dress." He gave a brass figurine of a rearing horse a half turn on the mantel, then flinched as if expecting some secret door to open. Hastily, he twisted it back.

"It doesn't seem to suit me." I glanced at the clock next to it, watching the pendulum swing in a steady rhythm.

Will tugged at his collar. "Me either. I had grown rather accustomed to seeing your ankles."

I playfully lifted my skirt enough to reveal the tip of my toe. He grinned and took my hand.

"You chose me," he murmured.

"What are you talking about?" I tilted my head, studying the intent expression on his face.

"I know you could have gone back, changed what happened with the fire, but you didn't." I tried to pull away from him, but he held my hand fast.

My guilt ate at me. I had sacrificed my family, for what? He wasn't willing to have me. He had made that clear.

"Meg?" I slowly brought my gaze to his. He brushed a kiss across the back of my hand.

"When I found out Rathford had taken you, I thought the worst. I thought I would never see you again." He pulled me closer. "I discovered I can't bear that thought."

I didn't know what to say. My heart dipped, then I felt as if I had wings once again.

He leaned in close to my neck. "I need you," he whispered so close to my ear. "I want you."

Pulling back, he peered deeply into my eyes. "Please say you'll have me, too. We can find a way."

My heart fluttered, then burst like fireworks on the fifth of November. "I love you, Will."

He turned my hand over and kissed my palm in answer. I smoothed it over his cheek.

"Whatever happens, I'm watching out for you." He kissed me, hard, fast, as he lifted me up and spun me around the room.

I knew he always would.

ACKNOWLEDGMENTS

I AM SO GRATEFUL TO EVERYONE WHO PLAYED A PART IN the writing of this book. First I have to thank my incredible editor, Anica Mrose Rissi, for all her hard work and her dedication to this story. Her talent has made me a better writer, and her enthusiasm has kept me a sane one. I also have to thank my agent, Laura Bradford. She said the things that needed to be said, even when it wasn't easy. She pushed me to make something great, then she championed it with passion. For that, I owe her my gratitude.

Several people helped me during the writing process, giving me support, encouragement, and a critical eye. My critique partner, Angie Fox, who deserves the title of Goddess of All Things Critique-y, put in an amazing effort both in her critiques and in her insistence that I slow down and get some sleep during the frantic nights when I considered sleep optional. Even with Angie's help, this book wouldn't have seen the light of day without the remarkable insight of Katie Wallace, who helped me find Meg's voice. I also owe my eternal thanks to her mother, Lisetta Wallace, for being the best English teacher I've ever had, and for looking the other way when I used to scribble stories in the back of my binder during her class. I also have to thank Jules, Julie, Vivi, and Kristie for their encouragement, and Tracey Stefureak and Hasna Saadani for helping keep the language authentic to England.

There is so much more than just writing involved with creating an amazing book. I'd like to thank Shooters Productions for their generous time and efforts to create a beautiful online presence for this book. I also want to give a special thanks to Julie, my assistant, for her help with any odd request I have thrown at her.

I appreciate the contributions of all of the agents associated with the Bradford Literary Agency who worked to bring this story to the widest possible audience. And finally, I have to thank all the people at Simon & Schuster who had a hand in bringing this book to the market. From the art department to marketing and metadata, I'm so proud to have you on my team.

Last thing, I swear. I have to give all my love to my incredible family, especially my husband, who put up with me crawling into bed too late for too many nights, mumbling about clockwork coaches and battling giant mechanical sea monsters. I couldn't do this without you.

Thank you all from the bottom of my heart.

Don't miss book two in the Secret Order series:

Rise of the Arcane Fire

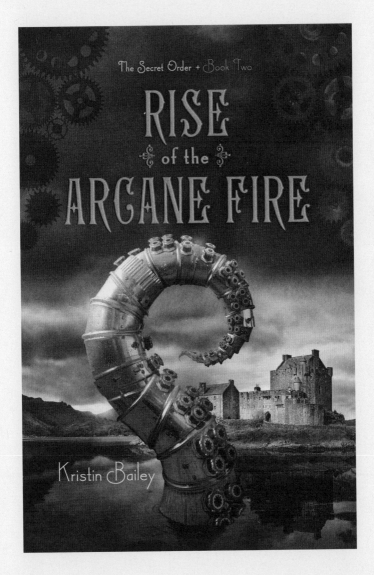

The Secret Order • Book Two

RISE
of the
ARCANE FIRE

Kristin Bailey

"HOP, DAMMIT," I MUTTERED AS I PUSHED BACK FROM the table and rubbed my burning eyes. The lantern flickered, nearly out of oil, and my entire body ached from hunching over the absurd little contraption before me.

It was hardly elegant. Or even whimsical.

The oddly shaped mechanical frog stared up at me with enormous eyes that I had fashioned from inky black marbles. It trembled, as if terrified of what I might do should it fail to obey. Eventually the cog in its back wound down without the frog budging so much as an inch.

Sighing, I blinked back my exhaustion, then glanced at the notes from one of a dozen books lying open on the table.

Finally I made one last attempt to adjust the spring in the left leg.

It was hopeless. I couldn't do this.

When I had become the shopkeeper for Pricket's Toys and Amusements, I'd known it was a very special place. While it may have seemed outwardly like a normal, if somewhat curious, shop in the heart of Mayfair, I knew it held a secret.

The former owner had been part of a reclusive society, the Secret Order of Modern Amusementists. The Order boasted a membership that included some of the finest minds in all of Europe, perhaps even the world. They would gather and challenge one another to great feats of invention, purely for whimsy—and also to line their pockets with a wager or two on the outcome.

I had seen some of the wonders the Order had created. They were haunting, often terrifying, but always beautiful. My own family had been part of the Order for generations. Both of my grandfathers had been high-ranking members. My father as well. But they had kept it all from me.

I supposed I couldn't blame them, considering that their involvement with the Order had led to their ruin.

If my adventures in the spring had taught me anything, it

was that genius often comes hand in hand with madness, and some secrets could kill.

There had been a string of murders within the Order about five years earlier. During that time, my grandfather had disappeared. His carriage had been found in the river, and by all accounts he was presumed dead. But that had hardly been the last tragedy to befall my family. A year ago I lost my parents as well, which forced me into destitution.

I had known nothing of my family's secrets when Lord Rathford took me into his household as a maid, claiming to be a benefactor. It turned out he'd only wished to use the master key my grandfather had left me, to unlock a horrible invention that had had the potential to destroy the entire world as we knew it.

It was fear of that invention that had driven Rathford's nemesis, Strompton, to murder. He would have stopped at nothing to keep the terrible invention from ever seeing the light of day.

The entire ordeal had been both terrifying and illuminating.

Now, even knowing the worst of the Order, I couldn't help myself. I wanted so badly to be a part of it. I took the frog in my hands and stroked my finger over the cool metal plate that formed the top of his head.

Perhaps that is why I'd taken over management of Pricket's Toys and Amusements.

Simon Pricket had been a gifted young Amusementist and a protégé of my father's. Tragically, he had also been a victim of the murderer. Before Simon's death, he had accumulated an entire library of prolific notes from his time as an apprentice, and then as historian and inventor for the Order. Reading them had been a revelation. Unfortunately, the elaborate texts only encouraged me to fancy myself an Amusementist.

It was an admirable, if futile, pursuit. After all, I had seen firsthand the wondrous machines my own family had built. During my adventures I had discovered a dome of stars hidden deep in the earth beneath an iron replica of Stonehenge, a labyrinth complete with a mechanical Minotaur, a set of gilded wings, and a clockwork ship set to do battle with a monstrous leviathan. Within the Order anything was possible, even tearing apart the fabric of time.

All this potential hung like tantalizing fruit before me, just out of my reach. Honestly, I didn't see the good of being born into a secret society of inventors if I couldn't make a measly toy frog hop.

I placed the frog back on the desk and rubbed the soreness from my neck. It wasn't as if dreaming about becoming an Amusementist would accomplish anything. I'd been born a girl, so I could never be part of the Order.

I could rail against the unfairness of it all, but it would be little use. I couldn't change what was. But no one and nothing could stop me from reading and tinkering in my own shop— except, it seemed, my own inability to create an insipid frog. I slammed my hand down on the desk, and the blasted frog bounced up into the air.

Wonderful.

A substantial lust for invention couldn't imbue me with comprehension of the finer points of compressing springs.

I slumped face-first onto one of Simon's journals, the mathematical scribblings turning into blurry patches of gray just beyond my nose. Simon had written that through mathematics, all the secrets of God's creation could be unraveled. If only those secrets could seep into my skull as I rested. I wanted to invent a machine that could accomplish *that*.

My eyes burned and I couldn't keep them open any longer, but of course I couldn't sleep. I could fall over from exhaustion, but I couldn't sleep. I hadn't been able to sleep for a week. Every time I let go and began to drift off, I saw the flames, heard the ticking clocks and shattering crystal.

I jolted upright out of habit.

The knot in my shoulder grew worse, and I tried to soothe the ache there. My body was wound tighter than the troublesome spring. I didn't feel I could eat, because, in spite of my appetite, everything I attempted turned sour and made me feel ill.

This was no sort of life for a sixteen-year-old girl. All the other girls my age fretted about dresses, and gossip, who invited whom to tea, and the latest society ball. Instead I spent every waking moment thinking about death—my own and the deaths of the ones I had loved.

My eyes pained me the worst of all. If I cried, perhaps they would burn less, but I couldn't bring myself to do it.

One year ago exactly I had fallen asleep in my father's clock shop on a night as unassuming as the one currently surrounding me. I tried, but I couldn't remember the book I'd been reading that night. I did recall that it had been the farthest thing possible from advanced mathematics but nearly as boring. It had been a frothy story, and I remember feeling the girl at the heart of it had been a mindless ninny. I don't know why I'd stayed up to read, other than the fact that, no matter how terrible a story is, I always must know how it will end. So much ended that night.

I couldn't recall falling asleep, but I did remember distinctly the moment I had woken.

It had been a crash that had startled me. I'd opened my eyes, then fallen out of my chair. Smoke like a heavy fog pushed down. I couldn't see the ceiling as I pressed my face to the Turkish rug and coughed until I feared blood would pour from my lungs. My eyes burned, tearing so badly, I could hardly see. The heat seared my skin like the fires of hell itself. I saw the flames flickering in the gallery and licking up the walls, turning the drapes to ash as they burned.

Like a horse, panicked and seeking safety in a burning stable, I crawled toward the stairs. Smoke poured up them and away from me, like a murky river flowing topsy-turvy along the ceiling, spilling up into our home above the shop.

I screamed for my parents. There was no answer.

The crystals of the clocks in the gallery shattered one by one with loud pops that sounded like gunfire.

I had to get out.

I dragged myself along the floor until I managed to escape out into the small courtyard in the back of the house. The windows from the upper floors burst from the heat, raining glass down on me as the flames roared out of them. I heard the clanging bell of the fire wagon as I searched the courtyard for my parents, then fervently prayed they had escaped out the front.

They had not.

The disaster left me alone and destitute in Lord Rathford's house of madness.

It wasn't until I uncovered Lord Rathford's dangerous plot to alter the fabric of time that I discovered the true culprit behind the fire.

Rathford's time machine allowed me a glimpse into the past, and in it I witnessed a man with a clockwork mask that covered half his face. He was in the gallery of my father's shop at the moment it burst into flames.

I stopped Lord Rathford and his terrible machine and also exposed Lord Strompton as the real murderer of Simon Pricket and several other Amusementists. But it was all for naught, because the man who had killed my parents was still at large. He had hunted me across the English countryside trying to capture my grandfather's master key.

He was still hunting me.

I didn't think I would ever sleep again.

Something rattled in the front of Pricket's shop, a distant tapping, like a wooden bead dropped onto the floor. It brought my thoughts back to the present moment.

I twisted in my chair, immediately alert. Holding deathly still, I listened for any sound at all besides the frantic thumping of my heart. I slid my hand beneath the table and withdrew my pistol from the compartment hidden there.

It felt heavy in my hand as I stood from the table and stepped toward the secret door that led from my workshop to the toy shop out front. The sound could have been nothing, only a rat most likely. I heard something thump.

That was no rat.

With my heart in my throat, I readied the pistol, feeling the strain in my pinched shoulder and praying I didn't have to use the weapon. My insides twisted into knots as I stepped into the toy shop.

The door to the workshop closed behind me with a soft *snick* and appeared once more as a high shelf of picture books and tins of toy soldiers to the left of the counting desk.

"I'm armed, and I will fire," I warned the silent shop. Dawn was beginning to break, the first dim light casting the room in eerie shadows. My hand shook, but my resolve did not.

The marionettes hung from the ceiling, their faces staring down on me like macabre grimaces of contorted men at the gallows.

I drew my gaze away from them as I searched for a single thing out of place.

The bell hanging from the front door swung like the slow pendulum of a clock. I even thought I heard a soft ticking.

"Miss Margaret!"

I wheeled toward the door to the living quarters behind the toy shop, my heart leaping into my throat. I brandished my pistol at the tiny old woman before me.

Mrs. Brindle, the housekeeper, screamed and dropped a tray laden with a pair of teacups and a plate of cheese. It crashed to the floor.

I immediately laid the pistol on a shelf and rushed to her side. She had her hand clutched to her chest.

"Mrs. Brindle, oh my goodness. I'm so sorry." I propped her up. Her wrinkled face had gone ashen. Dear Lord, I hoped I hadn't just sent the eighty-year-old woman into an apoplectic fit. She was the favorite nursemaid of Simon Pricket's widow. I had met Lucinda Pricket while on the trail of the murderer, and she had become my best friend. Mrs. Brindle's death would probably not be received well.

"For love and mercy, child," Mrs. Brindle scolded. Her arthritic hands shook as she carefully righted her nightcap. "What are you doing with that horrible thing?"

"I thought I heard a burglar," I said, though that seemed to pale in comparison to the truth of the matter. I feared murder. *My own murder.*

I helped poor Mrs. Brindle up, her thin white hair standing out at odds from beneath her cap. For as much as we both pretended she was there to look out for me, I knew the opposite to be true. After losing her usefulness as a nursemaid, she had been destitute. She needed both a home and a salary in her dotage, so Lucinda had hired her on as the housekeeper and an informal chaperone for me. I didn't mind in the least, and was simply glad for her company.

"Well, dear, if it was a burglar, best let him have what he's after. A fine young girl such as you should never take on something so base as a pistol." Showing the resiliency that had served her well through eight decades of life, she began cleaning up the fallen tray as if nothing had happened.

I couldn't quite grasp her logic. I was to become a victim of burglary, or worse, so as not to debase myself by holding the weapon? My recent brushes with death had changed my outlook on many things, especially propriety. I had discovered a newfound sense of practicality when it came to saving my life.

Thankfully, Will understood. In fact, he'd been the one

who'd taught me to use the pistol. He didn't like leaving me alone with only Mrs. Brindle, and occasionally her son Bob, for protection. My hands shook as I helped Mrs. Brindle with the tray.

Will had been the groom for Lord Rathford while I had been a maid serving in his house. I had conscripted poor Will as an often unwilling partner in my quest to discover the truth of what had happened to my family. During that time he had proven himself a brave, devoted, and clever companion. I touched my lips. Not to mention an amorous one.

It didn't hurt that he was handsome as the Devil, with dark hair, and eyes as still and fathomless as a moonless night.

Will had accompanied me to my parents' graves the first Sunday of every month since our return to London. Though my fear at the thought of an intruder in the toy shop still stuck in my throat, anticipating Will's arms around me filled me with warmth. When he held me, the world felt right and no danger could touch me.

Once again I thought I heard the soft *tick, tick, tick* of a clock.

It must have been a trick of my mind, the old memory of the clocks amid the flames. I was slowly losing my sanity.

Mrs. Brindle touched my arm, pulling my attention back

to the task at hand. "Have you slept at all?" she asked, her faded eyes too perceptive.

"Of course," I lied.

Mrs. Brindle shook her head slowly. "Don't fuss with this mess. I'll set it right. Kate will be in later to help straighten things upstairs. Go wash your face and share a cup of tea with me."

"Thank you." In spite of her words I found myself bending to gather the ruined tea. Mrs. Brindle was lively for her remarkable age, but I always felt inclined to care for her, much like a dutiful granddaughter would. I had few memories of my own grandmothers, and in my own simple way it made me feel as if I had a family again.

As I lifted the tray to the counting desk in the corner, I glanced at the small picture frame I kept next to the ledger. Frozen in time, my grandfather laughed as he demonstrated a floating top to a young boy and girl. He looked so alive. I felt as if I could touch his image and set it in motion, bringing him back. He was the only true family I had left.

I had seen proof that he'd faked his death to escape being murdered. He was out there somewhere. For the past several weeks I'd been waiting for word from him. I had thought that once I'd unraveled the conspiracy to kill anyone who'd aided in the construction of Rathford's time machine, he would return. Yet the days continued to pass, and there was no sign of him.

I closed my eyes and prayed that no misfortune had befallen my dear Papa, and yet I knew. The man with the clockwork mask had had something to do with his disappearance. I had to find my grandfather. Wherever he was, I had to somehow reach him and bring him home.

ABOUT THE AUTHOR

Kristin Bailey grew up in the middle of the San Joaquin Valley in California. In the course of her adventures, she has worked as a zookeeper, a balloon artist, and a substitute teacher. Now she is a military wife and the mother of two children and several very spoiled pets. Find out more at kristinbailey.com.